The Widows of Westram

Widowed by war...tempted by new flirtations!

Lady Carrie and her sisters-in-law, Lady Petra and Lady Marguerite, each tragically widowed on the same day by the same battle in Portugal, have had time to come to terms with their circumstances.

Now these three beguiling widows aim to seize the day and build their own destinies—in life, and in the realm of romantic liaisons...!

Find out what happens in Carrie's story:

A Lord for the Wallflower Widow

And look out for Petra and Marguerite's stories coming soon!

Author Note

In each and every book, I try to find some little part of Regency everyday life that might be new to you in addition to the usual glitz and glamour of the balls, jewels and gorgeous gowns. This time you meet a real elephant and visit a typical English fair of the time. I do hope you enjoy Carrie and Avery's story because I am busy writing about Petra just for you.

If you want to know more about me and my books, visit me at annlethbridge.com. There you will find links to social media, books and my newsletter. If you would like to get in touch, write to me at ann@annlethbridge.com. I love to hear from readers.

ANN LETHBRIDGE

A Lord for the Wallflower Widow

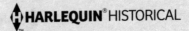

Recycling programs
for this product may
not exist in your area.

ISBN-13: 978-1-335-52296-2

A Lord for the Wallflower Widow

Printed in U.S.A.

www.Harlequin.com

In her youth, award-winning author **Ann Lethbridge** reimagined the Regency romances she read—and now she loves writing her own. Now living in Canada, Ann visits Britain every year, where family members understand—or so they say—her need to poke around every antiquity within a hundred miles. Learn more about Ann or contact her at annlethbridge.com. She loves hearing from readers.

Books by Ann Lethbridge

Harlequin Historical
and Harlequin Historical *Undone!* ebook

It Happened One Christmas
"Wallflower, Widow...Wife!"
Secrets of the Marriage Bed
Rescued by the Earl's Vows

The Widows of Westram

A Lord for the Wallflower Widow

The Society of Wicked Gentlemen

An Innocent Maid for the Duke

Rakes in Disgrace

The Gamekeeper's Lady
More Than a Mistress
Deliciously Debauched by the Rake (Undone!)
More Than a Lover

Visit the Author Profile page
at Harlequin.com for more titles.

This book is dedicated to Lilly, a very special young lady who recently came into our lives. Lilly, you may never read Grannie's stories, but provided you grow up a strong, sensible woman like your mother, you will make me very proud.

Prologue

April 1812

Redford Greystoke, Earl of Westram, forced himself not to look away from the three black-clad, heavily veiled ladies arraigned before his desk. It broke his heart to see them. Beneath those veils hid three beautiful young women. Two were his sisters, the other his sister-in-law. All of them widowed on the same day, at the same hour. Their husbands had been absolute idiots. Their loss left him numb.

From being an earl with a brother as heir and a spare hopefully in the offing, he'd become the last male member of his family with three destitute women to support. The very reason for their presence here and the reason for the animosity filling the air.

'You *will* remain under my roof,' Red repeated firmly. 'There is no more to be said on the matter.'

'Redford.' Lady Marguerite, his sister older than him by two years, had taken the role of spokesperson. She spoke quietly enough, but nevertheless with underlying heat. 'You cannot tell us where we shall reside.'

The trouble with widows was that they thought of themselves as independent women.

'I can, if I am to foot the bill.' Damn. Now he sounded like a truculent schoolboy. 'Let us be clear, ladies. I do not have the funds to set you up in your own establishments, whether I might wish to do so or not. You will reside with me in Gloucestershire until your period of mourning is over. At which time, I will be more than happy to open the London town house from where we will set out to mingle with our fellow peers.'

Lady Petra, his other sister, glared at him. Despite the veil hiding her face, he knew exactly the look directed his way when she was crossed. Petra was a master of glares. 'If you think I could ever marry anyone else...' A handkerchief in a black gloved hand disappeared beneath her veil. She sniffled.

He mentally cursed. 'No one is forcing you to do anything. If next year you do not wish to attend the Season, or go to balls, you may stay at home.' But knowing women as he did, he had no doubt they'd be bored within a few months of isolation in the country and begging to attend a ball or Almack's.

His sister-in-law, Carrie, the woman he hoped like the very devil was carrying his brother's heir, put an arm around Petra's drooping shoulder. 'It is all right, lass,' she said softly.

He liked Carrie Greystoke. A great deal. She was a practical no-nonsense woman, though she must have had a momentary loss of reason when she'd agreed to wed his harum-scarum brother. Fortunately, since her husband's death, she had been a rock of good sense in the eddying currents of grief and shock.

Sometimes he thought she was almost too calm. The

kind of calm that he suspected hid quiet desperation. He forced the thought aside. All three women were baulking at his proposal and he needed to marshal all his faculties if he was to prevail.

'Pluck up your courage, Petra,' Marguerite said. 'No need for tears because a bunch of idiots went off and got themselves killed.'

Marguerite had also wept on his shoulder when the news had been delivered. The fact that she now had her emotions under control was a very good thing. He hoped.

Petra, who had lost not only her husband and lover but her very best friend in the world, buried her head on Carrie's shoulder and sobbed.

Red wanted to bury his head in his hands and weep, too. For a few short weeks, he'd thought he was finally able to see his way clear of the debt left him by his father. Until the earth crumbled from beneath his feet, leaving this gaping abyss. He still didn't know what had sent these women's husbands off to join Wellington's army. Some sort of wager was the only explanation he'd been able to glean from their friends. Whatever it was, it had been the most nonsensical ridiculous prank— He cut the thought off. There was nothing he could do about the past. The future was his concern now.

The thing that had shocked him the most was the extent of Jonathan's debts. They had eaten up every penny and more of the wealth brought into the family by his marriage to Carrie. Red still could not believe he had not known that his brother had dipped so deeply in the River Tick.

And what his father had been about, letting Red's two sisters marry men without prospects, he could not imagine. Except that his father had been overindulgent where his daughters were concerned, giving them whatever their hearts desired. Which was why they were being so dashed difficult now.

'I think it would be best if you would let us at least try to manage on our own,' Carrie said, over his sobbing sister's head. 'We won't be a burden on you, Westram. I promise you that.'

If Carrie supported his sisters' mad scheme, then he was lost. Sensible and down to earth and as stubborn as they came, she would never give in. Perhaps it would be best if they learned first-hand that they were like babes in the woods when it came to the real world. Then they would listen to reason. His reason.

He threw his hands in the air. 'As you wish. I will give you the period of your mourning to try this experiment. I can afford very little in the way of allowances.' He shot Carrie a look of apology. 'I am so sorry, but all the money you brought to the marriage has gone to pay Jonathan's debts.' Jonathan had also charmed her father into handing over what should have been her widow's portion to invest in what his brother had called a sure thing on the 'Change. If her father had talked to Red beforehand, he would have disabused him of the notion. And maybe Jonathan would still be alive today. 'I would replace what my brother misappropriated, if I had it. I do not. Perhaps in time…' He tailed off, sick at heart. His sisters were no better off. He was appalled that their husbands had left their affairs in such disarray. He sighed. 'I will give you the use of Westram Cottage in Kent provided you can keep yourselves on that property within your allowances.' He glared at them. It was the only way he could maintain his dignity. 'I will be checking.'

They'd be back knocking on his door within a month.

Marguerite rose. Carrie did likewise, helping his younger sister to her feet. As always, he was taken aback by the woman's height compared to that of his sisters. His family tended to be on the short side.

'Thank you, Red,' Marguerite said, her voice warmer than it had been since this discussion had started. 'You will not regret it.'

Oh, yes, he would. Of that he had no doubt.

The ladies filed out.

Red poured himself a brandy and swallowed it in one gulp.

Chapter One

April 1813

Carrie Greystoke carefully dusted each shelf, as she had done every morning since the little shop had opened three days before. She replaced what she considered the shop's *pièce de résistance*, a sumptuous leghorn bonnet decorated with handmade flowers and cherry-coloured ribbons, in the window and took up her position behind the counter. Hope however, was beginning to fade.

In the three days since the doors of First Stare Millinery had opened not one customer had entered the little shop. If she didn't sell something soon, they would likely have to admit defeat. The thought of going to the landlord to admit her error in thinking she and her sisters-in-law could sell the product of the hard work they had put into the bonnets these last few months was humiliating.

Mr Thrumby, a friend of her dead father's, had taken a chance in renting her the shop. For her father's sake. Perhaps if it had been located on Bond Street rather than the less fashionable Cork Street… But then it would have been far too expensive. As it was, they'd had to pool all of their meagre resources to pay the first month's rent on this narrow little establishment. Shelves lined one wall, displaying bonnets on little stands. The glass-topped counter behind which she stood had been an extravagance, but was an absolute necessity to display the painted fans, lacy gloves and embroidered slippers also made by her sisters-in-law.

After an hour, she slumped on to the stool. Perhaps she should rearrange the window again? What on earth was she to tell Petra and Marguerite? They would be so disappointed when she returned home in two days' time with nothing to show for their efforts.

A shadow fell over the window display.

Carrie straightened and pinned a smile on her lips.

The shadow passed on. Her heart sank.

'I be back, missus.'

Jeb, their young ruddy-faced lad of all work at Westram Cottage, had brought her up to town the day before the shop opened. It was he who had built the shelves and carried in the counter she had purchased in a down-at-heel shop in the Seven Dials. He'd also helped her furnish the room she used as lodgings at the back of the shop, since it was too far for her to travel home to Kent each evening.

Marguerite had not been happy about this last arrangement, but had given in when Carrie agreed to come home to Kent with Jeb as her escort every Saturday night in order to attend church with them in the morning. They planned that she would return on Monday afternoons with new stock for the shop.

Not that they would be needing any new stock. They still had all the old stock left.

'Did you deliver all of the flyers to the addresses I gave you, Jeb?'

'Yes, mum.'

The flyers had been another costly idea they could ill afford, but she had to get the word out about their offerings somehow. An advertisement in the newspaper would have reached more people, but was horribly expensive.

Unfortunately, she had no way of knowing if the flyers had got into the right hands. Perhaps she should go and stand at the entrance to Hyde Park and hand them out herself to passers-by. Not just any passers-by, but ladies of quality with good fashion sense.

It might work.

She would go about five this afternoon. Fortunately, she was still largely unknown to society as she had not been introduced to very many people of the *ton* before her hasty marriage to Jonathan. In addition, their wedding had been a tiny family affair, because her father had been at death's door. Why Jonathan had even singled her out... She squashed the thought and the accompanying pang.

Face it, Carrie. He'd chosen her because he'd been looking for a way out of his money troubles. Somehow Father must have learned of this circumstance and, worried about her future once he passed away, had made Jonathan an offer he couldn't refuse. Carrie had known none of this when she'd arrived in London before the Season began. Jonathan had been pointed out to her by her aunt when she went on her first carriage ride in London. He'd bowed to her and she'd agreed with her aunt that he really was a most handsome gentleman. The next day he'd arrived at her door on a morning call and a few days later had proposed.

Everyone had said it was love at first sight. She'd been a complete fool to believe such nonsense.

In hindsight, it was as plain as the nose on her very plain face—he'd only married her to get himself out of debt. If she had known, she would never have agreed. Not even to please her dying father, who had been thrilled to see his daughter become one of the nobs. She certainly hadn't expected her bridegroom to take to his heels the morning after the ceremony. No doubt he couldn't stand the thought of living with his plain, middle-class, gruff wife. That had hurt dreadfully. Worse yet, he'd not even done her the courtesy of coming to her bed on their wedding night.

That particular rejection had hurt to the core of her soul. And still did, when she listened to her sisters-in-law giggle about the joys of the marriage bed during the long winter evenings at Westram Cottage when they'd been working on fabricating the hats and bonnets they now hoped to sell. Not that she'd ever told them the truth about her wedding night.

'Put what is left on the counter, Jeb, please. It is time for you to return to the cottage. I am sure the other ladies have all manner of things for you to do.'

Jeb scratched at his unshaven chin. The poor fellow had been required to bed down with the horse in a stables some distance from the shop, since there was no place for him to rest his head here.

'Are you sure, mum? I don't like leaving you here alone. A bed of iniquity Lunnon is. Me ma said so.'

'I will be perfectly fine. The locks you have added to the doors and the bars on the windows will keep me quite safe. And Mr Thrumby's man is more than a match for any intruder.' Mr Thrumby's man guarded the back entrance at night.

Jeb's expression remained doubtful, but she kept hers firm and unyielding.

'As you wish, Mrs Greystoke.' His formal use of her married name was his way of administering an admonition. But it was worse than that. It was a lie. She never really had been Mrs Greystoke. Not properly. Little did anyone know the use of her married name made her resentment of her husband burn like acid.

She forced her mind back to more mundane topics. 'I will see you back here on Saturday afternoon.'

He touched his forelock and left.

Now she really was on her own.

She slid open the top drawer of the counter, removed three of the lacy embroidered handkerchiefs and put them in the front window. Handkerchiefs were not as expensive as bonnets. A cheaper purchase might lure someone in. She shifted the bonnet to present a more intriguing angle and returned to her stool.

One sale. Then she would be sure she was on the right path.

Lord Avery Gilmore, younger son of the Duke of Belmane, stepped out into the street and blinked in the light of mid-morning. The porter of the gaming hell where he'd spent the last many hours slammed the door behind him. Avery grinned. His night had been reasonably successful. His pockets were plump enough to ensure not only that there would be food on his sister's table for a few more days, there would plenty left over for coal for his fireplace and a bottle of really fine brandy.

He never came home empty handed. After his father had thrown him out of the family for refusing to marry the woman Papa had chosen, he'd had years of living by his wits on several continents to hone his skills at the gambling tables. Last night and into this morning had been more successful than usual. Perhaps Lady Luck had turned her smile his way.

Which was a good thing. All these years of living abroad, he'd become adept at supporting himself, but having learned of his sister's struggles from his older brother, he now felt financially responsible her, too. At least until her husband could earn enough to support his family as a barrister, which would hopefully be soon, since he had recently been called to the bar and accepted for a pupillage in chambers.

Finally, after last night, Avery could truthfully tell Laura not to worry about money, at least for a while.

Blithely, he strode for his lodgings, but halted at the sight of a very pretty bonnet in a window polished to a mirror-like shine. A cleanliness one didn't often find in the backstreets leading off Bond Street. He crossed the street to take a closer look, avoiding the dollops of horse manure and the vagabond lounging in a doorway. Fellows like that would cut your purse in the blink of an eye if you weren't careful.

Avery knew all about cutpurses and their ilk. The owner of the Ragged Staff, the establishment he'd just left, had accused him of being a fraudster, because he had so easily seen through the house's ploy to trick him out of his winnings. For a moment, it had looked as if he might have to fight his way out of the hell, but for the interference of some of the other customers, who were only too happy to see someone win for a change.

Pigeons for the plucking they might be, green as grass, too, but *they* were also gentlemen.

Avery wavered a little on his feet as he stared at the bonnet displayed in the window. He shook his head to clear it. Too much cheap brandy, though he was nowhere close to foxed. His unsteadiness was more from lack of sleep, though he had no doubt he would have the devil of a headache later. He squinted at the hat. The violets and primroses decorating the crown were not real, as he'd thought at first, but silk. He didn't want the hat, but he did want a posy to offer to Mrs Luttrell later. The poor little pet pined for such marks of attention. Would silk flowers raise her spirits?

The confection blurred. Dash it. He was a little more in the bag than he had thought. He really needed to go home to bed. But he also needed a gift…

Silk flowers lasted longer.

No doubt they would also cost a great deal more. Still, Mimi Luttrell would be more compliant with such a mark of attention. And for once he had blunt in his pocket.

He entered the narrow shop.

A tall, remarkably tall, young woman rose to her feet behind the counter. Her face was not pretty exactly, but handsome, with fine grey eyes and a mouth that begged to be kissed even as she frowned. Why was she frowning?

Gad, she really was tall. Not quite his height, but close to it.

'Good day, sir,' she said, her voice pleasantly deep. 'How may I be of service?'

He stared at her in surprise. Outwardly, she looked like a shop girl in her dun-coloured gown and prim cap, but she sounded like a lady, for all that there was a trace of the north in her accent.

Plush full lips pursed in disapproval. 'Is something wrong?'

He dragged his gaze from her mouth to her face. Brought his mind back to the task at hand. He gave her his most charming smile. 'Nothing wrong at all. I simply had not expected to find such a lovely lady brightening my morning.'

The frown reappeared. 'It is after midday, sir, and this is a ladies' millinery shop. Perhaps you mistake where you are?'

He swayed on his feet, surprised by her lack of response to his smile. He had smiled, he was sure of it. 'I beg your pardon, but I certainly do know where I am. Your shop has a remarkable array of very fine bonnets.' That compliment ought to cheer her up. 'And you, I notice, have remarkably beautiful eyes.'

Astonishment filled her face. 'Sir—'

Clearly, he was not up to snuff this morning, or else the lady was not of a flirtatious bent. 'How much for the violets, madam?'

The floor shifted uneasily beneath his feet and he propped a hip against the counter.

Warily she backed up, her expression puzzled. 'Violets?'

'Yes, violets. In the window.'

'There are no— Oh, you mean the ones on the bonnet. They are not for sale.'

Everything was for sale for the right price. 'I'll give you sixpence.'

Her eyes widened. A hint of desperation lurked in

their depths. Grey depths. Grey depths, encircled by a smoky line around the edge.

He waited for her acceptance.

She shook her head. 'I am afraid it would ruin the look of the bonnet.'

He blinked. Had she really turned him down? Well, there was a surprise.

'You can soon make a new trimming.' He waved at the other bonnets. 'Put one of those in the window in the meantime.' He peered at one festooned with rosebuds. 'This is just as pretty as the one in the window.' A wave of dizziness hit him and he rested one hand on the counter for support, hoping she wouldn't notice.

A hand sporting a wedding ring flattened on the counter as if to steady it against his weight. He felt a surge of disappointment at the sight of that ring. Really? No. He was just disappointed that she wouldn't sell him the posy.

'All right. I'll give you a shilling.'

Now who was desperate? And why? He could just as easily buy a posy from a flower girl. There was one on every corner. Except that something told him that this silk posy would be received with a great deal more pleasure. And he never ignored his well-honed instincts of a veteran gambler. Yes, he relied on his skill and never played foolish games of chance, but there was also that certain something that told him when to bet high and when to hold back. And right now, it had a feeling about those flowers.

Another frown shot his way. 'I will not take advantage of a man obviously in his cups. There are plenty of fresh violets for sale on the street at this time of year.' She made a shooing gesture with her arms.

Why the devil was she being so intractable? 'Fresh?' he scoffed. 'I'll be lucky if they last until this afternoon.' He leaned forward, giving her his best friendly smile. 'I need to make a good impression. Those flowers are better than real ones.'

She eyed him askance. 'If you want to make a good impression, you will need to sober up first, I should think.'

'Rather direct and to the point for a shop girl, aren't you?'

She coloured faintly. 'If there is nothing else...'

'I am not leaving until you sell me those flowers.'

'Then you must buy the bonnet.'

Aha! So that was the game she was playing. 'I can't imagine you get many customers stuck away here on this side street. Isn't it better to have a shilling in your hand than no sale at all?'

She closed her eyes briefly. He felt uncomfortable as desperation won out over what had been a very ethical response to his demand. Sadly, he'd been right. Everything did have a price.

'Very well. I will sell you the violets.' She came around the counter. He moved back to allow her to pass in the narrow confines of the shop. Once more he was struck by her height and now got a look at what could only be described as a sumptuous figure. As she leaned over to remove the hat from the window, he ogled the swell of her derrière, its curves beautifully outlined by the dark fabric of her narrow skirts. Surprisingly, for all the fabric's drab colour, it was of the finest quality of cotton.

Which was strange for a shop girl.

He squeezed back against the shelves as she returned to the counter with her prize.

She took down another bonnet to place in the window, not the one he had suggested, he noted, but a summer hat with gauzy yellow ribbons and a cluster of cherries adorning the upturned brim.

Once she was satisfied, she returned and removed the violets from the bonnet and wrapped them in tissue paper. 'I hope your lady is suitably impressed.' She held out her hand. 'One shilling, please.'

The dryness in her voice struck him on the raw. Clearly, she thought the gift paltry. He glanced down at the wares on display in the glass case. 'How much is that handkerchief? The one embroidered with violets.'

'Thruppence.' She smiled for the first time since he had walked into the shop. It changed her whole face from plain to lovely. Not pretty, exactly. But...lovely. He blinked.

She pulled the drawer towards her, withdrew the delicate square from the case and laid it on the counter.

Another wave of exhaustion washed through him. He forced his spine straight. Besides, he'd already spent quite enough. Silk violets for a shilling? He must be more foxed than he'd thought.

'I'll take it, Mrs...'

Again, a wash of colour rose up her face. 'Greystoke.'

Greystoke. The name sounded familiar. Propped against the counter, he watched her fumble in the drawer. She pulled out a calling card which she wrapped inside the tissue paper along with the handkerchief. 'In case you should know of anyone who might be interested in one of our bonnets. They are of the finest workmanship. Perhaps your wife...' She smiled encouragingly.

Once more he found himself staring at her in a be-mused fashion. 'I am not married.'

She glanced at the neatly wrapped package. 'I see.'

'Those are for a special lady of my acquaintance.' Hell, why had he felt the need to say such a thing? The recipient of his purchases was none of her business. 'A very special lady.'

'Of course.' Her voice held not a scrap of interest. She tied the package with a ribbon.

He bowed and hand over his calling card. 'It has been a pleasure doing business with you, Mrs Greystoke.'

Out in the street he glanced through the window to see Mrs Greystoke rearranging her display of handker-chiefs and watching him from the corner of her eye. Making sure he departed post-haste, no doubt.

He clapped his hat on his head and marched off.

A spray of silk violets for a shilling. He hoped like hell Mimi Luttrell appreciated the sacrifice.

But he would tell her about the bonnets. Because Mrs Greystoke was right. Even in his inebriated state, he could tell they were of the finest quality.

Whatever hopes Carrie had harboured that Lord Av-ery's purchase would result in a swarm of ladies inter-ested in hats had died over the following two days. He hadn't bought a hat, he'd merely pillaged its decoration. The hat, *sans* violets, now resided on the highest shelf, there to languish until her return to Kent.

There it remained, a constant reminder of his whee-dling smile and beautiful brown eyes rimmed with the longest eyelashes she had ever seen. Disastrously beauti-ful brown eyes with gold flecks scattered like sunbeams across them. Not to mention how he towered over her, which so few men did. Dash it all, she did not want to think about Lord Avery, the younger son of a duke, she'd realised later, having properly read his calling card. A wealthy young man she should have tried to convince to buy a dozen embroidered handkerchiefs instead getting flustered and wrapping up one. She'd made a proper mull of it, as her father would have said.

The idea of returning to the ladies at Westram with nothing but the grand sum of one shilling and thruppence and a ruined bonnet had given her nightmares. Her handbills had not brought in a single customer and she dared not use any of these meagre funds to print more. All in all, the shop in which she had placed such high hopes was a failure.

They would be able to afford one more week's rent from what little funds they had saved over the winter before she had to close the doors. It was so frustrating. If the ladies of the *ton* saw these bonnets, their original design, their craftsmanship, she had no doubt they would snap them up. But how was she to accomplish it?

For the third time that morning she rearranged the items beneath the glass counter top, putting lacy gloves beside the chicken-skin fan Marguerite had painted with a pastoral scene. The bell above the door tinkled. She straightened. Her jaw dropped. 'Lord Avery?'

He bowed. 'Mrs Greystoke.'

She glanced behind him. There was no sign of the very special lady he had mentioned. 'How may I help you?'

'I have need of another of your fripperies.' He scanned the hats.

Blankly she stared at him. 'This is a millinery shop, my lord. You bought the one and only violet nosegay in the shop and I have no intention of demolishing any more of my stock for a whim. However, I would be more than pleased to sell you a hat in its entirety. What you do with it afterwards would be your prerogative.'

Oh, dear, that was not the way to treat a customer. Especially the younger son of a duke. But really!

'It is hardly demolished.' He gave her that heart-stopping crooked smile that had flustered her the first time he'd gazed at her. He looked even more handsome this morning than he had the other day. His lovely brown eyes were clear and bright, his jacket unrumpled, his dark brown hair carefully ordered. And that smile… It was doing devastating things to her insides. 'And besides,' he continued, 'a hat is far too personal item for a gentleman to purchase. In my experience, a lady needs to try on several bonnets before she can decide on one. Do you let your husband buy your hats?'

'My husband is dead.' She clamped her jaw shut. Now why had she told him that? And in such a blunt manner, too. He might think she was interested in him and before she knew it he'd be taking advantage. That was the sort of thing men did. It had been drummed into her at Mrs Thacker's Academy for the Daughters of Gentlemen.

His expression changed to one of sympathy. 'I am sorry.'

Why should he be sorry? She meant nothing to him. But he was right about him buying his lady a hat. Most women did prefer to choose their own. There was something very intimate about the purchase of a hat and it was decidedly perspicacious of him to realise that particular fact. Clearly the man knew women.

A suggestion was in order. She gave him a tight little smile, wishing she knew how to be a little more charming. 'Perhaps you could bring her with you and let her choose.'

He gave a low chuckle, a deep rich sound that seemed to stir things up low in her belly. 'Perhaps one day. In the meantime...'

'Well, I doubt any lady would be pleased to receive the same gift, even if it is in a different colour and form.'

His brow clouded. 'No. You are right.'

'What about a pair of gloves?' She brought out a pair and set them on the counter.

'Too practical.'

'An embroidered pair of slippers.' She laid several before him.

'Too mundane.'

'Not these. The workmanship is the finest you will see anywhere.'

He shook his head. 'I would prefer something more...'

'Romantic?' She smiled sweetly.

'Unique.'

'What about a fan?' She spread two hand-painted silk fans, showing off the delicate paintings, one of a ballroom scene and the other of the countryside.

He picked one up, opening and closing it and inspecting the painted sticks. 'Very nice. Are they imported from the East?'

'No, my sister-in-law makes them.'

'She is a talented woman.'

Carrie smiled. She loved to hear her sisters-in-law complimented. She'd been an only child and the idea of having sisters thrilled her.

He stood there, staring at her mouth as if he had never seen a woman smile before. Her body flushed warm. Goodness, but the man was a flirt.

'Your special lady will love using it,' she said firmly. 'It is sure to be admired by all her acquaintances.'

He gave her a sharp look. 'And put me in her good graces?'

She nodded encouragingly. 'Of course.'

'How much?'

'Half a crown.'

His lips thinned. 'That's a little steep, don't you think?'

'Is the lady not worth it, my lord?' She flicked it open. 'Nevertheless, because you are a repeat customer, I am willing to sell it to you for two shillings.' That was sixpence more than the price she and the others had agreed upon, but the man's need seemed urgent. And her own needs were pressing in.

'Very well. Two shillings it is. Though I feel I am getting the worst of this bargain.'

It was not good for a customer to feel that way. 'You will not see another fan like this one anywhere, I assure you.'

'I see another right there.' He pointed to a third fan.

She spread it open. On this one, the leaf was a pale blue silk and showed a scene of the ocean at sunset. 'It is not at all the same.'

He grinned. 'You have me there, Mrs Greystoke. Very well, I will take this fan for two shillings.'

He dug out his money pouch. 'I hope you will recommend my shop to your lady,' she said as calmly as possible despite the rapid beating of her heart. Was it him making it beat so fast? Or merely the idea of finally making a sale? She wrapped the fan in tissue. 'When she is next in need of a hat.'

'I most certainly will. Indeed, I will mention your shop to every one of my acquaintances.'

He bowed and left with the little package tucked under his arm.

Carrie could not help admiring his lithe male figure as he disappeared through her shop door. He was so masculine. Despite his elegant tailoring, he looked athletic and fit. He'd no doubt be an excellent lover. She blushed at the unbidden thought. It was his flirting that had made such a wicked thought about a man she scarcely knew occur to her.

She was a woman, wasn't she? And her thoughts were her own. As long as they remained merely thoughts, she was doing nobody any harm.

What would it be like to have such a handsome gentleman paying attention to one?

Lord Avery would no doubt be a master of the art of flirtation. And she had never been the object of a gentleman's attentions. Not even her husband's.

A sigh escaped her. She was such a fool. No doubt Lord Avery would never even think of her again, let alone mention her little shop to anyone.

She looked in the tin cash box. The grand sum of three shillings and thruppence stared back at her.

The Westram ladies were going to be so disappointed.

Chapter Two

'What do you think?' Mimi Luttrell batted her lashes at Avery, her pale blue eyes soulful, her lips pouting provocatively.

He stifled the urge to yawn. Mimi would run a mile if he so much as hinted at anything sensual between them. She had agreed to this little outing in his company because her husband preferred the hunting field to escorting her to shops and balls. She wanted to feel appreciated, that was all. And perhaps wake her errant husband up to the fact that she was a desirable woman.

It was strange how differently the English husband regarded the position of cicisbeo to those on the Continent. In Italy a man would see it as a compliment that his wife garnered the attention of a young attractive gentleman. He would even participate in funding said gentleman, provided the *affaire* was conducted according to the rules. In England, such financial arrangements were despised by noblemen who liked to guard their wives, pulling up their drawbridges as if they were castles.

It had certainly worked that way with Lady Passmore, the first lady whom Avery had endeavoured to charm on his recent return from the Continent. Her neglectful husband had hot-footed it all the way back from Scotland to stake his claim on his wife and hadn't been far from her side ever since.

To Avery's surprise, the whole thing had also been financially rewarding, both in terms of her eternal gratitude expressed in her effusive thank-you note accompanied by a parting memento he'd sold for a goodly sum and with the commissions from the merchants where he had taken her to shop, the latter being the same sort of arrangement he had entered into in Italy where he'd been living until recently.

There, in Venice, he'd fallen into the role of cicisbeo quite by chance, having at first been attracted to the lady in question, only to discover there were financial benefits to be reaped from what could only be described as a platonic relationship, and all with the approval of the lady's husband.

Here in London, he was walking a much finer line between husband and wife, but Lady Passmore had been so delighted with the results of her innocent flirtation with Avery that she'd advised Mimi to contact him about a similar 'arrangement' to see if it worked on her dilettante husband, too.

And he was happy to oblige, as long as Mimi shopped in the places he recommended and did not expect him to come to her bed, since socially that would put him beyond the pale.

'I prefer the blue.' He'd picked out the fabric because he had known that it suited her perfectly.

Mimi frowned at herself draped in the material in the looking glass. 'Why?'

He gazed at her silently.

She glanced over at him and gave a trill of laughter. 'Really, Ave, darling. Please explain.' Again, she fluttered her lashes.

Unfortunately, Mimi's girlish tricks were a little too cloying for his taste. He much preferred the stern looks he encountered in a certain millinery shop. And the very rare smile he was able to coax from its owner.

Madame Grace, the dressmaker, pursed her lips as if trying to hold back words.

Avery had no trouble interpreting that look of disapproval. Madame Grace knew that this lady was married to someone else. The dressmaker likely thought he was a libertine, if not something worse, but that was because she did not understand that his goal was to bring the lady's errant husband home to her side, not drive a wedge between the couple. If Mimi's husband did not show up in a day or two, the man didn't deserve his wife. But he would since he did not yet have his heir and his spare. He certainly would not want another man poaching on his turf, at least until that duty was completed. And knowing the minds of men, it would be a long time before her husband strayed again.

While Madame Grace might pout about giving him his cut of what Mimi spent in her shop, she knew where her best interests lay. Why should he not be paid for the extra business he brought her way?

Not that these arrangements brought him a huge income. They merely helped augment his winnings at the table.

Avery leaned back in his chair in the fitting room at the back of Grace's shop and smiled lazily at the woman staring at her image. 'Because that blue shade brings out the colour of your eyes, my dear, and the lustre of your

skin. The rose colour you have there does not complement, rather it shouts your best features down.'

Her lips formed an O of surprise. Again, she peered
into the mirror and turned this way and that. 'How clever
you are, Ave.' She turned to the dressmaker. 'Let me see
the first one again?'

Madame Grace swathed her in the pale blue fabric,
pleating it artfully so it displayed well.

Mimi nodded slowly. 'I see what you mean. I'll take
it.'

Behind her, the dressmaker heaved a sigh of relief
and Avery knew exactly how she felt. Sometimes ladies
spent hours looking in the mirror and bought nothing.
But Madame Grace should know better than to worry
about one of Avery's ladies. They never left her establishment without placing an order.

Oddly, he used to enjoy accompanying a woman
shopping, but more recently it had simply become a
chore. He gave Mimi a broad grin of approval. 'Where
do you want to go next, Puss? Slippers?'

Ladies loved their shoes and the cobbler made a
healthy profit that he was more than happy to share
with Avery.

Mimi stroked the pale blue fabric. 'Which bonnet
would I wear with this?'

He stilled. An array of exquisite bonnets popped into
his mind. But he did not have an arrangement with Mrs
Greystoke. Indeed, he'd been doing his best to ignore the
fact that he had ever met the woman, because he found
her far too intriguing. A distraction. Yet, despite his best
efforts, he kept thinking about her smile.

Why hadn't he offered her the same arrangement he

had with other merchants? Was he concerned about what she would think about him? Why would he even care?

'Ave?'

Mimi's peevish tone brought him back from the recollection of a tall stern-faced woman to the dressmaker's shop. He gritted his teeth. He hated it when Mimi called him Ave. It was presumptuous and demeaning, but she was his sister's bread and butter and as such her irritating little foibles had to be tolerated.

'Yes, Sweetling?'

'I don't have a bonnet that will go with this fabric.' She touched the rose fabric, now discarded on the counter. 'I do have one with pink ribbons.'

The lady did love pink. He recalled that particular hat with an inner shudder. It was hideous. Not in the first stare of fashion either. 'You wish to drive out in a brand new carriage dress wearing a bonnet you must have worn at least five times?'

Mimi winced. 'You think people would notice?'

'Other ladies would certainly notice. The gentlemen would not give a fig, I suppose.'

She grimaced. 'But the ladies will mention it to the gentlemen and they will rib George about not providing for his wife. I won't have them belittling George.'

Mimi was really fond of her husband in the strange way of the *ton*.

'A bonnet it is then,' he said. 'I know just the place.' He winced inwardly. He really was going to do this, then? Take her to visit Mrs Greystoke? Where he wouldn't make a penny in commission. He must have porridge for brains. Except he wasn't thinking with his brain if the surge of warmth in his veins at the thought of seeing her again was anything to go by. 'Afterwards,

we will see new half-boots to complete the ensemble.'
And put a few coins in his purse.

Mimi put her arm through his. 'Perfect.'

Trailed by Mimi's maid, they strolled down Bond
Street, looking in shop windows until they passed a milliner's shop. Mimi pointed at a jaunty hat with a huge
feather. 'What do you think of that one?'

'It really isn't you.'

'It is all the crack. It might look better on.'

'We can come back if we don't find anything else.'

For a moment, he thought she would refuse, but she
shrugged. 'Very well.'

When he turned off Bond Street, she frowned. 'Really, Avery? Where are we going?'

'Not far. This shop has the best hats for really decent
prices and if you purchase one, you won't see another
hat like it anywhere.'

Her face lit up.

Finding something unique but not outrageously priced
was always the trick. There was nothing worse than ar-
riving at a ball or a drum and discovering another lady in
the exact same gown or riding Rotten Row and meeting
a lady wearing the same carriage dress or hat.

Ladies set great store by such things. Whereas most
men were happy wearing black coats and buff pantaloons with the occasional idiosyncrasy of a fanciful
waistcoat.

He opened the door to Mrs Greystone's establishment
and ushered Mimi in.

As far as he could tell not a single bonnet had been
sold since his last visit two days ago.

'Good morning,' she said, eyeing him askance.

'Good morning,' Mimi said.

A strange look passed across Mrs Greystoke's face as she took in his companion. An expression she quickly masked with a bright smile.

'This is Mrs Luttrell,' Lord Avery said.

Mrs Greystoke dipped a curtsy. 'How may I be of service, madam.'

'I need a hat.'

Amusement danced in Mrs Greystoke's dove-grey eyes. 'Then you have come to the right place.'

Avery felt a surge of gladness that he had brought Mimi here. He'd recognised the shadows in Mrs Greystoke's eyes the last time he was here. Desperation. He just hadn't wanted to acknowledge he didn't like it. He had enough responsibilities as it was.

Nevertheless, the idea that she was desperate had weighed on his shoulders. And he was glad he had the means to do something about it, even if it did leave him a bit short of funds.

Mimi pulled forth the scrap of blue fabric Madame Grace had cut off the bolt. 'This is the fabric for a new carriage dress. What do you suggest?'

Avery wedged himself in a corner by the counter and let the two women have at it. His part would come later, when a decision was to be made. In the meantime, he could not help but compare the two women. Mimi, a sweet English rose at first glance, but with all the experience of a married woman, and Mrs Greystoke, not exactly pretty, but striking and strangely innocent.

Greystoke. Now why did he keep thinking that name sounded familiar?

Lord Avery's special lady was older than Carrie had expected and apparently a widow to boot, but pretty as a picture, nonetheless. The sort of woman she would have expected to attract him, if she was honest. Carrie helped the lady remove her hat and brought down three bonnets that she thought would suit the lady's face and complement the fabric.

A maid eased in through the door. Mrs Luttrell frowned. 'Boggs, I am sorry, but you need to wait outside. There really isn't room in here for another person.'

The maid, who was all of eighteen, looked worried. 'Yes, mum.' Her accent came from the north. She started to back out.

The sound of someone from her home county gave Carrie an odd feeling in her stomach. A bit of the same feeling of homesickness she'd experienced when she'd first arrived in London to go to school at around the same age as the maid. She'd been sent to a young ladies' academy to acquire a bit of polish, as her father put it.

'Your maid can wait in the back room,' Carrie said. 'This is not the best of streets for a young girl to linger on.'

'Thank you, mum,' the maid said with a look of relief.

Mrs Luttrell gave Carrie a sharp look. 'That is very kind of you, Mrs Greystoke. I can certainly vouch for Boggs's honesty.'

'Indeed.' Carrie smiled kindly at the girl. 'Perhaps you could make us all a cup of tea while you are waiting.'

The girl beamed. 'That I can, mum.' She glanced at her mistress. 'That is, if you agree, madam.'

'It is a wonderful idea.' Mrs Luttrell picked up a bonnet Carrie hadn't suggested. 'What about this one?'

Carrie tried not to frown at the choice. 'If you wish to try it on, you may, but I think you will find it hides your face and, with a pretty face like yours it would be a shame.'

'Do you think so?' She turned to Lord Avery. 'What do you think, Ave?'

He gave her an indulgent smile and for a moment Carrie wondered what it would be like to have a man smile at her in that warm lazy way.

'I think Mrs Greystoke knows what she is about, Pet,' he said. 'Trust in her judgement.'

Mrs Luttrell put the bonnet aside and picked up one of Carrie's suggestions. 'May I try this one first.'

Carrie helped her put it on. She tied a neat bow and directed Mrs Luttrell's attention to the looking glass.

Mrs Luttrell viewed herself from various angles with pursed lips.

Carrie held her breath. This was it. This was her chance to get this shop found by ladies of the *beau monde*. Oh, she could tell that Mrs Luttrell was not a diamond of the first water, or a member of any of the first families of the *ton*, but she wore her clothes well and other ladies would admire her, if she wore the right hat.

After a couple of minutes, Mrs Luttrell turned to Lord Avery. 'What do you think, Ave.'

'I think you should try them all, before making up your mind. I like that one very much, but another might suit better.'

How very odd. Most men hated shopping.

So the lady tried on all three. When she reached the last one, Lord Avery straightened. 'I like them all,' he said. 'The last two looked equally good on you, Mimi. Whichever one you pick you cannot go wrong.'

Carrie did not agree with him. She preferred the one Mrs Luttrell had chosen to put on last. 'The one you have on now suits you particularly well,' she said, not wishing to argue with his lordship, but wanting the lady to make the right choice.

Lord Avery picked up his cup and sipped at his tea. He'd put a great deal of sugar in it, Carrie had noticed.

Mrs Luttrell turned this way and that and then also took a sip of tea. 'I am sure I cannot decide between this one and that one.' She pointed to the first one she had tried on.

'Take them both,' Lord Avery suggested.

Carrie stared at him. Surely, he was jesting?

Mrs Luttrell frowned.

Dash it! She was going to refuse them both now. 'Truly, the one you have on suits you best, madam. It is perfect for this time of year. I am sure you will be doing a great deal of driving out now the weather is changing for the better.'

'You are right,' the lady said.

Carrie breathed a sigh of relief.

'But if I am doing a great deal of driving out...' she turned towards Lord Avery and batted her lashes '...then I *will* need more than one bonnet.'

Lord Avery nodded. 'I should say so.'

'Then I will take them both.'

Carrie snapped her mouth shut. Showing her surprise was not the way to do business. 'Let me wrap them for you, while you finish your tea.'

In short order, she had both bonnets wrapped in tissue paper and in their boxes, while Mrs Luttrell drank her tea and chatted with her companion.

Carrie waited for them to finish their conversation. 'Where would you like me to send the bill, Mrs Luttrell?'

She hated the idea that she was not to be paid right

away for the purchase, but it was the way the *beau monde* did their business. Hopefully, Lord Avery could afford such extravagance.

'Send it to my husband,' Mrs Luttrell said and handed over her card.

Shocked, Carrie could only stare at her for a second or two.

Mrs Luttrell didn't seem to notice her surprise, but Lord Avery had a naughty twinkle in his eye. The wretch. He knew Carrie was shocked all the way to her toes. Her back had gone stiff and her smile had frozen solid on her lips.

Glancing at the address, she put it in a drawer for safe keeping. As soon as they were gone she would write up the bill and have it sent round to Carlin Place. She could only hope that Mr Luttrell approved of his wife's purchases while in the company of another man.

More to the point, what did that make Lord Avery? Her lover? How very shocking. And disappointing…

'Oh, look, Ave, darling, there is another of those pretty fans. It is similar to the one you bought for me.'

'Each one is unique,' Carrie said, aware her voice was terser than she would have liked. Was she really such a prude? It wouldn't be the first time she had heard of a man taking an interest in another man's wife. She had just thought it happened behind closed doors, not flaunted in the faces of respectable people.

'I have received a great many compliments on it, you know.' Mrs Luttrell stared down into the cabinet. 'Now I can tell everyone who asks where it was bought.' She gave Carrie a sharp look. 'As long as there are no more exactly the same as mine.'

'I will guarantee there is not, Mrs Luttrell,' Carrie said. 'Or I will gladly refund your money.'

The woman nodded in approval. 'Boggs,' she called out.

The maid materialised from behind the curtain. 'Yes, mum.'

'Pick up the boxes. We are leaving.'

'It is all right, Mimi, dearest,' Lord Avery said. 'They are two bulky for Boggs. I'll carry them.' He bowed to Carrie. 'Thank you, Mrs Greystoke. I wish you good day.'

Mrs Luttrell waved a hand. 'Yes. Thank you. You can be sure I shall let everyone know where I purchased my hats.' She frowned. 'Though it would be better if you had a more fashionable address.'

They left the shop, making it feel suddenly very empty. Carrie herself felt empty. Surely it was nothing to do with the knowledge she'd gained about Lord Avery? It must be to do with the excitement she'd experienced in making her first real sale.

Now she had good news to take home. It was such a relief.

'How did we do?' Petra's voice rose to a squeak.

Carrie removed her bonnet and gloves in the hall. It must be so hard for the other two waiting at home, wondering if all their hard work had been appreciated. 'Not too badly for our first week.' Much to Carrie's astonishment. 'We have covered next week's rent with a little left over for supplies.'

It was almost four in the afternoon, her back ached from the long drive home and yet she could not help feeling proud.

Marguerite popped her head around the drawing room door. 'I thought I heard the cart. Petra, for heaven's sake let her pass. Carrie, come and sit down and have a cup of tea. You must be worn to the bone.'

She was, but she was also exhilarated by their success.

She hung up her spencer, then joined her sisters-in-law in the drawing room. She sank into the most comfortable chair in the room beside the hearth. Bless them, they had saved it for her. She loved having sisters.

Petra brought her a cup of tea and somehow managed to hold back her questions until Carrie had taken a sip.

'Well?' Petra exploded.

'We sold two bonnets, a fan, a handkerchief and a posy.

Petra frowned. 'Only two bonnets.'

'Two bonnets are better than none,' Marguerite said, in prosaic tones. Clearly, she was also disappointed. Some of Carrie's excitement dissipated.

She forced herself to sound cheerful. 'I am sure the lady who purchased them will tell her friends and then we will have trouble keeping up with the demand.'

'It is a wonderful start,' Petra said, clearly trying to hide her doubts. She gazed at the tea tray. 'Are those shortbread biscuits, Marguerite. Isn't that a bit extravagant?'

Her older sister looked embarrassed. 'I only made a few. We need a treat now and then. And see, I was right. We have good news to celebrate.'

Petra pointed to the hat box. 'What is in there.'

'A hat. I removed the decoration for a gentleman who wanted it for a posy.'

'A posy? How very odd,' Petra said, giving her a sharp look.

Carrie felt the heat rise to her cheeks. Why would

talking about Lord Avery make her blush? 'I thought so, too. Actually, I think he was intoxicated.' She'd seen her father and uncle in their cups often enough to recognise when a man was more than a trifle warm. She put up a hand at their shocked expression. 'He was never impolite, simply a little slurred in his speech.' As well as wavering on his feet. 'He said he wanted it for a special lady. At that point, I had sold nothing. Better to sell a bit of trim than nothing at all.'

'Very wise, I should say,' Marguerite said. She opened the box and drew out the hat. 'It is easy enough to replace the...' She raised an eyebrow in question.

'Violets,' Carrie said. Violets for a special lady indeed. Mrs Luttrell was a very pretty woman. Dainty and delicate, not unlike Carrie's sisters-in-law. The sort of woman Carrie had always envied. And while Carrie could not approve of Mrs Luttrell's closeness with Lord Avery, she could certainly understand why she would attract a handsome lord. Perhaps it was difficult for a woman to ignore such a charming man's attentions and hard for him to ignore such a pretty lady if she was lonely.

Carrie, being plain and gruff and unattractive, would never catch the eye of a man like Lord Avery. She would be far better to focus her thoughts on making a go of this venture instead of indulging in stupid flights of fancy about a handsome gentleman. Such dreams would only lead to further humiliation.

'Which hats did you sell?' Petra asked.

'The chip straw and the blue shako,' Carrie said. 'Unfortunately, the shop is a little bit further from Bond Street than I realised. There is not much passing traffic. It is going to take a while to build our clientele.'

'But you think it will build?' Petra asked.

'I hope so.'

The ladies fell silent, thinking about the consequences of failure, no doubt.

'What we need is something really different,' Carrie said, thinking about the lovely Mrs Luttrell again and how she'd seized upon the idea that no one would ever carry the same fan as the one Lord Avery had given her.

'What sort of something?' Marguerite asked.

'Lots of places sell bonnets, though ours are unique and beautifully styled,' Carrie hastened to add. 'But we need an item ladies cannot purchase elsewhere.'

'I have no idea what you are talking about.' Marguerite looked thoroughly puzzled.

Petra looked intrigued.

'Perhaps something a little risqué,' Carrie said, her face immediately fiery.

'Risqué?' Marguerite pursed her lips in disapproval. 'We don't want to attract the wrong sort of customer.'

They already had. Carrie bit her tongue to stop the words from forming.

'Don't be prudish, Marguerite.' Petra said. 'We don't care who buys the hats, do we? If we can't make a go of this, we'll all be shipped back to London to live with Westram. And all he wants to do is marry us off. The thought of another marriage…' She shuddered.

Carrie frowned. She'd always thought Petra's reaction to marrying again quite odd when her first marriage had been so happy. Perhaps when one found true love, one could never face the prospect of another man.

Still, they had all agreed that none of them wanted to marry again.

So they needed to make a success of their shop. Carrie swallowed. 'I was thinking perhaps of something for the boudoir. Something feminine and alluring.' Something a gentleman like Lord Avery might want to buy for a special lady. 'Something a wife might buy to re-kindle her marriage?'

The other ladies' eyes widened.

'That sounds…wicked,' Marguerite said, looking worried. 'I am not sure Westram would approve.'

'He won't know unless someone tells him,' Petra said sharply.

Marguerite stiffened at the less-than-subtle implication that she would go to their brother and tell tales.

'Well, let us put our heads together and see what we can come up with,' Carrie said quickly. 'We will do nothing unless we all agree.'

'You know,' Petra said, turning to Marguerite, 'Carrie knows far more about running a shop than we do. We should follow her advice.'

'You are right,' Marguerite said. 'Carrie, you must do whatever you think is best to make the shop a success. We will help you all we can.'

Their vote of confidence made her heart swell with pride. 'It is a joint venture, ladies. Together we can do anything.'

They toasted each other with their teacups.

Leaning back, Carrie sipped at her tea. She had no doubt that, between them, they could come up with something unique that would appeal to the likes of Mrs Luttrell.

'How is the garden coming along?' she asked Petra. The cottage had both a kitchen garden at the back and a large front garden full of roses. Petra had agreed to take on the task of providing vegetables and herbs for their table. She actually liked grubbing around in the dirt.

'Really well,' Petra said. 'It is too bad we have so little ground. I could do so much more.'

'I don't think you would have time,' Marguerite said. 'You already work your fingers to the bone on the hats.'

Carrie handed Marguerite the cash box. 'I sent the bill for the bonnets to the lady's husband.'

Marguerite looked inside. 'You will need some of this for change. The rest can go towards our household bills.' She rose to her feet. 'It is time to start on cooking dinner. After that we will see what we can come up with to bring more custom to the shop.'

'I've been working on hats all day,' Petra said. 'I need some fresh air. I'll go and do a bit of weeding.'

It seemed wrong that these ladies who had grown up with every privilege should be required to work so hard now and all because her husband had led their husbands astray. Or at least she thought he must have. She could not think of any other reason they had left with him to join Wellington's army.

She was determined to do her share to make up for it. 'I will fix the hat,' Carrie said picking up the hat box. 'After all, it is my fault it is spoiled.'

'We have two more finished for you to take back with you,' Petra said. She frowned. 'And I'll make a couple of extra posies in case that gentleman should return.'

Carrie's tummy gave a funny little hop. It had been doing that every time she as much as thought of Lord Avery. 'I doubt if he will,' she said and followed Petra from the room.

Chapter Three

Avery opened the door for Lady Fontly to pass into the milliner's shop. It had been two weeks since his last visit. He had forced himself to stay away, though he had encouraged Mimi to recommend the shop if anyone should admire her new hat.

As he entered, he was taken aback by the changes.

Rose-filled vases graced every open space not occupied by a bonnet or a lacy cap. There were two women in the narrow space between the door and the counter, a lady and her maid, being helped by Mrs Greystoke, and there were giggles coming from behind the curtain leading to the shopkeeper's private quarters. Maids having cups of tea, he assumed.

He turned to his companion. 'I apologise, Elizabeth, I did not expect it to be this busy.'

Lady Fontly, green-eyed and auburn-haired, beamed. 'How clever of you, Avery. I heard whispers about this place, but was unable to discover its location.'

He kept his expression blank. Whispers? About Mrs Greystoke? 'Then it is my pleasure to bring you here.'

The customer at the counter turned at the sound of his voice.

'Lord Avery?' Mrs Baxter-Smythe's eyebrows shot up and Avery inwardly groaned. 'And Lady Fontly,' she said with a sly smile. 'How very…surprising to meet you *both* here.' The widow cast him an arch look and her innuendo was perfectly clear.

Mrs Baxter-Smythe had made more than one attempt to begin a flirtation with him, but she was a widow. Avery had no truck with widows. They usually had brothers or fathers or distant cousins, who would see their role as protectors of virtue. And no matter how merry the widow, they were unlikely to pass up the chance to marry off a single relative to the son of a duke.

Avery bowed. 'Likewise, I am sure, Mrs Baxter-Smythe.'

The widow turned her gaze on his companion. 'I understand Lord Fontly is out of town at the moment?'

Elizabeth's cheekbones coloured. 'He has gone to the races in Newmarket.' She sounded a little too defensive.

'How you must miss him,' Mrs Baxter-Smythe cooed. 'And you only recently married.'

'Lord Fontly has a horse entered in a race,' Avery put in cheerfully. 'Not something even a newly wed husband should miss.'

Elizabeth recovered her composure. 'And he recommended Lord Avery take me shopping, since it is something he hates to do.'

Avery gave her arm a little squeeze of approval. Elizabeth had been hurt by her husband's departure so soon after their marriage, so he had suggested that a new hat might be just the thing to make her feel better.

He became aware of a pair of grave grey eyes watching the interchange between him and the ladies. It was the sort of considering look one might get from a tutor who realised you were not going to live up to your potential. Her eyes held curiosity along with a dawning understanding.

What did she understand? That he served as an escort when a lady's husband was absent? Did she think it was more than that? Let her think what she wished. Everyone else did. And naturally his special ladies never discussed him with others. They were married, after all.

'It seems everyone has discovered this place,' Mrs Baxter-Smythe said. 'Does Mrs Greystoke not carry the most beautiful hats you have ever seen?'

'I have not yet had a chance to look.' Elizabeth glanced around. 'But I must say at first sight they appear to be most attractive.'

'Each and every one is stunning,' the widow said. 'And do ask her about the other unique items she has for sale.' She pinned her eyes on Avery. 'I am having an open house next Monday. Afternoon tea. I would love to see you there.' She moved her focus to Elizabeth. 'If you are free, I would love you to come also, Lady Fontly.' The afterthought was a deliberate snub.

Mrs Baxter-Smythe was a denizen of the *ton*. For Elizabeth not to accept would put her on the fringes of society. Flirting with him was one thing, but declining to attend one of Mrs Baxter-Smythe's at homes was quite another.'

'I shall be delighted to escort you,' Avery said, smiling at Elizabeth, who dipped a little curtsy. 'If Lord Fontly is not back in time.'

'Oh, but of course,' the widow said. 'Your husband is welcome also, should he be home, if he does not think it a terrible bore.' She gave them a sickly sweet smile, squeezed past him and Elizabeth and left the shop with her maid trailing behind her.

A young woman he recognised as the wife of a prominent banker appeared from behind the curtain. Her eyes were dancing and her cheeks were bright pink.

A shop assistant appeared right behind her with a tissue-wrapped package.

At the counter, Mrs Greystoke smiled calmly and wrote up a bill.

Avery frowned. Why on earth would anyone go behind a curtain to try on a hat?

Mrs Greystoke gave Elizabeth a cool smile. 'How may I help you, madam? Is there something you would like to try on?'

'Elizabeth, may I introduce Mrs Greystoke, the owner of this establishment. Lady Fontly is looking for a bonnet.'

Lizzie pursed her lips. 'I am looking for a something summery. Something to wear on a picnic.' The picnic she'd planned for her husband's return. Avery had suggested it as a way to engage the twit's attention. The man had to be an idiot if he left such a pretty wife at a loose end during the Season.

'What about this one?' Mrs Greystoke lifted down a becoming wide-brimmed straw bonnet trimmed with strawberry leaves, flowers and berries. 'It is our latest arrival. It will see a lady through the hottest part of the summer and is ideal for both town and country.' She tilted one side of the brim upwards. 'It can be worn one of two ways and comes with three different colours of ribbon.'

Liz hesitated. 'It is lovely.'

Why the hesitation? 'Try it on,' he urged.

Mrs Greystoke tilted her head on one side and looked at her shrewdly. 'Or perhaps you were seeking something a little more intimate?'

Elizabeth blushed.

Lady Fontley was not as sophisticated as some of the other ladies he had taken under his wing, those like Mimi Luttrell whose husband had arrived home more than a week ago and made it plain his wife no longer needed an escort, much to Mimi's satisfaction.

He took Elizabeth's hand and raised it to his lips. 'What is it, Pet?' he asked in a low voice. 'I thought we wanted something that would make your husband look at you anew? Is the bonnet not to your liking?'

'It is beautiful, but—'

'I think Lady Fontly would like to inspect our other wares.' Mrs Greystoke gestured to the counter.

The last time Avery had looked at the items on display there had been neatly ordered fans and gloves and handkerchiefs. Now there were froths of lace and silk.

'Tansy, fetch his lordship a cup of tea,' Mrs Greystoke said. 'Unless you would prefer something stronger?'

Another change. An assistant. He found he did not like it for some reason he could not name.

'Nothing for me, thank you.'

Mrs Greystoke went back behind her counter and brought forth a flimsy robe of scarlet, edged in lace. 'This is a very popular style of *robe de chambre*, my lady.'

When she spread the garment out on the counter and put her hand between the layers of fabric, Avery almost swallowed his tongue. The robe was so sheer as to be almost invisible and there were strategically placed openings that were revealed as the lace trim fell to one side.

What the devil was Mrs Greystoke doing, showing garments like that to a respectable woman? All right, so Elizabeth had accepted his offer of escort in a fit of pique when her husband left town to go on yet another spree with his friends for the fourth time in a month. The poor dear was feeling neglected, but she was still a modestly brought up girl—

'What do you think, Lord Avery. Will Roger like it?' she whispered in his ear.

A man would have to be dying, or at the very least dead from the waist down, not to like the idea of the curvy Lady Fontly in such a shockingly revealing negligee. Unfortunately, all Avery could think about was seeing Mrs Greystoke in the gown. She was so lusciously tall, it would look far better on her than the petite Lady Fontly.

'Yes,' he said a little more tersely than he intended. 'It is deliciously wicked,' he added a little more warmly.

'Would you like to try it on, Lady Fontly?' Mrs Greystoke asked.

'May I?' Lizzie asked.

Mrs Greystoke smiled. 'You can use my private quarters at the rear of the shop. Tansy will be happy to help you.' She looked back at him. 'Gentlemen are not permitted.'

Liz looked relieved. 'Do you have it in any other colours?'

'We do. One for every day of the week.'

Liz giggled. 'Good lord. Really?'

Mrs Greystoke inclined her head. 'Really.'

Avery inhaled a breath. His forte was helping ladies choose outer garments that showed them off to advantage. Things such as this were best left to the women themselves. Or their husbands. He didn't want to be facing pistols at dawn over such a trifle. 'The colour you have there would suit you very well,' he said, smiling. 'Try it on. You can always try a different colour if you decide you do not like it.'

Elizabeth took the whisper of fabric and lace and followed the shop assistant into the back of the shop.

'And how are you, Lord Avery?' Mrs Greystoke asked.

Since there was now no one else in the shop he gave her his best charming smile. 'A little surprised, I must say.'

'At our new venture?'

Our? Who were the others? She had said her husband was dead. 'Yes. I thought you were a milliner.'

'Oh, we discovered a demand for something no one else was offering. We thought it a suitable addition to our inventory, since most of our customers are ladies.' She gave him a considering look and lowered her voice. 'How is Mrs Luttrell?'

'She is well, so far as I am aware.'

A crease appeared in her forehead as she considered the implications of his remark. He had the decided urge to kiss that little frown. To taste it with his tongue. To smooth it away with his thumb.

'If you should see her,' Mrs Greystoke continued, 'give her my thanks for sending her friends along. If there is ever anything I can do for her, I would be most happy to return the favour.'

Good old Mimi. She had kept her word, then. Was that the reason he had hesitated about returning here? Because he feared she might have not done so and that he would discover Mrs Greystoke more desperate than before?

'I will let her know, but I believe she is away at the moment. At a country house party in Sussex.'

'Oh, I see.'

What did she see? Ah. Did she think he was doing something underhanded with Lady Fontly in the other lady's absence? 'Yes. We parted on the most agreeable terms.' He emphasised the word 'parted'.

Her frown deepened and the disapproval in her expression said she had drawn some conclusions she did not like. He quelled a faint sense of hurt and the urge to explain. It was none of her business how he chose to support members of his family.

A moment later, Elizabeth emerged with a neatly wrapped package in her hand. She looked ready to explode with excitement. 'I love it.'

'Did you wish to purchase a hat also?' Mrs Greystoke asked.

'Yes. Yes, I do.'

They agreed on the summer bonnet Mrs Greystoke had already recommended and when she wrote up the bills, she wrote one to Lord Fontly. The other she wrote to Lady Fontly. 'In case you wish to keep it as a surprise,' she explained.

Or in case she wanted to wear it for Avery, he thought, feeling a little bitter at her misjudgement, despite knowing how it looked.

Mrs Greystoke handed him the hatbox. 'Enjoy your purchase.'

When she said those last words, she was looking at him. Oh, yes, she really thought him some sort of Lothario.

Fortunately, Elizabeth did not notice her misunderstanding.

Annoyed at Mrs Greystoke and feeling slightly ashamed of himself, he left the shop.

The next morning as Carrie swept the front step and the narrow path in front of her window, she could not help wishing the shop had a better location. Mr Thrumby had warned her more than once to keep her door locked and bolted at night and not to linger in the street during the day. Fortunately for her, he and his wife occupied the upstairs rooms, the stairs to which were reached by way of a hallway that passed her back door. He kept a porter on duty at that back entrance, both day and night, so there was always someone nearby who would come at her call.

Hearing the sharp tap of footsteps on the pavement, she lifted her gaze from her broom to glance up the street. A familiar figure strolled towards her. Lord Avery. Behind him a door slammed. The gambling hell Mr Thrumby had warned her about no doubt. There could be nowhere else he was coming from at this time in the morning.

Why *did* men gamble away their fortunes in such places? It was so utterly irresponsible. They ruined themselves and they ruined their families. They also gambled away their lives for the sake of some foolish bet. As her husband had. Furiously, she brushed at the paving slabs, as if she could sweep away the memory of her wedding night along with the news of his death in some terrible battle in Spain a few weeks later. She wanted no truck with any man who gambled.

As if she could sweep away Lord Avery along with the memories. Even if he was the most handsome, most charming fellow she had ever met.

He removed his hat and bowed. 'Good day, Mrs Greystoke.'

Blast. She had meant to whisk herself inside before he reached her shop. Hadn't she? She straightened and met his gaze. She couldn't believe how haggard he looked, how tired and drawn, and yet his usual charming smile curved his lips and his eyes warmed as they rested upon her face.

An answering warmth trickled through her veins. 'Lord Avery.' She couldn't believe how breathless she sounded. It must be all that vigorous sweeping.

'Up and about early this morning, aren't you?' he said.

She folded her arms across her chest and narrowed her gaze. The first time he'd visited her shop he'd been quite bosky. This morning he simply looked tired. 'As are you. *I* have to make ready for my customers.'

His smile broadened. 'Indeed. And here I am.'

She frowned. 'The shop is not yet open.'

His smile changed from charming to wheedling. 'Surely you will not make me come back later.'

'What did you want?'

'Another of your delightful posies, naturally.'

She sighed, but inside her chest her traitorous heart was galloping like a runaway horse. 'Come in, then.'

He followed her into the shop and she went behind her counter. She felt more comfortable, more in control when there was a solid piece of furniture between them. She spread out several little sprigs on the counter. 'These are all I have at the moment.'

He stared at the array 'Did you make any of these?'

What an odd question. 'I helped make the pink roses and the yellow sweet peas.'

'I'll take the roses.'

'I really would not recommend those for Lady Fontly. The yellow would be better for her colouring.'

He grinned. 'It is not for Lady Fontly.' He tucked the spray of flowers into his buttonhole. 'It is for me.'

'Oh,' she gasped. 'That was why...' Surely not.

He raised a brow. 'That was why what?'

Heat raced up her face to her hairline. 'Nothing.'

He chuckled. The deep rich sound sent a shiver down her spine and made her want to giggle like a girl not yet out of the schoolroom.

'It was why I asked if you had made any of them,' he said. 'I wanted something to remind me of you. I need cheering up today.'

He was flirting with her. She felt uncomfortable. Awkward. What was she supposed to do? Should she be flattered or annoyed? Better to ignore the whole thing than make a fool of herself. 'Will there be anything else, Lord Avery?'

He gave a little grimace. 'No. That will be all, thank you, Mrs Greystoke.'

She wrote up her bill. 'Why do you do it?' Oh, there went her brusque tongue again, asking questions regarding things that were none of her concern.

He leaned a hip against the counter. 'Do what?'

'Gamble. You must have been up all night, you look so dreadful.'

'That bad, hmmm?'

She nodded. She forestalled the urge to ask if he had won or lost, but he seemed so weary, she guessed it was the latter.

'I do it to keep the wolf from the door, Mrs Greystoke. To put food on the table. Coal in the hearth. To keep body and soul together.' He sounded bitter.

The son of a duke needing to earn a living? 'Surely...'

'Surely what?' His tone was suddenly dark, even a little dangerous.

She handed him the bill. 'I beg your pardon. It is none of my business.'

He glanced down at the paper in his hand and back at her face. 'You were going to ask why a man in my position, the son of a duke, needed to earn his living in such a manner.'

'Oh, please. I have no wish to pry.'

'My papa is a man with high expectations of his sons. I have disappointed him and therefore I am to make my own way in life.'

She knew all about parental disappointment. 'Why not engage in some sort of gainful employment?' She winced. Dash it, she sounded disapproving.

His lip curled and his smile became mocking. 'You sound just like my father.'

Mortified, she began to put the rest of the nosegays back in their places in the drawer. 'I beg your pardon. It is not my place to judge.'

The kettle on the hob began to sing. She raised her gaze to meet his. 'Would you like a cup of tea?'

He looked surprised. And then pleased. 'That is the best offer I have had in the last twenty-four hours. But I would hate to interrupt your morning.'

'It is no interruption. I went to sweep the step while I waited for the kettle to boil. Would you throw the bolt on the shop door for me? No lady goes shopping at this early hour.'

He did as she asked and then followed her behind the curtain into her private quarters. Very small quarters, she realised as his large form seemed to take up most of the space in the little kitchen-cum-sitting room-cum-dining room. And more recently a place for ladies to try on naughty night attire.

She winced. And then there was the alcove curtained off, where she slept. Perhaps he wouldn't notice.

'Please, sit down,' she said.

He took one of the two chairs at the small kitchen table while she busied herself with the pot and tea leaves.

'This is where you live?' he asked, his voice full of curiosity. 'All alone?'

'This is where I stay during the week while the shop is open. I go home at week's end to collect more stock.' She glanced over her shoulder to discover he was frowning.

'London is not a safe city for a woman on her own,' he said.

'I am perfectly safe. My landlord, Mr Thrumby, lives upstairs and his man keeps an eye on my safety.'

He looked less than satisfied. She hadn't expected him to care about her well-being. It surprised her and warmed her in odd ways. Something inside her chest seemed to soften.

She brought two cups of tea to the table along with milk and sugar on a small tray. 'Please, help yourself.' It was hardly the sort of elegant tea a lady would serve in a drawing room, but she was pleased to see him adding cream and sugar to his cup and sipping the tea appreciatively.

She felt bad for him. While he had not said in so many words that he had been disinherited by his father, clearly it must be the case. A gentleman such as he would have no trade, no skills, to fall back on, so it was no wonder he gambled. And then there were his special ladies. Mrs Baxter-Smythe's sly words returned to her mind.

A terrible idea entered her head. Terrible and exciting and awful. Terrifying.

So awful, yet so awfully tempting. She struggled to think of a way to phrase her question. Her request.

He leaned back in his chair with a boyish smile. A smile quite different from his usual practised charm. It made him seem more endearing. 'That is the best cup of tea I have had in a long time.'

As a general rule men like him, charming handsome men, made her feel uncomfortable. She always felt awkward, as if her arms were too long and her feet too big. Lord Avery, on the other hand, made her feel…womanly. Even attractive. She could not help beaming back at him. 'Thank you.' She took a sip of her own tea.

A friendly silence descended. It felt companionable. As if they had known each other for years.

She put down her cup. 'I wanted to ask you…'

He tilted his head in question. 'What?'

'I am not sure how to put it?'

'Ask away.'

'Do you also earn money from the ladies you escort to my shop?' The words were too blunt when she had meant to be tactful.

He stiffened. 'What makes you ask?' he said. His voice was calm, but his eyes were cold. Shuttered.

She repressed a shiver. Oh, dear, why hadn't she left well enough alone. 'Something Mrs Baxter-Smythe said.' Dash it, she should never have opened her mouth. She had spoiled everything.

His lips thinned. 'Mrs Baxter-Smythe is jealous because I do not count her as one of my special ladies.'

'Ladies you escort while their husbands are out of town.'

'Exactly.' He put down his cup. 'And, yes, they do pay for my services.' He picked up his hat.

He was going to leave and she still hadn't asked her awful question. 'Can any lady hire your...services?'

His eyes widened, then narrowed. 'Are you asking for yourself?'

Heat rushed all the way up her face to her hairline, but she was not one to hide behind a lie. 'I am.'

He put his hat down and shook his head. 'I am not sure I fully understand what it is you are asking me. The ladies I escort are all wealthy and married. Single ladies present too many complications since I am single myself.'

She twirled her cup on its saucer. Did he think she was looking for a husband? 'I am not seeking anything permanent, I assure you. I would prefer something...' She frowned and set the handle of the cup at the proper angle.

'Something?' he prompted. His voice held a distinct chill.

She glanced up. His lips were still a thin straight line. 'Brief,' she blurted. In for a penny in for a pound her father always used to say. 'One night. I am willing to pay, of course. Whatever the other ladies pay.' She still had a little of her personal allowance for the month left over.

His eyebrow lifted. 'Let me get this clear. You wish to pay me to bed you.' His tone was grim.

Embarrassment rushed through her in a hot tide. Oh, why had she said anything at all? But having done so, she pressed on, her cheeks hotter than fire. 'As you can imagine, there are particular disadvantages to being alone. I simply thought that...' She gave an awkward laugh.

'I do not bed my special ladies for money, Mrs Greystoke.' His tone was as dry as dust. 'I merely serve as their escort in their husband's absences. And since you do not have a husband, the arrangement would not work.'

He was trying to let her down gently, to couch his rejection in kinder terms. She didn't believe him for a moment. She had seen the looks that had passed between him and Mrs Luttrell. And Lady Fontly. She wasn't such a fool as to think the ladies merely wanted him to take them shopping.

Resentment spurted through her and a healthy dose of disappointment. She should have known all his flirting with her was nothing but a hum. 'You don't have to lie, Lord Avery. You can simply say no thank you.'

'You may, of course, think what you wish, Mrs Greystoke, but I would advise you not to listen to gossip.' He clapped his hat on his head and strode out of her shop.

Clearly, he viewed her offer as an insult. Something in her chest shrivelled.

'I win!'

The men around the table groaned as the young fellow opposite Avery laid down his cards and scooped up the guineas in the centre of the table. 'Waiter, more wine here.'

Astonishment broke Avery broke free of his reverie. He glared at the rapidly disappearing gold. Money he needed for Laura and her family.

'I've no luck tonight,' one of the other men said.

Another threw his cards down in disgust. 'I need a drink.'

The whist table broke up.

Avery stared at his hand. He should have won. His skill was legendary among London's gamers, which was why he had been reduced to gambling in hells like this one, where he would meet men who were not aware of his reputation. Amend that, he thought bitterly. His skill *had been* legendary. These past few days he'd been unable to concentrate. Not only was he losing at the tables, he'd been avoiding all of his social engagements, including a request from Lady Fontly to suggest a new hairdresser. He knew just the fellow who would have put a considerable sum of money in his pockets.

And now this.

The conclusion he'd been avoiding for the past few days became unavoidable. He needed to see Mrs Greystoke and get the dashed woman out of his head. He could not stop remembering the way she had looked at him when he had refused her offer. It wasn't the hurt in her eyes that haunted him, it was the acceptance.

She had expected his rejection.

He rose from his seat.

'What? Giving up already?' His opponent, Giles Formby, a young gentleman from Surrey, frowned. 'Don't you want a chance to recoup your losses?'

Avery shook his head. He wasn't such a fool as that. 'Another day.'

Craddock, the hell's owner, sidled up to Formby. 'You won't beat me so easily.'

Giles's opponents perked up.

'If you'll take a bit of advice from someone who knows gaming,' Avery said to the younger man, 'leave now, while your dibs are in tune. Come, I'll find you a hackney outside.'

Formby hesitated, then nodded. 'You are right. It is getting late.'

Craddock shot Avery a hard look. 'The night's young yet, gents.' His smile became oily as he turned it on Formby. 'Surely you ain't leaving yet, young sir? Not when lady luck is looking kindly upon ye.'

The young man glanced at Avery, who raised a brow. He didn't want to alienate Craddock, but nor did he want to leave a wet-behind-the-ears boy to the cardsharp's tender mercies. Avery won by skill, Craddock would use any means at his disposal to relieve the young man of the money he had won.

No one who did not pay for the privilege was supposed to win in this place. Including Avery, who paid a percentage of his winnings for a place at Craddock's tables. Avery had contributed a considerable sum of money over the past couple of months. He hoped Craddock would let him get away with leading the mark out of trouble, at least this once.

He leaned close to the young fellow's ear. 'I know a place where the wine flows free and a man can find himself cosy between the sheets.'

Giles swallowed. 'A brothel?'

Damn, but the boy was a fool. Had Avery ever been that innocent? 'A very exclusive place I know. Want to go?'

Giles nodded eagerly.

Craddock frowned, but let them leave without another word. No doubt he assumed that Avery had another plan to get his fingers on the boy's money, so he would be receiving his share later.

Outside in the brisk evening air, Avery pushed Giles into a hackney. 'Where do you live.'

Giles looked puzzled. 'I am lodging in Golden Square. Number three. Why?'

Avery gave the address to the driver.

'I thought we were going to a brothel?'

'You are going to a place where you don't have to pay for wine and you have clean sheets waiting. You will thank me tomorrow. And so will your parents.'

The boy looked chagrined at the reminder of his parents and then grinned broadly. 'Won't Pater be proud when I tell him I won. After all his warnings about gambling hells, too.'

'Only if you refrain from going to another,' Avery said drily. 'You were lucky tonight.'

'I know. And besides, tonight was my last night here. I am due home tomorrow. I'm on my way down from Oxford. I can't delay any longer or Papa will worry. He's not a bad old chap, but he does fuss so.'

Very lucky indeed. Avery wished he had a papa who cared enough to fuss over him.

'Buy a nice gift for your mama and buy a new waistcoat for yourself and go home.'

The boy sank back against the squabs, his expression thoughtful. 'Thank you, sir. I will.'

The boy might be naive, but he wasn't stupid. Avery wondered if he would have been so sensible at that age. He stepped back and the hackney coach clattered off into the night.

He strode down the street and turned into the alley that ran behind Mrs Greystoke's shop. There was an odd feeling in his gut. A sense he might be making the worst mistake of his life. The gold plate on the door identified the residence of a Mr Arnold Thrumby. He hesitated. Did he really want to do this?

Her expression, the instant acceptance of his rejection, swam before his eyes once again. If nothing else, he could not allow her to continue to believe she was not worthy of his attentions. Damnation and how the hell was he to do that? He'd just have to play it by ear. The way he always did.

He knocked.

After a few long moments, the peephole opened. 'Who be knocking at respectable folks' door at this time of the night?' a deep voice grumbled.

'A visitor for Mrs Greystoke. Lord Avery. I am expected.'

Hopefully the lady would not give him the lie. Though he would not put it past her to deny him entry. She was not like any other woman he had ever known. Which accounted for some of his fascination.

Footsteps retreated and a little later returned. 'She says you best come in.'

The elderly porter opened the door and stood back. 'At the end of the hall there.' He indicated with his thumb. He locked and bolted the door and sat back down at his post.

So much for her safety. The porter needed a swift kick somewhere it would hurt for letting a man visit the lady in the middle of the night.

The door to Mrs Greystoke's apartment stood ajar, allowing a small bar of light to escape into the corridor. He pushed it open and stepped inside.

She was sitting at the kitchen table facing the door, wearing an old brown woollen dressing gown pulled tight around her form. A heavy rope of brown hair curled over her shoulder and rested on her generous right breast. At her throat, a fragment of lace peeped out from the enveloping gown and skimmed the hollow of her throat. The scrap of frill was a nod to her femininity. And it was the most erotic sight he had ever beheld.

Slowly he raised his gaze to her face. 'Mrs Greystoke. Good of you to see me at this late hour.'

'Lord Avery?'

Her voice held a question, though her face was perfectly calm. A calmness she wore like armour to hide her worry. But the tremble in the hand that clutched her robe close gave her away.

He shouldn't have come. 'I don't suppose you would offer me a cup of tea?'

She stared at him for a long moment.

He really should not have come.

She rose from her chair, tall, magnificent, composed. 'Very well.'

Chapter Four

He wanted a cup of tea at this late hour? What did he think this was? A tea house? To calm her thundering heart, she busied herself with stirring up the coals and filling the kettle of water. To her mortification, she realised he was still standing with his back against the door. Watching her. And taking up far too much space in her little kitchen.

'Please,' she said. 'Sit down.'

He moved with cat-like grace across the small space and took the chair against the wall beside the kitchen table. It didn't help. His watchful presence unnerved her. She should have told the porter to send him away. Of course she should. But then she never did anything she was supposed to do. Except for marry Greystoke. And look what a mistake that had turned out to be.

He said nothing. Why didn't he say anything?

She was hopeless at small talk.

She kept her back firmly pointed in his direction, until finally there was no more excuse to avoid his gaze. She carried the tea tray to the table and set it down. She sat opposite and poured his tea. She recalled he liked lots of sugar and cream and put plenty in before handing him his cup.

'Thank you.' His deep voice resonated around the room.

'I—I don't have any biscuits, I'm afraid. I gave them all to Jeb. For his journey. To Kent. I haven't had time to bake more.'

He stirred his tea, took a sip. 'Excellent.'

She blushed like a schoolgirl at the compliment.

He leaned against the chairback. Relaxed. Confident. Elegant. Whereas she felt as if her hands were too large for her arms, like an ungainly colt.

'Was there something you wanted?' she blurted. So awkward. And her blush went from warm to scalding.

He put down his cup. 'I have been considering your proposal.'

The blood drained from her head. 'No. I mean I made a mistake. I wish you to forget it.'

A brow lifted. He tilted his head. 'I wish you would hear me out.'

She turned her face away. Embarrassed. Mortified. Angry at her stupid impulse. 'I beg you will say no more on the matter. You were clearly insulted by what I asked.'

'Mrs Greystoke, I apologise if I was rude. I ought to be used to the gossips by now.'

She drew in a shuddery breath. 'But I think ladies do not generally ask for your services so bluntly.' She tried a smile. It felt weak. She straightened her shoulders. 'Let us say I have changed my mind.'

'Have you?' His voice sounded wistful. Almost regretful.

Again the horrible blush. She'd done nothing but dream about the what ifs all day. What if she had flirted with him? What if she had enticed him? What if she had been someone other than Carrie Greystoke, daughter of a merchant and as blunt as a darning needle?

He reached across the table and took her hand, gently, lightly, his thumb brushing across the back of her fingers. Tingles shot all the way up her arm. She drew in a quick breath. Never had she felt anything so startlingly sensual. Her inner muscles clenched.

'Please listen to my proposition before saying any more,' he said gently. 'I am simply suggesting we get to know each other a little better over the next two weeks and see where the attraction between us leads. That way neither of us will be uncomfortable.'

Attraction. Between them? Had he really said that?

And two weeks? She had imagined a single night in his arms and a whole host of delicious regrets the morning afterwards. Two weeks? Goodness. Her heart picked up speed at the idea of a minute in his company, let alone fourteen days. 'How much would you charge?' Oh, stupid, *stupid* thing to say. So lacking in refinement. So horribly crass.

His lips tightened.

She waited for him to storm out again. Good. It was what she wanted. Dread hollowed her stomach. Against every particle of common sense drummed into her since childhood, she opened her mouth to apologise.

'Actually, that is not the way it works. My rewards are more indirect.'

She flushed as much at the innuendo as at the deepening of his voice and the intensity of his gaze on her face. If only he would come right out and say what he wanted. Instead of hinting vaguely and leaving her in the dark feeling awkward. 'As I said, I changed—'

He held up a hand, the one that was not still holding hers. She snatched that hand back and closed her fingers around the residual warmth as if she could somehow save it.

'Let me finish,' he said and amusement danced in his eyes. Not mocking, simply amused.

'Then please stop beating about the bush and tell me.'

His eyelashes lowered a fraction, hiding his thoughts. A small smile curved his lips. 'That is what I like about you, Mrs Greystoke. Your unfailing honesty.'

He liked her honesty, whereas she was ready to melt into a puddle every time he looked at her. This was clearly not a good idea, but she would let him have his say before she asked him to leave.

'Continue, then, but please recall the hour is late and I have an early start in the morning.'

His grin was cheeky. 'Very well. In a nutshell. This is my proposition. Since being seen in my company will increase your business, I will escort you around town in your lovely bonnets and you will pay me fifteen percent of any additional profits. Think of it as a fee for bringing new business to your shop. This is similar to the arrangement I have with other shopkeepers around town.'

Her jaw dropped. This was how he made money from his special ladies? Not from... Oh, heavens, he must think her terrible for asking him to... Oh, dear. 'So shopkeepers give you a commission on what the ladies in your company buy from them.'

'Yes.'

She frowned. 'But what you are proposing to me is different. You could make the same arrangement with me as you have with the other tradespeople.'

He inclined his head. 'I could. But it would be nowhere near as enjoyable as what I am suggesting. It allows us to kill two birds with one stone, as it were. We will explore the very obvious attraction between us, while introducing your product to ladies of the *ton* in a way that will spark their curiosity.' He shrugged. 'And if we discover we do not wish to deepen our acquaintance, at the end of two weeks we will go our separate ways, each of us better off financially.'

'Won't you being seen in the company of a mere shopkeeper be detrimental to your reputation?' Not to mention what Westram would say, were he to hear about it. Marguerite had decided it would be best not to tell him about them opening the shop. Or at least not until they knew it was successful. Once they were financially independent, there would be nothing he could do. They hoped. She also knew from his letters that Westram was currently out of town, busy on his Gloucestershire estate, so there was little danger of meeting him unexpectedly whilst out and about with Avery.

A cynical smile curved his lips. 'One thing I have learned with regard to being the spare to a dukedom is that one can do anything one wishes, except perhaps murder, and no one will say a word. Besides, there is no doubt in anyone's mind that you are a lady, despite your occupation.'

It was almost as if he *really* wanted her to accept his offer. A little flutter of anticipation stirred low in her belly. She was so very tempted to agree. And if it led nowhere, she would be no worse off than she was right now.

The lonely woman inside her longed to say yes. The shopkeeper immediately saw the flaw in his proposal. Honesty required her to speak. 'I would not know which sales resulted from such an arrangement and which did not.' At the moment, she wasn't making much profit at all. Just enough to cover Tansy's wages and the cost of further supplies. This could be the opportunity they needed to really catch the notice of ladies of the *ton*. What would her sisters-in-law want her to do?

She recalled Petra's words of faith in her abilities to make the shop a success. This would be a way of proving her right.

She forced herself to meet his gaze.

The corners of his eyes crinkled with silent laughter, as if he knew exactly what she was thinking. 'I trust you completely to do what is fair.' He smiled. A warm genuine smile that sparkled gold in his eyes.

She swallowed. It felt too intimate. She in her dressing gown, he with the shadow of a day's growth of beard on his chin. She had the urge to touch the stubble. To discover how it felt against her skin. And if she agreed to this, then she might just have the chance to do so.

He leaned forward, gazing into her eyes. 'Nothing else will happen unless you want it to.'

Her heart tumbled over. She was lost and did not care if she was never found. 'All right.' Her voice came out in a hoarse sort of croak.

He held out his hand. 'Then we have a bargain.'

To her immense surprise, she shook it. 'We do.'

Inside her stomach butterflies took wing. What on earth had she agree to?

He rose. 'I will pick you up tomorrow afternoon and we will go for a drive. Wear one of your bonnets.'

'Tomorrow?'

'It is your half-day closing, is it not?'

Breathless at how quickly things had moved, she nodded.

He picked up his hat and gloves. He gazed down at her. 'Do not look so worried, Mrs Greystoke. It will be fun.' He leaned forward and brushed his lips against her cheek and strode out of her kitchen.

Longing filled her. She wanted this. She touched her cheek where his silky lips had left a warm glow. It was the first time a man, other than her father, had kissed her. Small thrills chased along her veins, making her tremble.

She must have gone mad.

She wanted to run away and hide. She wanted to go with him, have him kiss her again.

Standing on the edge of a precipice must feel like this. Longing to leap, to fly into the void, but knowing that in the end all you would do was fall and get hurt.

Calm down, Carrie. This was first and foremost a business arrangement. An exchange of one thing for another, with additional possibilities. Surely she understood commerce well enough not to falter having shaken hands upon their bargain.

And besides, after getting to know her better, he might decide he no longer found her attractive.

Her heart sank. Her husband had certainly discovered her to be so unbearable as to prefer risking his life to marriage to her.

And if she did not take this chance, she would never forgive herself if another opportunity never materialised.

Every morsel of sense she had said she was treading on dangerous ground. Taking unknown risks, the way her father had. But she had opted for safety when she married Jonathan, only to discover she'd stepped into a quagmire of worry. How could this be any worse?

For heaven's sake, she was the one who had made the

proposal in the first place—was she now going to back away from the challenge?

She got up and began to clear away the tea tray. If she was going to go out and about with a nobleman in order to show off her bonnets, she would need something very different to wear. Fortunately, she had a whole trousseau of clothes bought before her wedding and never taken out of their wrappings, packed away in a trunk at her aunt's house. She would send for it first thing in the morning.

While it would likely all come to nothing, since it was unlikely such a handsome engaging man would truly find her attractive, she would endeavour to look her best for him and for the shop.

Avery wended his way through the traffic towards Mrs Greystoke's emporium the next day. Greystoke. He *had* heard that name before. It niggled at him. Surely if recalling the name was important, he would remember where he had heard it. And besides, it was a fairly common name, his memory might have nothing to do with her at all. He shrugged off his doubts as he pulled up at the end of the lane leading to the back door of her shop.

He tossed a coin to a lad loitering nearby. 'You know Thrumby?'

The lad nodded.

'Knock on his door and have the porter escort Mrs Greystoke out to me. Understand?'

The boy nodded and dashed up the alley.

A few minutes later, Thrumby's porter marched out with Mrs Greystoke. She looked more magnificent than usual. She had discarded her drab workaday gown in favour of an emerald-green carriage dress trimmed in black velvet and cut low over her generous bosom. Her hat, a spectacular confection trimmed with a pheasant feather tilted jauntily to one side. He could not have chosen anything better to show off her looks. He grinned and jumped down as she approached.

He took her hand and bowed. 'Good day, Mrs Greystoke.'

'Lord Avery.' She sounded a little breathless.

'I am not too early, I hope?'

'Not at all.' She was gazing wide-eyed at his vehicle, which was a very dashing high-perch phaeton.

'Will the height trouble you?' he asked, wondering if he should have borrowed his brother's brougham instead.

'Not at all,' she said. 'I begged Papa to buy me one just like yours, but he thought it far too frivolous.'

'You like to drive?'

'I do. Not that there have been very many opportunities.'

'Then you must drive this one.' Bart probably wouldn't mind, as long as they didn't overturn it.

She smiled and seemed to relax. 'I would like that, but not today. These gloves would not survive.' She held out her lace-clad hands for inspection.

A sensible answer. 'Very well. But next time wear your driving gloves.'

Her expression said there might not be a next time. What? Did she plan to give him his *congé* before they had as much as driven out once? Was it possible his charm had deserted him? Or had he somehow made a bad impression? Clearly, it was something he needed to rectify.

And not because he needed her money. Her shop was likely barely surviving. Any profit from their arrangement would be minimal. No. This was about making her see him, as a person, someone she would want to spend time with because of *who* he was and not just what he could do for her.

Though why he cared, he wasn't sure. He never had before. At least not much. Being the second son of a duke had quickly taught him that most people were interested in getting to know his father or his older brother and thought to use him as a stepping stone in that direction. Even the woman he'd loved had stepped on his heart when she'd accepted his father's bribe to marry someone else.

He pushed the thought aside. It was so long ago now, he scarcely remembered her face. Later, much later, he'd heard that she had died in childbirth, and he'd felt sad, but not as devastated as he would have expected. And Bart was hinting that, now Avery had returned to England, the Duke would like him to settle down and find a wife. More likely that was Bart's hope, since he was baulking at the idea of wedded bliss with the woman their father had chosen to be the next Duchess, poor fellow.

Well the Duke was going to be disappointed with regards to Avery. As soon as he was sure Laura's husband was financially able to support his family—and according to Laura that would be any day now—Avery would be off on his travels again. His brother would just have to do his duty. After all, he was the heir.

In the meantime, Mrs Greystoke required his full attention, because he was determined to fulfil the terms of their agreement and to bed her into the bargain, provided she remained willing.

Determined? The idea took him aback. With most of his ladies, he simply ensured they were happy doing what he wanted them to do. What was it about this woman that made him want to please her? Perhaps it was because she so rarely smiled.

As if she had some inner sadness.

He helped her up into the carriage. Her long legs made an easy task of the climb and afforded him a glimpse of a very finely turned ankle. He stifled the urge to curl his hand around the delicious curve of her lower calf. It was far too early for such intimate play. And while many of the ladies he escorted would laugh and take it as their due, this skittish woman would likely run for the hills.

He liked that. Her mix of modesty and boldness. After all, it was a bold woman who propositioned a man the way she had and all the while maintaining her dignity.

He returned to his seat and set his horses in a steady trot.

'They are beautiful steppers,' she said after a few moments.

'Yes. I made an excellent purchase five years ago.' When his dibs had been in tune. If Father learned that his brother Bart was now paying to keep Avery's horses in fine fettle, there would be hell to pay. And no doubt the horses would have to go.

They made their way through the usual rush of London traffic and out on to the open road.

'Where are we going?' she asked after a few minutes of watching the road.

'Hampstead Heath. There is a nice little tea house there.'

She tensed. 'Oh.'

He frowned at the doubt in her voice. 'I can assure you it is quite respectable. I thought you might feel more comfortable this first time, if we went somewhere quiet.

Somewhere we can talk and get to know each other better in comfort before we face the *ton* head on.'

Her shoulders relaxed. 'I see. Yes, I suppose it is for the best.'

Dash it all, what did she mean by that? He knew better than to ask, though. Females were notoriously fickle, but she seemed content to go along with his plan so he would leave it at that. No sense in forcing her to speak her mind. Hopefully today's outing would set all of her fears at rest.

'Where do you call home?' he asked, to divert her thoughts. 'I can tell you originate from somewhere in the north, but not exactly where.'

'I was born and raised in Nottinghamshire, but when I am not keeping shop I reside in a small village near Sevenoaks with my sisters-in-law. I have grown to like the south of England.'

An evasive answer if ever he'd heard one. 'My family hales from Wiltshire, near Salisbury. We have more than a few bishops in the family. Have you ever visited the cathedral there?'

'I have never been to Wiltshire.'

'It is devilishly flat in more ways than one.'

'I would love to visit Stonehenge.'

So, the lady knew her history and her geography. Unlike many of her peers. 'I would like to show you around. It is one of the strangest sights I have ever seen in the world.'

'Have you seen a great many sights in the world?'

'Yes, indeed.' He noticed that her tension diminished even more. The lady clearly did not like to talk about herself, but was delighted to talk about him. Another thing that made her unusual. Well he certainly didn't mind talking about his experiences, if that was what she wanted. At least for now. Eventually he would learn all her secrets. 'I have been to several of the great continents—Europe, India, Africa—but there are many places I have still to visit.'

'Where will you go next?' she asked.

'The Americas.'

'Oh. Is it your intention to go soon?' Her voice lacked any emotion, as if she didn't care one way or the other.

Her lack of interest stung. He kept his voice equally expressionless. 'As soon as I may.'

'What holds you back?'

He hesitated. Was there more behind that question than mere curiosity? Well, there was no need to hide the truth. His sister's runaway marriage had caused a lot of gossip just over two years ago—her husband, John, was so much beneath her—but these days hardly anyone remembered her existence. Not that Laura had ever had a come out, so while her name had been on everyone's lips, her face had been unknown. It was only their father who refused to let go of the past. After all, while Laura's marriage straight out of the schoolroom might have been impetuous, John came from a decent family, despite the fact that they had no money, and would make a fine barrister some day soon. It had taken him far longer to get established than it should have because of the Duke's interference, which is why Avery had returned to England to help. It still made him go cold when he recalled Father's threats against John. 'Family responsibilities mostly.'

Carrie swallowed a gasp. She thought he had assured her that he was a single gentleman, not one with a family to support. She had looked him up in *Debrett's Peerage* and it had said nothing about him being wed. Not him or his older brother. It had mentioned a married sister. To a commoner. Perhaps it was not the most recent edition.

Oh, dear, it seemed she had made a very bad error in judgement. 'Really.' Her tone sounded repressive. Disapproving. It expressed her feelings exactly.

He glanced her way. 'It surprises you that I would care about my family?'

'I—I didn't know you had a family.'

'Not much of a one. A brother and a married sister, whose situation was somewhat dire, although it has been improving lately.'

She frowned. 'You do not have a wife?'

'Heavens, no. I already told you I did not. I am not the marrying sort, I'm afraid.'

Oh! It was his sister he meant. Not a wife and children. The relief left her feeling weak. 'It is good of you to care about your sibling.'

He raised an eyebrow. 'Why would I not?'

'Oh, no, I didn't mean that. Of course you would. I was a little confused.'

He negotiated around a carter travelling at a snail's pace and cast her a smile. 'Come now, Mrs Greystoke, it is not like you to beat around the bush. What is going on behind that lovely face of yours.'

Lovely? She almost swallowed her tongue. She didn't know whether to be pleased by the compliment or annoyed by his analysis of her character. In the end, she chuckled and decided to tell him the truth. 'Well, when you said you had family responsibilities I suddenly imagined a wife and children squirrelled away deep in the country while you enjoyed yourself in town.'

He laughed outright. 'You really do not have a very good opinion of the gentlemen of the *ton*, do you?'

'Oh, I do not paint them all with the same brush, but you have to admit, it is not an unheard-of situation. I was warned about it very carefully at the seminary for young ladies I attended. Sadly, I have found it to be mostly true.'

He stared at her for a second, then turned his attention back to his horses as they came up on another lumbering trade vehicle. A coal dray this time. Once they were safely past the obstruction he shifted slightly as if wanting to see her face better. To look her in the eye, as her father would have said. 'Who are your family, Mrs Greystoke? Your name has a familiar ring, but I have not been back in England long and I never did take much notice of such things before I left.'

'I told you, my family are merchants in Nottinghamshire.'

'And your husband's family. Why are they not caring for you, instead of sending you out into the world to earn a living?'

'My husband's family helps as much as they are able.'

Why she did not want to tell him about Westram, Petra and Marguerite, she was not sure. Perhaps it was because she feared Avery would be shocked to know she had dragged Westram's sisters into trade when the nobility frowned so much on that sort of thing. She did not like the idea of the *ton* ridiculing the Earl either. The poor man was doing his best in the face of such a terrible family tragedy.

He glanced up at the sky. 'It seems we are to be lucky with the weather today, Mrs Greystoke.'

Carrie winced. How she hated the sound of her husband's name on his lips. 'Do you think…would you mind calling me Carrie? All my friends do.'

'Carrie,' he repeated. 'Short for Carolyn or Caroline, I assume.'

She gave a short laugh. 'I wish it was. No. My name is Carrington. My father wanted a son. He picked out the name before I was born and refused to countenance another when he discovered I was a girl. It was his mother's maiden name.'

His smile held commiseration. 'I am named for some long-lost ancestor, too.'

'I like the name Avery.'

He grinned. 'Good, then that is what you shall call me and we will forget all about the Lord thing and the Mrs thing.'

'In private,' she warned. There was no doubt her association with a well-known rake was going to get back to Westram eventually. She should not have agreed to these outings, but on the other hand, how was she ever to become a woman instead of a spinster?. Fortunately, she did not have to worry about pleasing Avery, the way she would have to please a husband, and could just be herself. Blunt brusque Carrie. After all, in a roundabout way she was footing the bill for his time.

An odd sense of disappointment filled her. A feeling that she would have been just a little bit happier if he was escorting her, not for financial gain, but simply because it pleased him to do so.

Such foolishness. Yet he had said he found her attractive. He had also called her face lovely.

Had he said those things because she was his business associate? Or because he flirted without thinking?

Whatever it was, she was going to enjoy it while it

lasted. If Westram decided to put his oar in…well, she would deal with that when it happened.

No sense in crossing bridges before you came to them.

For the rest of the drive they talked about things he had seen on his travels abroad. The sights of Rome and Florence. The ruins in Greece. Some of his adventures involved avoiding the ongoing war between Britain and France. The time passed quickly and pleasantly and they were soon drawing up at a tea house on the edge of the heath near the village of Hampstead.

'What a lovely spot,' she remarked as he helped her down.

He looked pleased. 'I am glad you like it.'

There were other carriages outside the shop. Carrie braced herself for the scrutiny of strangers, while hoping like mad there was no one either of them knew.

This was it, then. Her first clandestine meeting with a man. *So what?* a little voice whispered in her ear. *You are a widow. You can do whatever you wish.*

She straightened her shoulders.

He smiled and offered his arm. 'Shall we?'

They entered to the tinkle of a little bell above the door.

A lady in a prim cap and apron bustled forward. 'Lord Avery. How lovely to see you again. Your usual table?'

'Yes, please,' Avery said.

His usual table. Again, there was that unaccountable feeling of disappointment that he had brought other women to this spot. She squashed it flat. His other ladies were why she had chosen him in the first place. She'd known from the first what sort of charming flirt he was. Why would she expect anything different? In truth, she did not know what to expect at all, so she should just put aside her worries and enjoy the experience. It wouldn't likely happen again.

An older couple seated in an alcove off to one side looked up as they entered a parlour scattered about with round tables covered in white cloths, some with seated guests. Each table bore a little vase containing a single rose.

Strangely, the older couple glanced at them with curiosity in their gazes, but not, thank goodness, recognition, before returning to their tea and quiet conversation. Carrie breathed a sigh of relief. There was no one here either of them knew and even if some of them recognised Avery, it would not mean anything.

She gave herself a mental shake. What was she thinking? The whole idea was for people to recognise them, to admire her bonnets and to come to the shop. Indeed, that was why she had worn this very fetching hat.

The woman led them to the table in the centre of the bow window. It looked out over a small garden full of flowers and gave way to the distant view of London's spires.

'What do you think?' Avery asked, once they were seated.

'It is charming.'

Avery smiled. 'Not to mention that they have the best cream cakes in all of London.'

'That we do,' their waitress said, beaming. 'Shall I bring you the usual assortment, my lord?'

Avery glanced at Carrie, clearly asking for her opinion.

'Whatever you think,' she replied.

'Yes, the usual assortment,' he said to the woman.

'What sort of tea would you like?' the woman asked.

This time he gestured to Carrie. 'You choose.'

He really was a lovely man. While she might not know what sort of cakes were on offer, she did know her tea. 'I would like Oolong,' she said.

'Good choice,' Avery approved.

The waitress bustled off.

Avery smiled at her. 'Tell me about your family.'

'I am an only child. I mentioned before that my father wanted me to be a son, but my mother never had any other children after me. It was a great disappointment to them both. They would have liked a large family. Is your family large?'

'There are three direct descendants of the Duke. My older brother, then me, then my sister. But there are hundreds of relatives scattered across Britain and France.' His mouth twisted wryly. 'At least it seems so. Every time I go anywhere someone claims kinship. I would like you to meet my sister, Laura. We are very close.'

'I don't believe that would be appropriate. Do you?'

'Why not?' He lowered his voice. 'I think she'd like you. She married against my father's wishes, so he cut her off. She's just as *de trop* as me in polite circles.'

'How very cruel.' Her own father had been the opposite. Far too doting. Suffocating, almost.

The waitress appeared with a tea tray.

She set it in front of Carrie and scurried away. Carrie inhaled the fragrant steam. 'This is very good tea.'

'Not once have I been disappointed.'

Carrie poured.

The woman returned with a tiered plate piled high with confections. They looked delicious.

'I put extra of your favourites on there, my lord,' she said with an indulgent smile.

He grinned like a small boy given a treat. 'You are a wonder, Mrs Bentlock.' He looked at Carrie. 'Let us hope we have the same taste in cakes.'

'Personally, I never met a cream cake I didn't like,' Carrie said laughing at his eagerness.

Mrs Bentlock dipped a small curtsy.

'I can see I will have to watch you,' Avery said, his eyes twinkling. 'Or you'll be eating all the best ones.'

She laughed. It took her by surprise. It seemed he was one of the few people who could surprise a laugh out of her. She wasn't used to his sort of teasing. But she liked it.

Using the silver server, he carefully lifted a confection on to her plate, cream and strawberry jam layered between flaky pastry. 'Try this one.'

She took a bite. It melted in her mouth. She closed her eyes for a moment as she savoured the burst of strawberries and cream, and the explosion of buttery pastry. She swallowed. 'Oh, so delicious.'

She became aware of his gaze watching her mouth with an intensity that caused her insides to tighten. He brought his gaze up to meet hers and the desire in them took her breath away. Heat rushed up from her chest all the way to her hairline.

His lips curved in a sensual smile. 'I am glad you like it. It is my favourite of them all.'

He picked the same kind and took a large bite with white even teeth before it got anywhere near his plate. He managed it without creating a single crumb on the pristine white tablecloth, whereas she had managed a veritable avalanche of pastry flakes on and around her plate.

'I can see you are an expert.'

'I am. My mother used to bring us here when we were children as a special treat. The Duchess did not approve of crumbs. The secret is to inhale, just a little, as you bite.'

'I would be more likely to choke,' she said, eyeing the last mouthful on her plate.

'Mother did not approve of choking either.'

He spoke with such seriousness, she had a feeling there was more to his words than he was saying, yet he looked perfectly cheerful. Perhaps he was making a joke? Unsure how to respond, she sipped her tea.

He put a different sort of cake on her plate. A scone with more of that lovely jam and cream in the middle. 'Wait,' she said, smiling at him. 'I haven't finished the first one yet.'

He grinned. 'You have to keep up or I'll be hogging them all to myself.'

'Aha, a challenge. I can tell what you must have been like as a boy.'

'I had to be quick. My brother is three years older than me. He could make short work of a plate of cakes. Laura and I had to guard our plates, too, or he'd filch from them as well.'

'It must have been fun.'

His gaze shadowed. 'We did have fun upon occasion, though being the heir and spare to a duke is a serious business.'

'I would imagine so.' Since it seemed like a bit of a painful topic she decided to change it. 'You mentioned that you visited India. What was it like?'

'Like?'

'Well, I do know that it is hot and that the people are exotic and different, since I have read about it in books, but I have never met anyone who has actually been there.'

'It is exotic and different.' He squinted as if looking into the distance. 'The heat is extraordinary.'

'Like a hot summer day?'

'Not even close. The air is like a wall of steam pushing against you in the middle of the day. And it smells different. The spices used in their foods lingers in every breath. It is crowded and noisy and since everything is in the local dialect, one is confused and awed. I spent a lot of time simply watching it all.'

'Did you see any elephants?'

'Elephants? Yes. They are everywhere. They are used the way we use horses, more or less. For farming, pulling heavy loads, carrying people.'

She ate the scone. 'Oh, my goodness, that is so good, I don't know which I prefer now.'

'Then try this one.'

He plopped a jam tart with a blob of cream right in the middle on to her plate.

She took a bite. Again, the pastry melted on her tongue. 'Oh, my.' She sighed. 'Are elephants as big as they appear in books?'

'A book cannot do justice to the size of them, I'm afraid. Such a massive body, so much strength, all carefully controlled by their mahout.'

'Mahout.' She liked the taste of the word on her tongue. 'I would like to see that. Did you ever ride one?'

'I did. Several times. The local Sultan was most insistent on showing the son of a duke every courtesy.' He sounded a little bitter.

'Was it uncomfortable?' she asked, trying to understand his sudden change of mood.

He seemed to relax at her question. 'It took a bit of getting used to, I must say. One is an awfully long way from the ground. And, my Lord, how it sways. Like a ship in a heavy swell. The stomach takes a while to settle down. Although I must say I prefer an elephant to a camel any day of the week.'

She laughed. 'Don't tell me you have ridden on a camel, too?'

'All right. I won't.'

He was teasing her again. She tapped his foot with the toe of her slipper and gave him a mock frown. 'Tell me.'

His eyebrows shot up. 'Eat the last cake and I will.' He placed it on her plate. This was a little round sponge cake with its top cut to look like little wings sprouting from a dollop of cream.

She poured them both another cup of tea and dutifully ate the cake. It was so light, it was like eating fresh air. 'Absolute heaven,' she declared. 'Now tell me.'

'Very well,' he said, chuckling. He covered her hand with his where it rested on the table. The warmth of his skin was a delicious shock. Her toes curled inside her slippers. Never had a man touched her so intimately. She had the strange urge to lift his hand to her mouth, to brush her lips against the hairs on the back of his knuckle, to feel the weight of it in her palm. She swallowed a gasp of surprise and looked up to again find that intensity in his gaze that made her breathless and sent little thrills running along her veins.

'Yes, what?' she managed to say, more or less in a normal voice.

'I did ride a camel. But they are unpleasant beasts, constantly grunting and moaning their displeasure. They also spit.'

She grimaced. 'They spit at people?'

'It is a form of aggression or defence, I believe. Their owners take great delight in putting the unwary traveller in the line of fire.'

He looked so disgruntled, she couldn't help laughing. 'One spit at you?'

'He caught me right in the eye. It stung like the blazes.'

She shuddered. 'I think I will avoid them, then. Though I'm hardly likely to meet one in London.'

Out of the corner of her eye, she noticed that the other couple, were leaving. The woman was looking at them. It seemed as if she intended to approach. She said something in a low voice to her companion and he shook his head as he responded, not looking their way at all, since all his attention was focused on the woman at his side. He gave her a look so full of warmth and affection, it made Carrie's heart stumble. It seemed to envelop the woman like an aura. Like some warrior of old offering his lady protection. It was...beautiful.

The woman gave a light laugh and as she passed their table she offered Carrie a smile of encouragement. Carrie blushed and dropped her gaze. No doubt the woman thought they were married, or at the very least betrothed. If she knew the truth, she would likely be horrified. Assuming she and her companion were married.

If they were married, they were certainly happy and that made her feel strangely glad.

'More tea?' she asked Avery.

He shook his head, eyeing the empty cake plate.

'You were right, these are the best cream cakes I have ever tasted.'

'I'm glad you enjoyed them.' He sounded very pleased with himself.

She could not help wondering how many other women he had brought to this spot. The owner certainly seemed to know him very well. Something unpleasant twisted in her chest, causing a pang. Really? She was feeling jealous? Or possessive? When she knew this was nothing more than a temporary arrangement cooked up between them?

The pang became a sharp ache behind her breastbone. Ridiculous. She'd had her chance at marriage. Look what a failure she had been. She would do better to devote herself to helping her new family. They had welcomed her with open arms and they deserved her full attention. This thing with Avery was merely a fling, if it turned out to be anything at all. A brief one at that.

He gave her a smile, as if he sensed her unease. His usual charming smile. The one that made her toes curl in her slippers and stole her breath. It was warm and lovely, and touched her heart in unexpected ways. How could it do that?

She had been letting the longings she'd tried so hard to suppress sneak out into the light. She really must not do that. Not with this man. Or any other. She would only get hurt.

He tilted his head. 'Tell me about the most interesting thing you did as a child?'

'Interesting?'

'Yes. Some adventure that stays in your mind as a fond memory.'

Most of her childhood had been a rather serious affair. But… 'I remember going to Goose Fair with Father and Mother. It is held every year in Nottingham Town Square in September.' She smiled at the recollection. 'We went because we needed a new gardener and a supply of cheese for the winter. Father said it was the only place all the best local cheeses were to be had. I was more interested in the fairings on the stalls and the entertainers. I remember, we bought bunches of ribbons from a tinker for me and Mother. There were jugglers and mimes and you had to keep your hand on your reticule because of all the pickpockets. And then there were the geese. Hundreds of them. They made such a racket.'

'Oh, yes,' Avery agreed. 'Fairs are great fun. It was grand mingling with all the locals. Bart and I used to go to one near our estate every year. And when we were older we used to sneak off from our tutor to watch the boxing matches. I won quite a bit of money off him betting on the outcome.' He smiled fondly.

She wasn't sure if his smile was for the memory of the fair, or the recollection of the money he had won. She wanted to think it was the former. 'I only went that once.' Mother had died not long afterwards. Father had never been so jolly again.

Avery grinned at her. 'I sometimes forget the fun parts of growing up. I haven't thought about those fairs for years, and though I have attended many a boxing match they were all between professional fighters. In those days it was local lads, most of whom we knew.'

She had not thought about that day in years. It was a good memory and she could not help smiling at him. 'Well, I think that was my most adventurous afternoon. It certainly doesn't come anywhere close to elephants and camels.'

'Have you ever been sailing?'

'No.'

'Fishing?'

'No. I grew up in the middle of Nottingham. There was no opportunity for such things.'

He laughed. 'I suppose not. Perhaps one day I could—' He broke off.

There would never be a one day for them. To fill the awkward pause, she glanced around the table. 'I could not eat another bite or drink another mouthful of tea, could you?'

'No, indeed.' He gestured to Mrs Bentlock to bring the bill and after he had paid her, he helped Carrie to rise. It was not long before they were tooling back along the road towards London.

Chapter Five

Avery felt unusually contented. Perhaps it was the good weather. But more likely it was the company of the woman at his side. There was something about her calm air of contentment that settled his constant urge to be on the move.

'Do you think they were married?' Carrie asked. 'The older couple in the alcove?'

Startled by the wistful note in Carrie's voice, Avery glanced at her face and caught a look of such longing it shook him to the core.

'Probably not,' he said rather more brusquely than he had intended. 'They looked too happy.'

The light in her face went out. Damn. He had not meant to be so forthright, but he certainly didn't want her getting romantic notions of a long and happy life together.

He didn't want a wife. A family tied one down. Look at how he was forced to kick his heels here in London for Laura's sake. And perhaps just a very little for Father's, though the old man would never acknowledge his presence in town. Not unless Avery gave in to his ducal demands and married a woman of the Duke's choosing.

Which went full circle around to the disappointment on Carrie's face.

She shifted in her seat, putting distance between them, and he instantly regretted the loss of intimacy that had been growing between them. He should have been a little gentler, but he could not afford to give her the wrong idea. Then another reason for her interest in the couple occurred to him and he felt worse.

'Do you miss your husband?'

Her expression changed. Stiffened. Becoming more remote.

Hell, why had he asked her that? His usual easy manner around the ladies seemed to have deserted him entirely.

'We were not married very long,' she said coolly. 'He—died a very few weeks after we were wed.'

He frowned. 'You did not know him beforehand? It was not a love match?'

'It was arranged very quickly.'

'His death must have come as quite a shock, then?'

She nodded.

Damn. It was like pulling teeth trying to get any information from this woman. Perhaps he should leave well enough alone, but something drove him on. The need to understand what made her so sad beneath her outward appearance of complacency. At least his talk of his travels had made her forget her unhappiness for a while, for her laughter had been genuine. And then she'd had to start on about marriage.

Resentment filled him. Resentment that even if he wanted to, he could not afford to marry. Not that he did. The very thought appalled him. He liked his freedom. No, the real resentment was against his father for forcing the issue. He shoved his feelings away, they were not worth the bother, and focused on Carrie. On her sadness.

'May I ask how he died?'

She hesitated as if trying to find a way to express what ought to have been a simple answer. 'He died in battle. At Badajoz. Shortly after we married.'

The mists in his brain dissipated in a flash. Now he recalled where he had heard the name Greystoke. It had been a huge on dit a week or so before he came home. Laura had told him all about the three noblemen who had gone off to war and been killed in Spain, leaving the house of Westram in complete disarray.

An abyss seemed to open up at Avery's feet. 'You are Westram's sister-in-law.' He could not help the note of accusation in his voice. This was bad news indeed.

She tensed. 'I am.'

'Why in heaven's name did you not tell me?'

Her spine straightened. 'I do not see how it is relevant.'

'And what the hell is Westram about, letting you keep a shop like some common merchant's wife?' Leaving her around for men like him, or worse, to prey on, for heaven's sake. Or leaving her around to trap some unsuspecting nobleman into marriage. God help him, had he really fallen into such a trap?

'I am some common merchant's *daughter*,' she said icily.

'You are related to a peer.' He could not help his fury. 'The settlements—'

'Are hardly any of your business.' She stared ahead of them. 'What a wonderful view.'

So, she was not prepared to discuss her husband with

him. That was fine. He had no wish to become embroiled in her personal circumstances.

The sister-in-law of an earl. This was why he never pursued single ladies, even if they were widows. He'd certainly jumped in with both feet in this instance. What the hell was he to do? End it, right here and now, would be the most sensible course of action.

Dammit it, he didn't want to. Not yet.

He was surprised by his reluctance. Normally, he would have no such qualms. But then, it was a matter of honour. A gentleman never went back on his word. He'd just have to find a way to handle it so he did not find himself leg shackled.

Carrie didn't know whether to feel miserable that he had discovered who she was, or relieved. She should have told him right at the beginning. Guilt gnawed at her stomach. Guilt that she hadn't been honest when she prided herself on speaking the truth, along with disappointment that he was clearly going to end their association before it had properly begun.

Nor could she imagine going through this again, asking another gentleman to be her lover, only to be rejected. She shuddered inside; the thought of asking another gentleman made her feel ill. Positively humiliated. She should not have asked Avery either. At least he had been a gentleman about it. Instead of turning her down flat or leaping into her bed for some exorbitant sum, he'd proposed a different sort of arrangement, with the possibility of more being left in the hands of fate. But what the 'more' might entail she wasn't quite sure and hadn't liked to ask.

But she had offered him money and since he was a

gambler, like Jonathan, he no doubt would expect to be paid, just as he expected her to pay him for helping her sell her hats.

She pinned a calm expression on her face and observed the passing view as they drew closer and closer to the fringes of the city. Once they reached her little shop, they would never have to see each other again. A sense of loss filled her chest. It was surely only because she knew she would never attempt anything like this again. It was all just too demeaning.

The silence between them became oppressive. Nothing she thought of to say sounded right in her own ears. How did one put an end to such a contract anyway? It was highly embarrassing. For them both.

'I'm sorry I was sharp with you,' he said quietly as they passed the first smattering of houses at the edge of the city.

'Not at all,' she said, trying to sound as if she didn't care. 'I never should have approached you in the first place. I doubt it will make the slightest difference to the success of the shop.'

His eyes widened. 'You are giving me my marching orders?'

Oh, dear, was it not permitted to end such an arrangement? Not even one that had been vague in the extreme?

'I thought that now you know who I am, you would not wish to be seen with me. I quite understand.'

His eyebrows crashed down. 'Why would you think such a thing?'

She took a deep breath. 'I know what the gossips say about me. That after one night with me, my husband found me so unappealing, he left for the battlefields of Spain.'

He stared at her. 'Who on earth told you that?'

She shrugged, trying to hide her hurt. 'It is common knowledge.'

He glared. 'I've certainly never heard it said.' Damn. He hadn't been in London at the time. And Laura would never have been so unkind as to pass along such malicious gossip.

'Well, if you must know, it was my aunt-in-law. She had been against the marriage, the moment she heard of it, and refused to attend the ceremony. She visited Westram as soon as she learnt the news of Jonathan's death. She was not reticent in speaking her opinion. Poor Westram did not know where to look.'

'He should have looked her in the eye and told her to mind her own business.'

Avery sounded strangely furious.

'She was only repeating what she had heard. And you mustn't blame Westram. He is a good man.'

'Then what is he about letting you and his sisters set up a shop in town?'

'We are widows and Westram has nothing to say in anything we do.'

Avery turned on to Bond Street, his face set in grim lines, but he seemed to accept what she said about her brother-in-law.

No doubt Lord Avery would now want to end their agreement. And his vague offer to see where their attraction led had probably simply been a way not to hurt her feelings. She really wasn't cut out for this sort of thing. She knew nothing about flirting or enticing a man. She always managed to put her foot in her mouth. 'I think it best if we do not see each other again,' she said flatly, anxious to have an end to her shame and embarrassment as soon as possible.

'Do you, now?'

'Yes. I do. I am finding the whole thing terribly uncomfortable to say the least. I must ask that you never speak of what I asked of you to anyone else. It was all a foolish mistake.'

He stiffened, his hands tightening on the reins so much one of his horses tossed its head.

He pulled up at the spot where he had picked her up. 'I don't have time to discuss this right now. I have another appointment. Nor can I leave the horses to take you inside.'

'I can manage to walk a few steps to my door,' she said calmly, while her nose and eyes burned as if they wanted to cry. How very stupid.

'I will visit you later this evening.'

She took her courage in both hands and glanced at his face, which was still set in grim lines. It was exactly the same sort of face she had seen on her husband on the day of their wedding. 'No,' she said firmly. 'I will not be at home this evening.'

'You are out?' he said. 'Or just not at home to me?'

'I don't see what difference either one makes.' She jumped down on to the pavement.

Her dress caught on the carriage door. His gaze widened as it landed on a good deal of her exposed leg. Snatching it free, she shot him a glare. 'Thank you for a wonderful afternoon.' She marched up the alley.

And that was that. The sound of his horses' hoofs gradually receded. When she could hear them no more, she knocked on the door to let the porter know she had returned.

* * *

The next morning passed for Carrie as if the clock's hands were weighted. For some reason, though the shop was busy, time seemed to hang heavy. Likely because sleep had evaded her the previous night. Too many images of Lord Avery escorting one of his special ladies to some ball or another. Which was ridiculous. She had hated the two balls she had attended, so why should he not go with someone else?

Balls were the worst form of torture for a girl on the outskirts of society, unless she was really pretty or good at flirting and making herself noticed. She had only attended a couple in London before her father became seriously ill and not one young man had invited her to dance. Another reason she had accepted Jonathan's proposal so quickly. Marrying him had been a way to escape the humiliating rituals of the marriage mart. If only she'd known that her father had more or less bribed him to come up to scratch, maybe she would not have been so quick to accept it as a way out.

No, she was much better off staying home. And besides, she wasn't ever going to see Avery again, was she? She had ended things very handily. It was far better being the one to bring things to a conclusion than to be the recipient of rejection. And she couldn't imagine that *his* feelings would be hurt.

At least she'd had the courage to speak her mind.

Then why didn't she feel the slightest bit courageous? Indeed, it felt more like she had run away. Dash it all, she wished she'd never met the man.

She sighed.

'Is everything all right, missus?' her assistant Tansy asked, looking up from where she was tying a bow on one of the bonnets. The girl was turning out to be a treasure. She had a flair for arranging things.

'Why would it not be?' Carrie asked.

'That is the second time you have sighed in as many minutes,' Tansy said, looking worried. 'Perhaps you need a cup of tea. We've been so busy this morning and I don't think you even had breakfast.'

She hadn't. She'd felt too miserable for food.

But she could not be presenting a long face to her customers. That was the surest way to get a reputation as a sourpuss. Shopping was supposed to be a pleasant experience.

She forced a smile. 'You are right. A cup of tea is in order for both of us. I'll go put the kettle on the hob.'

She left Tansy in charge of things and went through the curtain. A cup of tea would cheer her up. And she would not let herself think about Lord Avery ever again. Or at least not enough to make her sigh.

She stopped abruptly and blinked as she found him ensconced at her kitchen table, his hat and gloves set in the middle like a centrepiece, his long legs sprawled out into the middle of the floor.

Her heart hit a gallop in a second flat. 'Lord Avery. What are you doing here?'

'Waiting for you.'

'How did you get in?'

'The porter. He knows I'm a regular visitor. I simply needed to cross his palm with a bit of silver.' He offered her a wheedling smile. 'I thought you might prefer it, to my entering by the front door.'

She took a deep breath. Had she smiled back? Oh, surely not. 'As I said yesterday—'

'We had a good time yesterday did we not? I enjoyed

it immensely and I thought of somewhere you might like to go today.'

'I cannot go anywhere today. The shop—'

'Your Miss Tansy can manage perfectly well for an hour or two.'

'An hour or two?' Her voice rose. 'Certainly not.'

'I also came to apologise.'

She stiffened. She did not want him to apologise. She did not want any of this.

Chapter Six

Avery had thought it would be a simple thing. Show up. Smile. Tell her he was sorry for yesterday's argument and they could move on. It was how it had gone with other women in the past. Clearly not with this one.

'Carrie, I truly am sorry. Being the son of a duke, I am a prime target for women on the marriage mart.' That was what his father had said about Alexandra, the woman he'd thought he'd loved. Back then he hadn't wanted to believe it. Now he wasn't so sure. 'When you…' He hesitated. She had not lied about who she was, but she had certainly been evasive. 'When you did not reveal your relationship to Westram immediately, I jumped to the wrong conclusion. I should have known better.'

Her expression eased. A fraction. 'I still do not think this…' she waved vaguely between them '…is a good idea. I should never have brought it up. And I would appreciate if you would forget all about it.'

Damn. Much as he did not want to, he gathered himself to rise and leave. A wicked thought entered his mind 'You are actually going to break our contract?'

She stared at him blankly. 'Our contract? I made you an offer. I am withdrawing from it.'

'Oh, no. I offered you a contract. We shook hands on it. In this very room.'

'I brought the matter up first.'

'I rejected your offer. You took mine. Is that the sort of dealings the members of the *ton* can expect from the owner of this shop?' Blast. That really wasn't so very kind, was it, making it sound as if he might ruin her reputation? He wouldn't, of course, but he could see from the doubt in her face she wasn't sure. That hurt.

But needs must. He did not disabuse her of the notion. Instead of backing down, as he ought, he maintained an implacable expression.

'If I recall correctly,' she said, 'we were to decide whether we found each other *mutually* attractive. I—'

He jumped in before she could say something delightfully blunt that could not be got over. 'We agreed to give it two weeks while we see if we can increase your sales.'

She pressed her lips together.

He pushed ahead. 'I am asking you to come with me for an hour or two, that is all. So I can prove I am serious about my apology. It is only fair.'

'Fair?' An unwilling smile curved her lips. 'Who are you to talk about fair? You simply want your own way.'

Relieved, he grinned. 'Comes of being the younger son of a duke, I'm afraid.'

'Then being the younger son of a duke is bad for one's character,' she pronounced grimly.

He stood up and bowed. 'I will not argue that point. Shall we go?'

She glanced down at herself. 'I cannot possibly go out with you like this.'

'What you are wearing is perfect for this expedition of ours. This time it is not about showing off your hat and we will not see anyone who knows either of us.'

She frowned. 'What on earth can you mean?'

'You will see.'

Curiosity won out over caution, as he had hoped it would. Guessed it would, actually, given her lively turn of mind. 'You should probably wear a shawl, though. The wind is a little cool and while it is not far to walk, I do not want you catching a chill.'

'We are walking?'

'It will not take long.'

She stuck her head back into the shop area. 'Tansy, I am going out for a short while.'

She then took down a shawl from the peg on the back of the kitchen door and shook her head as if admonishing herself. 'Very well, then. Let us be off.'

A slight doubt niggled somewhere in the centre of his chest. If he was wrong about this, no doubt it would be the very last he would see of her. But he was not wrong.

He escorted her to the Strand by way of Piccadilly. He was pleased to discover that she did not dawdle and that it was very easy to match his long stride to her steps, because she was also tall. Of course, he knew why she was striding out—she planned to have this expedition of theirs over as quickly as possible.

The Strand was busy with traffic and pedestrians, both fashionable and common folk, but as they neared his objective, she glanced his way. 'Where are you taking me?'

'Just a few more steps.'

He drew them to a halt outside the Exeter Exchange.

She wrinkled her nose at the strong smell of animals. 'You are bringing me to a menagerie?'

'Yes.' He paid at the wicket and ushered her in and up the stairs. 'There is someone I want you to meet.'

The stiffness disappeared. 'I have heard of this place,' she said. 'They have all sorts of exotic creatures, I am told. How did you know I had never been here?'

He smiled. He really liked how she used her brain. He led her through a doorway into a vast room. 'Because of this.'

The vast room contained cages down its length, a tiger in one, a lion in another, other beasts that she would have lingered in front of if he had not hurried her along. It was the cage at the far end to which he directed her attention.

'An elephant!' she exclaimed.

An attendant came up to them as they reached it. 'Chunee his name is, ma'am…sir. An Indian elephant. He weighs seven tons, if you were wondering.'

Carrie looked at the creature with an expression of awe. 'He is enormous. This is the sort of elephant you rode in India?'

'Yes, though they were draped in scarlet and gold cloth and had a *houda* on their backs. A sort of seat with a canopy.'

She frowned. 'Is he dangerous?'

'Not a bit,' the keeper said. He grinned, exposing brown teeth. 'Though you do have to watch out for his tusks. And I am very careful to keep me feet out of his way when I clean out his stall. Wouldn't harm a soul, he wouldn't. Got a sixpence, sir?'

Avery handed over a coin.

'Remove your glove and hold out your hand, flat like, ma'am.'

Carrie looked a little worried.

'It will be fine,' Avery said. He'd done this himself, but was not going to spoil her surprise.

Carrie took off her glove and reached out, palm up. The keeper put the sixpence on it. 'Now stand very still.'

The animal uncurled its trunk and it glided out from between the bars.

Avery held his breath.

Carrie didn't dare breathe as the sinuous grey nose waved in front of her. She risked a quick peek upwards into the beast's eyes and was surprised how small they seemed in such a large head. There was a glint of amusement in those dark orbs and suddenly the fear went away. No creature who could smile in quite that way could possibly mean her harm.

She steadied her hand and watched in awe and delight at the tip of his snout, no trunk, found her fingers. A blast of wet warm air across her skin made her jump, then a sort of suction and the trunk retreated. The sixpence was gone.

'Did he eat it?' she asked in surprise, watching the animal curl up the proboscis and put it in his gaping red mouth.

'Ah, not he,' the keeper said smugly. 'He's no fool. Hold out your hand again.'

Once more, the trunk came through the bars. This time it dropped the wet sticky coin in her palm. She closed her fingers around it. The elephant's nose didn't retreat as it had before, but reached out to touched her cheek. Again, she felt that strange sense of suction.

She froze.

'It's all right, ma'am. Just his way of smelling you. Much like a dog does.'

'Can I touch him?' she whispered.

'If you wants,' the man said.

'Don't be afraid,' Avery said. 'He won't hurt you.'

She raised a hand and patted the grey wrinkly skin. It was rough to the touch and warmer than she expected. The trunk curled around her hand in the oddest way.

'He likes you,' the keeper proclaimed. 'There's not many that's brave enough to touch him.'

The animal shifted on its enormous feet and that's when she became aware of the chain around one of his ankles. 'Why is he chained?'

'A precaution, ma'am. That's a big beast.'

Chunee flapped his ears as if listening to their words. He released her hand and the tip of his trunk wandered down her length all the way to her toes. He blew out a breath and she once more felt heat and moisture against her ankles through her stockings.

A small boy escaped his nursemaid and ran up beside them. He had a sixpence in his hand, but when the elephant reached out to take it, the lad threw it and hared off.

Carrie watched, fascinated, as Chunee used his trunk to search through the straw until he located the coin. The sensitive tip of his trunk curled around it. Once more, she held out her hand and he dropped it in her palm.

'It is amazing, isn't it,' Avery said, 'that such a large animal can be so delicate. I have seen them pick up logs ten men would be hard pressed to lift and push over a tree as if it was kindling. And heaven help you if you make one angry. They can run faster than we can. And their charge is ten times worse than that of a bull.'

Carrie swallowed. The very thought of him getting loose... 'Does he ever come out?' she asked the keeper.

'He does, when he's performing in the circus. We keeps him here between times.'

A strangely sad feeling came over her. 'Do you think he's happy?' she asked Avery.

He looked surprised and frowned. 'He's well fed. He is well cared for. I don't see why not.'

She wanted to believe him. She really did.

He blew out a breath. 'You are right, Carrie. I doubt if he is truly happy. But, then, are horses truly happy? Or cows? He is very well cared for as you can see. Better cared for than some of those I saw in India, in fact.'

She reached out and rubbed the elephant's nose. It made a strange rumbling sound down its trunk. She jumped, but did not move away, just kept rubbing and the volume of the sound reduced.

'It sounds like the purr of a very large cat,' she said.

'I heard them make that sound in India when they greeted each other. He sees you as a kindred spirit.'

She liked that idea. She rubbed her hand higher up his trunk and he blew out a loud breath. Kindred spirit to an elephant.

'He makes that noise when I washes him,' the keeper said. He grinned. 'He really likes his bath. So he must really like you.'

'How long do elephants live?'

'A very long time. Fifty or sixty years, I'm told,' Avery said.

'Extraordinary.'

They walked back along the cages and a pacing tiger

snarled. She leapt back. Avery put his arm around her waist. 'Steady on. It can't get out.'

She laughed self-consciously. 'I know. He startled me, that is all.'

'Well, now you have seen an elephant, I suppose I should return you to your shop.'

She had forgotten all about the shop.

'Thank you for bringing me. It was a lovely surprise.' In fact, when she thought about it, no one had ever given her such a lovely gift. Avery was not only charming and attractive, he was thoughtful, too.

Avery guided Carrie out into the street. He had thought she would be delighted to see a real-life elephant. He still wasn't sure if he was completely forgiven, however. It would now be up to her to make the first move. He certainly wasn't going to force the issue. If she really did not want to have any more to do with him, then so be it. It was her decision. The fact that he enjoyed her company, that he liked her, was neither here nor there.

They walked in silence for a while.

'I'm sorry—'

'I'm sorry—'

They both spoke at once and they both laughed.

'You go first,' he said.

'I am sorry I got angry yesterday. You were right. I should have told you who my family is. It is just that Westram would not like the idea of his sisters as shopkeepers and milliners and I did not want to further antagonise him should he discover it. He would not be pleased were he to learn of our…association either. He is really quite stuffy about things.'

Avery would be stuffy about such things, too, were

Laura to enter into such an arrangement with a man like him. Damn it.

'And that is why you decided we should not see each other again.'

She nodded.

'I was going to apologise for my harsh words regarding your chosen profession. There is nothing wrong with it at all, I was simply surprised Westram allowed it. And apparently he does not, if you are keeping it a secret from him.'

'In our opinion, Westram has enough troubles without being burdened with the care and feeding of three widows. I must tell you that he was perfectly willing to do so until we married again. But since none of us wishes to ever be wed again, we could hardly impose on him to be responsible for us the rest of our lives. The bonnets, the shop, provide us with a means to be independent.'

'You wish never to marry again? Not ever?'

'Never.'

He ought to be dancing a jig at the news. Instead, he felt some sort of strange regret. He pushed it aside, focused on what was important. 'So my concerns of yesterday are completely without foundation.'

'Yes.'

They turned on to Piccadilly. 'Then there is no reason why we cannot continue as we agreed.'

'To share in the profits, if business increases.'

He frowned. 'And to see where our mutual attraction leads. I can assure you my attraction to you has not lessened these past few days.'

She flushed scarlet. 'But—'

'Has your attraction to me dwindled?' He might as well get to the heart of her hesitation. A lady had a right to change her mind about a fellow. In his experience, they also often said yes when they really meant no, or they pretended one thing was wrong when it was really something else. Yet he did not think Carrie was that sort. Up to now, she had always been brutally honest.

She made a funny little sound.

He peeked around the brim of her bonnet to see her face as red as a peony. 'Carrie?'

'No,' she said. And walked faster. 'Much as I do not want to, I still find you attractive.'

He forced himself not to laugh. 'Well, I will take that as a compliment.'

She snorted.

At that he laughed out loud.

She rounded on him. 'What is so funny.'

He touched the tip of her nose with a finger. 'You are, my sweet. And I adore you for making me laugh.'

A smile touched her lips. 'You are impossible. You know that.'

'I am. But in the meantime, all is forgiven and we will continue where we left off.'

'How can I say no? Clearly, a man who is able to conjure up an elephant in the middle of London is worth a second chance.'

He had the feeling there would not be a third. For a brief moment, he wished he had not made a bargain with her to do with profits and money, but then he remembered Laura's anxiety about next month's rent and he shrugged off the sentimental notion. But he did hope the attraction between them would blossom and they could find something more than simple financial gain.

And that was a shock.

But why not? She did not want to marry any more

than he did. He believed she had spoken the truth on that matter, she had been so vehement. So why should they not enjoy each other to the full?

He delivered her to her back door and kissed her hand before knocking. 'Drive out with me tomorrow, in Hyde Park?'

She looked anxious. 'Are you sure that is a good idea?'

'If we are to promote your wares to the *ton*, it is.'

She swallowed. 'You really are wishing to continue with our arrangement?'

'I am.' Her obvious reticence puzzled him. After all, even if he had changed the terms somewhat, this had been her idea. Unless... 'Are you saying you are ashamed to be seen with me?' The idea gave him a strange feeling in the pit of his stomach.

She looked horrified and he felt a sudden surge of relief. 'Of course not.' She straightened her shoulders. 'I worry that potential customers might not approve of my driving out with you, me being a shopkeeper.'

He frowned. 'You are Westram's sister-in-law.'

She shook her head. 'I have been in mourning most of the time since I married until just before opening the shop. My father died within days of the wedding and then my husband... No one really knows me as anything but a milliner. Even though they must all know the story of my husband's death, I doubt anyone would associate a mere milliner with the Earl of Westram and he is also currently out of town, so we will not meet him either.'

He had a feeling there were things she was not telling him, but he did believe she thought members of the *ton* would look down on her and he didn't like it. 'Well then, they need to know you are the best milliner in town and to do that we need to flaunt a few of those hats of yours.'

She shook her head at him, but one of her rare smiles graced her lips. 'Well, since it seems you will not take no for an answer, I will drive with you in the Park tomorrow.

He grinned. 'Wonderful. I will come for you at four.' He banged on the door.

The porter opened it and once Avery saw she was safely inside, he strolled off. To his surprise he realised he was whistling.

What was he thinking? He stopped at the end of the alley and glanced back. Great heavens, was he actually looking forward to showing her off to the *ton*? Hmm. It might be a little of that, but surely it was more about winning. It was not in his nature to simply give up on something he wanted.

Though he had given up on his father, had he not?

That was different. It was his father who had given up on him. And when the old man heard Avery was squiring a shopkeeper around town, he hoped it would give the old curmudgeon a few sleepless nights.

He glanced at his watch. It was early yet. Time enough to visit with Laura and her husband, before going to the new hell that had opened in St James's. The stakes were said to be the highest in London.

Chapter Seven

Ensconced beside the dashing Lord Avery and tooling through the streets of Mayfair, Carrie felt as if she looked down upon the world. It was the very first time she had been driven by a gentleman in Hyde Park and it felt wonderful. She felt wonderful. Feminine and somehow cherished.

Of course, she knew it was only his excellent manners that made her feel that way. Theirs was for the most part a business arrangement, after all, but he played his part to perfection and she was determined not to put him to shame. Hopefully the carriage gown she had chosen to wear today was suitable for the occasion.

He grinned at her. 'You look lovely.'

Good heavens, could the man read her mind, or was the fact that she had butterflies dancing in her stomach showing on her face? 'Thank you.' She hoped she sounded confident, instead of grateful for every crumb of kindness sent her way.

'That bonnet should draw a few eyes,' he said approvingly.

Oh, he was talking about their plan, not actually complimenting her looks. 'It is one of Petra's best efforts yet, it is called a *chapeau à la Salamanca.*'

'Clever, naming it after a battle and the military style is all the rage right now. It suits you.'

They turned through the gates into the park. Carrie was immediately struck by the vast numbers of people jostling for position. Not only were members of the *ton* in their elegant equipages vying for attention, but there were hawkers selling everything from roasted chestnuts to violets. She tried not to stare wide-eyed like some country bumpkin.

'Is this your first foray into the fashionable hour?' Avery asked, amusement in his voice.

Hmmm. Clearly, she had failed to look suitably bored. 'It is.' Now she sounded rather grim, as if he had asked her if it was the first time she had been tortured.

There had been a number of firsts coming her way ever since she'd met Lord Avery. Her first assignation at a tea house. Her first glimpse of India through the eyes of someone who had been there. Her first look at an elephant and now her very first drive in Hyde Park.

Then there was also the first she was anticipating with a mix of excitement and terror. Although that one was not yet a certainty. Her mouth dried at the thought of making love with Avery. She really wasn't sure she would be able to drum up the courage to go through with it, either, should the opportunity appear on her horizon.

A carriage drew up beside them going in the opposite direction.

Mrs Baxter-Smythe and a young girl. 'Why, how delightful, Lord Avery.' She glanced at Carrie and her eyes widened in shock, her mouth opening and closing like a landed fish. 'Mrs Greystoke,' she finally managed to say. 'Imagine meeting you.'

Carrie imagined hundreds of eyes suddenly focused on her sitting beside Lord Avery. A man known for libertine tendencies with other men's wives.

Lord Avery leaned forward and gave the girl beside Mrs Baxter-Smythe an easy smile. He held out a hand. 'I don't believe we have met. May I say how delightful you look in that hat.'

It was one of the ones the Mrs Baxter-Smythe had purchased in Carrie's shop. How clever of him to notice.

The girl blushed and looked adorably confused.

Mrs Baxter-Smyth looked horrified. 'Sukie, this is Lord Avery. Belmane's younger son. And his companion is Mrs Greystoke. Alfred, drive on!' The coach lurched forward.

'How...rude,' Carrie said looking back over her shoulder at the stiff-backed Mrs Baxter-Smythe, who was clearly lecturing her daughter.

Lord Avery chuckled softly. 'It is well known that I have no intention of taking a wife. Therefore, Sukie's mama is being suitably protective of a daughter barely out of the schoolroom.'

'You did that on purpose,' Carrie said and she could not prevent herself from smiling at the mischievous twinkle in his eyes. 'Poor girl. She'll be dreaming of you when she goes to bed tonight.'

'And her mama will remember that I liked the hat.' He gave her a quizzical look. 'Will you be dreaming of me, I wonder?' he asked with a teasing note in his voice.

'Certainly not.' Heat rushed to the roots of her hair. She hadn't meant to sound so brusque, but his question had touch her on the raw. She had been seeing his face in her dreams since the first day they met.

He laughed, sounding not at all put out, and manoeuvred around a couple of carriages whose owners had stopped to chat. 'I shall dream about you.'

'What a bouncer,' she scoffed.

He cocked an eyebrow. 'My dear Mrs Greystoke, you clearly underestimate your allure to the poor male of the species. Look at the way that fellow is staring at you.'

Indeed, another gentleman walking along the grass beside the carriage path was eyeing her through his quizzing glass. His female companion elbowed him in the ribs.

'I hope,' she said, a little more stiffly than she had intended, 'that he was admiring my hat.'

'I doubt it. Most gentlemen do not notice such things except in the most general of ways. They notice the lovely face beneath the brim. The slender neck supporting the confection. The luxurious curls framing the enchanting expression.'

The heat in her face said she must be positively scarlet at such fulsome compliments. 'I assume you are talking about the young lady by his side,' she said repressively.

'He wasn't looking at that young lady through his quizzing glass.'

'Foolish man,' she muttered.

'Do you mean him, or me?'

'You. You dolt.'

He laughed out loud, a deep, rich, happy sound that sent the butterflies in her stomach racing along her veins to dance in the tips of her fingers. How did he make her feel so utterly weak at the knees with a laugh? It wasn't right.

They reached the end of the Row and he expertly turned the carriage around without coming afoul of any of the many vehicles around them making the same difficult turn. Others weren't so fortunate. A landau and a barouche had their wheels locked, much to the amusement of a couple of children.

As they started back down the Row, they came face to face with the lady and gentlemen whom they had seen at the tea shop on Hampstead Heath.

The lady recognised them instantly and smiled and waved before leaning over to point them out to her escort.

Without thinking, Carrie waved back.

'Who the devil is that?' Avery asked.

'It is the couple we saw out at Hampstead. Surely you recognise them.'

'I didn't look that closely. I was too busy looking at you.'

Carrie's mouth dropped open.

'I was,' he said with a shrug.

'You, sir, are a terrible flirt.'

The admonishment seemed to cheer him. 'That I am.'

He drew up beside a carriage containing three very pretty young ladies, all blonde and all dressed in the height of fashion, with a woman who was either their companion or their mother.

'Mrs Greystoke, meet Miss Gideon and her sisters Lydia and Evelyn.' Miss Gideon stared intently at Carrie and she felt prickles dart down her back the way she always did when other daintier women took in her size. 'What a beautiful bonnet,' the girl exclaimed. 'Where did you buy it?'

Oh. The merchant in Carrie bustled to the fore. 'From a shop on Cork Street, First Stare Millinery.'

'It is stunning,' one of the other girls said. She frowned. 'Mrs Luttrell mentioned that shop to Mama, I believe.'

The chaperon looked up. 'She did, Miss Evelyn. A day or so ago.'

'Mother thought the address a little out of the way,' the oldest girl said. 'I think it would be worth it, if it sells hats like that one.'

Her own headgear was not nearly as nice as the one Carrie wore. 'We have lots of styles suitable for all events and weather,' she said and could not keep the pride from her voice.

Avery bowed. 'Excuse us, ladies, we are causing a traffic jam.' He set his horses in motion.

Carrie bit her lip. 'Did I press too hard? Do you think they will come to the shop?'

'Of course, they will. Everyone in London knows that my ladies wear only the most elegant of creations.'

'Then this drive has been worth it,' she said, relaxing.

He made a sound like a cross between a laugh and a groan. 'Then let us go home.' He turned on to Park Lane and set off at a spanking trot. 'I do hope you gained some personal pleasure from our drive,' he said, his eyes twinkling as he glanced her way. 'I know I did.'

Oh, yes, the man was a terrible flirt. And a man who did not take anything or anyone very seriously.

A good thing, surely. She certainly did not want to take him too seriously either. Once their time was up, they would likely never meet again. A pang squeezed her heart. A sense of loss. Apparently, she was becoming attached to him. That really would not do.

'I was wondering if you would like to come with me to the theatre tomorrow night?' he said. 'A chance to wear another of your elegant hats.'

The theatre. Another first. Longing filled Carrie, but obligation made her shake her head. 'I go home tomorrow afternoon.'

Something inside her warmed when he looked disappointed. Something she tried to douse with cold water and cold logic.

Laura looked tired Avery thought as she greeted him with a hug. 'Where is that disgraceful husband of yours?' he asked cheerfully, but perhaps a little too pointedly. It was gone nine at night.

'Working. As usual.' She sighed. 'Lannie, bring tea to the parlour, would you?'

The elderly maid took his coat and hat and disappeared into the back of the house. A very tiny house in Golders Green.

He handed over his previous night's winnings.

'You shouldn't,' Laura said, looking torn. 'John doesn't like it.'

He liked his brother-in-law, mostly, but John did not like him passing along his winnings at the tables. The man found it hard to accept that he was not yet providing a good enough income to support a wife and child.

'Don't tell him, then.'

Laura shook her head. 'We do not keep secrets from each other.'

They had married for love. Their father, his Dukeliness, had not approved the match, but Laura and John had gone ahead anyway. Once John built his practice up now that he had passed the bar, his income would increase substantially. Until then Avery would continue to do what he could for his sister and to hell with what John thought.

'I promise you, I won this honestly and no one was left destitute upon the parish.'

She smiled. 'I hope you kept enough for yourself this time.'

Laura had come to his lodgings unexpectedly and found it freezing cold. She had been most indignant that he had given all of his winnings to her and left himself without sufficient funds to heat his room. He had promised he would never do such a thing again.

'I did. And how is my nephew, the estimable Derek?' Derek was nearly two years old and the reason Laura had been required to wed so precipitously, despite her father's insistence that she could marry as he dictated and pass the child off as her husband's. Or not. He had said no one would care as long as they became part of the ducal family.

Sadly, he was right.

But despite the bullying and threats from her father, Laura had run off with John. And was now cut off from any financial support from that quarter. But John was getting more and more clients and soon would be on his feet, according to Laura.

Avery could not wait for that day to come. Then he would be free to return to his travels. His wanderings, as Laura called them. And yet, unexpectedly, at least for the moment, he was in no hurry to leave London. A certain Mrs Greystoke continued to hold his interest, though he could not figure out why. Perhaps it was the thought of that magnificent figure unclothed and beneath him. No doubt once he had had his wicked way with her, he could move on to pastures green. If the war continued the way it was going, soon all of Europe would be open to travel.

The thought left him feeling hollow. Almost homesick. He pushed the sensation aside. He had no home here in England.

'Derek is asleep, bless him,' Laura said, her face lighting up.

The maid brought the tea tray and some shortbread biscuits which Avery wolfed down.

'Haven't you had dinner?' Laura said disapprovingly.

'Not yet. I thought I'd go to the chop house when I left here.'

'You will not.' She rang the bell and the maid returned. 'Set the table for one and bring Lord Avery some stew.'

'I can't eat John's supper,' Avery protested.

'You can and you will. Besides, there is plenty enough for two.'

Avery grinned. 'Bossy.'

'Stupid.'

Once he'd eaten and was leaning back in his chair, thoroughly replete, Laura gazed at him over the top of her knitting. 'I gather you have a new lady friend?'

His heart stilled. He kept his face bland. 'I have several friends who are ladies.'

'Don't be obtuse, Avery. I'm your sister. A statuesque brunette has been seen on your arm on more than one occasion. I still have contacts among the *ton*, you know. Who is she?'

Laura had always been popular among her peers because she never put on airs. Her closest friends hadn't abandoned her, despite her fall from grace, either.

'One of my shopkeepers fits your description. Perhaps

it is she of whom you have heard.' Laura knew about his other form of income in the vaguest of ways.

Laura frowned. 'You don't usually parade shopkeepers in Hyde Park. You really are intent on getting your revenge on Papa.'

Good Lord, the visit to the park had been only yesterday. News travelled fast. 'Heard about that, did you? She is a lovely woman. Runs a milliner's shop in Cork Street. You should look in on her. Her hats are true works of art.'

'Harriet's godmother said she's seen you with her twice now. She said the lady was strikingly handsome.'

Good lord. It was a small world. Harriet was Laura's oldest and dearest friend. Her family had gone against the tide of opinion by supporting Laura's decision to marry a mere lawyer, despite the ducal fury. And Harriet's godmother was right, Carrie was striking and quite lovely when she smiled, though the lady herself did not seem to think so. Indeed, he often had the feeling Carrie felt that she was some sort of antidote.

'I don't believe I know who Harriet's godmother is. What is her name?'

'Countess Longacre. She and her husband are leaving town tomorrow, so Harriet said. They were passing through London on the way to their property in the north and stopped for a few days to visit friends.'

He had forgotten how small London really was, or at least the London of the *ton*. Everyone was connected to everyone else.

He missed that about England. Until now, he hadn't realised just how alone he had been these past few years. How lacking in companionship. Being with Carrie had somehow brought it to the fore.

An odd pang pierced his chest. 'Well, believe me, it is nothing but a business arrangement.'

Despite being settled beside the hearth with her sisters-in-law around her, Carrie could not stop her mind from wandering back to Avery. Had he gone to the theatre alone, or with someone else? She couldn't help hoping it was the former.

Petra peered at her over the hat she was decorating. 'There is something different about you, Carrie. What has happened?'

Marguerite put down the book she was reading out loud and glanced from one to the other. 'Different how?'

Oh, dear, she might have guessed Petra would suspect something; the girl was just too perceptive for her own good. 'Yes,' she said, hoping she did not sound defensive. 'Different how?'

Petra pursed her lips. 'You look…happier. There is a glow about you that was not there before.'

A glow? 'I am just pleased that things are going well with the shop, I suppose.'

Marguerite set the book aside. 'It is wonderful,' she said, thoughtfully. 'I am astonished, to be honest, given how many established milliners there are in London.'

'None of them have a flair for uniqueness the way you do,' Petra said. 'I am not at all surprised.'

Marguerite had the most amazing ideas, but it was Petra who was able to bring them bring them to life. She was an excellent needlewoman.

'It is not only the hats,' Carrie said. 'The lingerie is very popular too. We are nearly sold out.' Glad that Petra had accepted her explanation, she forced her mind to turn to business. 'I am guessing we will need double the number of nightgowns next week. Or more.'

'Oh, dear,' Petra said. She looked at Marguerite. 'I don't see how we can possibly double our output *and* produce more hats if they are also selling as well as you say.'

The hats were more expensive and ladies usually only purchased one or two per Season, but they were purchasing the nightgowns by the half-dozen. 'We will need to employ some women from the village to help.'

'Oh,' Marguerite said dubiously. 'So we are to start a factory? I am not sure Westram would approve.'

'Pooh,' Petra said dismissively. 'He never comes near the place. He won't know anything about it. Besides, they don't have to come here to work. We can provide them with the materials and the instructions and they can make them in their own homes.'

Carrie nodded. 'And I cannot see why Westram would object should it ever come to his attention. The additional income to the families will encourage his farm labourers to remain in the village, instead of them departing to work in the factories up north.' The cotton and wool mills were gobbling up workers across the country, leaving farms with fewer and fewer men to tend to the land.

'I can also limit the number of gowns sold to each lady,' Carrie suggested.

Marguerite frowned. 'Why would we want to do that?'

'Because then they will pay a higher price for them,' Carrie said.

'Or they will go elsewhere,' Petra warned.

'No one else will provide what we provide,' Carrie said with a certainty that caused the other two ladies stared at her.

'Quality and uniqueness.'

'The two things that are important to the *ton*,' Petra agreed. 'And for that they will pay outrageous sums, too. We will have to keep coming up with new ideas, though, Marguerite.'

Marguerite opened her sketchbook. 'I will see what I can do.' She glanced over at Carrie. 'I agree with Petra, though. There is something different about you.' Her expression changed. 'Do not tell me you have met a man?'

Carrie felt her face heat. 'I—'

'You have,' Petra squealed. 'I knew it! When are we going to meet him? What is his name? Are you—'

'Stop!' Marguerite said, staring at Carrie intently. 'Can you not see you are embarrassing the poor girl? If she doesn't want to tell us, that is her business.' She bit her bottom lip. 'You will be careful, won't you, Carrie? Men are such fickle creatures.'

And you couldn't get more fickle than Lord Avery. Which was why she had picked him. She groaned out loud. 'I have entered into an agreement with a gentleman. He is part of the reason our business has improved so rapidly. But—'

'Are you lovers?' Petra asked.

Carrie's face burned. 'No!'

'But you would like to be.' Petra's face lit up. 'Oh, Carrie, how wonderful. The first of us to have a gentleman caller. I am proud of you.'

Surprisingly, although Petra had seemed so devastated by the loss of her husband, she had been the one to suggest that they might entertain gentlemen once they were out of mourning, should they so desire. She seemed almost anxious for her sisters to enjoy the delights of the marriage bed, as she had called them when they had discussed the matter.

'I am not sure I am quite ready for that sort of thing,' Carrie said awkwardly, unwilling to say too much about Avery in case it should all come to naught.

Petra sighed. 'I can understand that. I am certainly not ready for it myself, but you had so little time with Jonathan. It doesn't seem right that your youth should be wasted just because—' She bit her lip and waved a hand. Oh, dear, was she going to cry again?

Marguerite pressed her lips together. She had been more reticent about the whole idea of them being merry widows, but then she was the oldest sister and had very strict notions of propriety. On the other hand, it had been her idea to convince Westram to let them live quietly in the countryside as independent women. And she had agreed that as such they should be able to do whatever took their fancy. Provided they were discreet.

'Marguerite, tell Carrie about the local squire,' Petra said. 'He is a bachelor.'

'A most disreputable one, too.' She visibly straightened. 'I would sooner hear about this man of yours, Carrie.'

Hers. The thought carried a lovely warmth with it. Well, he was hers, for the moment, she supposed. Carrie shared as much as she dared, but said nothing about him being the son of a duke, leaving them with the idea that he was some sort of merchant.

She felt a little uncomfortable about doing so, but they would never meet him and in a few days their little affair would be over. Indeed, it might never amount to much of anything at all.

Carrie collapsed, exhausted, in her little sitting room. Avery had been right, their brief foray into society together had brought curious ladies to her shop. There had been a constant stream of customers since midday and not one of them had complained about the prices. Indeed, it seemed the more exclusive and expensive the shop, the better they liked the wares. She really hoped Petra's idea of employing women to help with making the nightgowns worked, or soon they would completely run out of items to sell.

She pushed to her feet, filling her kettle with water and putting it on the hob. Something else unexpected was the way she had looked up with hope in her heart at every tinkle of the shop door bell. And the way her heart had dropped each time when the jaunty figure of Lord Avery had not been the one stepping through her door.

She just wished she had told her sisters-in-law the truth about him. That she had offered him money to become her lover. But how was she to explain that, while he'd been kind enough to pretend take her out to tea and to visit an elephant, somehow she had the feeling he was doing it because he was reluctant to take matters between them any further? He was simply being kind.

One thing was certain, whatever happened in the end, being seen in his company had definitely helped the business. He had certainly earned his finder's fee and for that she would be eternally grateful.

Tired to the bone, she removed her cap and pulled the pins from her hair, while she waited for the kettle to boil. She removed her shoes and put on the slippers Marguerite had embroidered for her as a Christmas gift.

A knock sounded on the door.

A breath left her in a rush. She bolted upright. Heavens above, was he here now? She glanced in the mirror, realising that her hair was a tangled mess hanging down her back, and her face was pale. She pinched her cheeks to bring a bit of colour to them.

'Mrs Greystoke? I have your supper here.'

Supper. How on earth could she have forgotten? Mrs Spate cooked her dinner at the same time as she cooked for the Thrumbys. Carrie felt so tired, she simply hadn't been hungry enough to tell the woman she was ready for dinner. She got up and unlocked her door. The middle-aged cook brought in a tray and put it on the table. She was so thin and angular, no one would ever guess she was an excellent cook, except perhaps the redness in her cheeks from bending over a hot stove might give her away.

'There you go, ma'am,' the woman said with a smile. She put her hands on her hips and eyed Carrie up and down. 'And mind you eat it all. Mrs Thrumby's orders.'

Her landlord's wife was a motherly sort and seemed to see it as her duty to keep an eye on Carrie.

Carrie inhaled. 'It smells delicious. I am starving.' She was, too. She just hadn't noticed.

'I'll send the girl down for the tray later.'

'Thank you.'

The woman bustled out and Carrie pulled up her chair to the table. It did smell delicious. There was a juicy pork chop with apple sauce, a bowl of clear soup, fresh baked bread, and buttered carrots and parsnips. And a little bowl of rice pudding for dessert. A meal fit for a queen.

She tucked in heartily. She had never been one to pick at her food. Finally, full to bursting, she put all the dishes back on the tray, leaned back in her chair and closed her eyes. She simply needed a minute or two, then she would put the tray outside the door.

A soft knock startled her awake.

Her gaze took in the tray of empty dishes. Darn. She had not yet put it outside. 'Coming,' she called.

The door opened instead.

There, looking elegant if a little damp, was Lord Avery. He grinned.

She gasped and put a hand to her hair. 'I thought you were the maid from upstairs come to collect the tray.'

'Sorry. No.'

'I— Oh,' She blinked to clear her head.

'May I come in? Your porter recognised me and let me find my own way.'

'Of course.' She got up and picked up the tray.

He took it from her hands. 'Where do you want it?'

Finally, her brain started to work instead of wanting to drink in his sartorial elegance. 'Outside the door.' She certainly didn't want the maid coming inside to fetch it while he was here.

While he put it outside the door, she ran frantic fingers through her hair, trying to coax it into some sort of order.

He closed the door and gave her another of his beautiful smiles. 'I am sorry, I should have sent around a note telling you I would call in, but it wasn't until I found myself close by that I thought of it.'

She was ridiculously pleased to see him, though she wished she had changed into something nicer. She gestured to a chair. 'May I offer you tea?'

He hesitated, his gaze searching her face.

The bottom dropped out of her stomach. One look at her in disarray and he was wishing he had stayed away.

Then he crossed the room and took the chair. 'A cup of tea would be lovely.'

Relieved, she stirred up the fire to heat the water

more quickly. 'I am sorry I do not have anything stronger to offer.' She ought to get something in. Wine or port. Brandy?

'Tea is most welcome.'

He had such lovely manners, she turned to face him with a smile.

'I cannot stop long,' he said, looking slightly uncomfortable.

What? Oh, he had said he was close by. He had not intended to stay. He must have seen from her face how pleased she was to see him and was simply pandering to the gruff widow who had to pay for a man's company. A pang squeezed her heart. She turned back to making the tea, determined not to show she was in the slightest bit hurt.

'I have some biscuits if you would like some,' she said over her shoulder, as she poured the water over the tea leaves.

'No, thank you. I have a dinner engagement.'

'Oh, I hope this won't make you late?' she said cheerily.

'Not at all.'

She brought the tray to the table and set it down between them.

'You look tired,' he said.

A polite way of saying she looked as if she'd been pulled through a hedge backwards. If only she hadn't pulled all the pins out of her hair. 'The shop was extremely busy today. You are going to be very pleased with our increase in profits.' She hoped she sounded businesslike and not hurt. Fortunately, he was not looking at her, he was stirring the sugar she had put in his tea.

'I am glad it is going well.' He looked up, smiling. 'But you must be careful not to run yourself ragged.'

The hedge turned into a shipwreck. 'Oh, I am used to hard work.'

He nodded. 'Still, do not overdo it.'

'I won't.' The man was unusually solicitous. It was part of his charm. No doubt his special ladies really appreciated how attentive he was. She pushed back the jealous thought. She had no right to be jealous.

She wanted to ask him where he planned to go for dinner, but resisted the urge. It was none of her business. Even a wife would hesitate to ask her husband such questions, at least according to her aunt who, on the morning of Carrie's wedding, had tried to give her some advice about the sort of things a wife might expect from a husband. Leaving the next day for Portugal had not been on the list.

'I did have a reason for coming here this evening.' His jaw flickered. He looked a little less sure of himself than usual.

Oh, this was it, he was going to end their arrangement. She steeled herself. 'What is that?' She made herself smile, a thing of carelessness, though her lips felt stiff and her chest tight.

'I wanted to ask if you will you drive out again with me on Wednesday afternoon.'

Wednesday would be the second half-day closing day he had asked her to do something with him. The pain of thinking of saying goodbye was replaced by a lightness out of proportion to the invitation. 'You think we should go to Hyde Park again?'

'No. I think we have accomplished all we set out to do. This will be purely pleasure.'

She tried not to let his words sound like more than they were. He was being kind, that was all. He did say he wanted them to get to know each other better. This was part of it. 'Where will we go? Back to the tea shop?'

He shook his head. 'It is a surprise.'

She didn't always like surprises. Sometime they were not very pleasant. But… 'Very well. Wednesday afternoon. What time?'

'Noon, if you can manage it?'

'I can. Tansy can manage for the hour or so before the shop closes.'

'Good. I'll be off now, then.'

To her surprise he leaned in and kissed her cheek.

She was still touching the spot his lips had caressed when the door to the street closed behind him.

Chapter Eight

Avery found himself whistling as he knocked at Carrie's door on Wednesday afternoon. He was a few minutes late. He hoped Carrie wouldn't give him a bear-garden jaw, but he'd had a little more trouble borrowing the carriage than usual. His brother had caught him in the carriage house and had futilely wasted precious minutes trying to persuade him to visit with their father.

Avery had been very tempted, but when he asked if the old fellow actually wanted to see him, Bart had looked more than a little tense. 'Somebody has to make the first move towards a reconciliation,' he had mumbled.

'That's all very well,' Avery had replied. 'The question is whether he will throw me out on my ear when I tell him I still have no intention of marrying to please him.'

'Dammit, Avery, you don't have to say that, you could just say you simply are not ready yet. Give him some hope of winning, at least. You know what a stubborn, prideful man he is.'

'I am not going to lie to him.'

Bart had looked ready to throttle him. 'If you don't act soon, you might never get the chance to make things right with him.'

A cold shiver had run down his spine. 'Is he that ill?'

'I don't know. The doctors will tell me nothing. On his orders.'

'I'll think about it.'

Bart sighed. 'Please do.'

'Now, may I borrow your carriage? I have an appointment.'

For a moment, Avery had thought his brother was going to say no, perhaps as a way to try to bring him to heel, but then he merely waved a hand, a gesture of assent.

'You usually take the curricle.'

'I need the town carriage today.' He wanted a bit of privacy. 'I'll have it back by seven at the latest.'

'Do not rush on my account,' his brother said. His voice sounded a little thin. 'I'm too busy for gallivanting.'

'All work and no play made Jack a dull boy,' Avery quipped, but his brother was already out of the stable doors and heading for the house. He wasn't sure whether he'd heard him or not.

Perhaps he should have followed Bart in and tried to make his peace with his father. But he knew Papa very well. An apology would not suffice. Only obeying the ducal edict would make the old autocrat happy.

Thrumby's porter was used to Avery coming and going and did no more than touch his hat and nod when he admitted Avery.

Carrie opened her door the moment he knocked. She looked delightful in a rich burgundy-and-black-striped carriage gown with a shako-styled hat set at an angle and sporting a net veil that skimmed the bridge of her nose and made her look mysterious, and elegant. Only a tall woman could carry off such a look.

'You look…magnificent.'

She looked surprised. 'Why, thank you, my lord.' She tipped her head to one side. 'Since you didn't say where we were going I was not sure what to wear.'

'That outfit is perfect for our destination.' He frowned at it. 'Or it will be if…' He checked the hem and smiled. 'Good, there is a loop to hold up your hems. I wouldn't like your gown to become soiled.'

'So, we are walking, then?'

'We will be, once we get there.'

She laughed and shook her head. 'No use trying to tease it out of you, I see.'

He laughed. 'None at all. Shall we?'

He escorted her out to the carriage and they climbed aboard.

Laughter was still bright in her eyes. 'Shall I try to guess?'

He crossed the small space between them and sat at her side, put one arm around her shoulders and gave her a grin. 'Now that would be a waste of your breath.'

She gazed up at him, her grey eyes questioning, her full lips parted, tempting him to discover their softness and plumb the sweetness of her mouth. He lowered his head a fraction, holding her gaze, seeking her permission. Heat rushed through his veins. His body tingled.

Her breathing quickened as if the air within the carriage had become too thin, her full bosom rose and fell in the most delectable way, yet there were shadows in her eyes. A slight furrow in her brow. She was worried. Unsure.

He did not want her anxious or afraid. He wanted her joyful and happy. Desiring him as much as he desired her. But it was far too soon for that. Knowing women as he did, he was not entirely surprised at her reticence. They had met each other only recently, but even in that short time he had learned she was not the careless sort.

Kissing her now, as much as he wanted to, might well have her fleeing for the safety of her family. He took a deep breath and, ignoring his body's demands for more, he gave her shoulders a light squeeze, careful not to crush her pretty hat. How marvellously well she fit into the crook of his arm.

The tension in her body eased and they gazed out of the window in companionable silence for a time. Something else he liked about her. The lack of incessant chatter. The aura of calm that surrounded her, now she wasn't fearing his intentions.

'Are you ever going to tell me where we are going?' she asked when they had left the outskirts of town. 'This is certainly not the way to Hampstead.'

'You are right. But you will see where we are going when we get there. I really want it to be a surprise.'

'A nice one, I hope.'

'It is certainly intended to be. It isn't too far, I promise.'

Soon they entered the village of Paddington and drew up near a village green crowded with people and stalls as he had been promised. He breathed a sigh of relief.

Carrie sat up straight, then turned in her seat to face him. 'It is a fair!'

'A rather small one, I'm afraid. Would you like to take in the sights?'

She shook her head at him. 'You are a very surprising man, Lord Avery.'

'I simply aim to please. It is nowhere near as grand as the Goose Fair in Nottingham, but I thought it might amuse you for a while this afternoon.'

He climbed down and helped her out. She hooked her arm through his and gazed about her with bright eyes and a smile on her lips. At the sight of her pleasure, his heart swelled in the stupidest of ways. 'What would you like to do first: visit the stalls, ride on the merry-go-round, or watch one of the side shows?'

She laughed with delight. 'You mean us to actually ride on the merry-go-round?'

'Naturally.'

'Then let us do that first.'

It was what he would have chosen, too. He guided her across the green to the far side where the merry-go-round held the place of honour in amongst a milling crowd.

Now she was faced with the whirling structure, Carrie's heart picked up speed. Would she dare? But with Avery's gentle pressure at the base of her spine, it seemed she had little choice. After her bold words, she certainly wasn't going to back down.

Avery paid for their tickets and they waited in line for their turn. As she looked about her, she realised there were very few people present whom she would call gentry. The patrons looked like shop girls on their afternoon off, or labourers, plus an assortment of very rough characters who looked like they would cut your purse or your throat with equal enthusiasm. She shifted closer to Avery, who put an arm around her waist.

A tall, skinny, middle-aged man in an old-fashioned frock coat and a top hat wandered over to the line in which they stood. He removed his hat and beamed. He opened his arms wide as if he was meeting a group of old friends. 'Ladies and gents, lassies and lads, I offer you a wonder of nature not to be missed. Did you ever wonder what the future held? Did you ever want to improve your fortune at the tables, or know which horse to bet on in a race? Madame Rose can tell you all this and more. All you need to do is cross her palm with a bit of silver and you will gaze into the future.'

'Can she tell me where to find a handsome husband?' a young woman further up the line called out. Her friend giggled and nudged her with her elbow.

'She will answer whatever you ask her,' the barker said, drawing closer to the two girls. 'She'll give you a love potion if you wants.'

''Ow do we know she's not a fraud?' the other girl said. 'She's a gypsy, isn't she?'

The barker smile widened. 'She tells you things about you no one else knows. You'll see.'

The girls whispered to each other and checked their meagre store of coins. The queue shuffled forward. Soon it would be her and Avery's turn for the merry-go-round.

Carrie's stomach lurched when the barker's toothy grin focused on her next. Avery gave her a little squeeze. 'We will visit you a little later, friend.' Avery had a certain presence about him, a confidence that brooked no argument.

The man's friendly grin wavered a bit, but he bowed and moved on.

Carrie let go a sigh of relief.

'Would you like to have your fortune told?' Avery asked.

Did she really want to know her future? What if she didn't like what was in store? 'Would you?'

'I wouldn't mind knowing the outcome of the New-market cup,' he said. 'I'd be set up for life.'

Gambling. Her stomach churned. He might think a wager on a horse race was harmless enough, but she knew better. Jonathan had gambled away a huge amount of money Westram could ill afford and then married her to help pay off his debts. He'd ruined not only his own life, but impoverished his sisters and his unwanted wife. And then he'd had the gall to take his own life by flinging himself into battle because he'd never wanted to marry her in the first place.

In trying to explain what had happened to all her father's money, Westram had said that in his opinion some people got so caught up in the excitement of winning, they could not stop even when they lost. It was some sort of compulsion. A compulsion that had hurt too many people in Carrie's opinion.

One man of that sort in her life was one man too many, if they did not care whom they hurt.

'I would far sooner let the future be a surprise,' she said quietly.

He laughed. 'Don't be such a stick in the mud.'

'You don't really expect her to tell you the outcome of a horse race, do you?' Heaven forefend he risked his money based on such things.

'Her guess is as good as mine. Come on, Carrie, it is only a bit of fun.'

He seemed so cavalier about the whole idea. It didn't

sit well in her stomach, but who was she to spoil the day? 'All right. We'll go after this.'

They shuffled forward again and watched the two shop girls whirling around, their giggles rising to shrieks the faster the two men in the centre of the contraption pushed against the spokes. And then it was their turn.

They sat side by side on the seats of a replica of an open carriage, while another couple mounted a goose and a gander and a mother and child mounted a couple of gaily painted horses. It turned slowly at first. Avery put his arm around her waist to steady her and the world around them passed by in a blur. Carrie closed her eyes.

Beside her Avery laughed, clearly enjoying the sensation that made her stomach feel queasy. She forced her eyes open and gradually managed to pick out things as they rushed by. A girl selling ribbons. A donkey giving rides to children. The colourful awnings of the stalls. She grinned at Avery and then giggled, resting her head on his shoulder and enjoying the sensation of closeness in the rush of movement.

The roundabout slowed and came to a stop. Avery helped her down. Strangely the earth beneath her feet seemed to keep moving. She staggered a few steps while he held her tight. Finally, the world stopped spinning and everything was back to normal.

'Are you all right?' he asked.

He sounded concerned. She gave her head a little shake. 'Yes, I think so. That was fun.' She glanced back over her shoulder. 'Thank you. I would never have dared to get on there by myself.'

'You look a little pale.'

She put her palms to her face. 'Do I? How odd. My

stomach was a little queasy at first, but I did become used to it.'

He took her hand. 'What would you like to do next? Look at the fairings?'

Glad he hadn't suggested the fortune teller, she nodded. 'I need some ribbons for the shop. Perhaps they will have something suitable.'

They walked along the row of carts and barrows some of which were set beneath striped awnings. There were all sorts of things for sale. Lucky hares' feet, ribbons of every colour, trinkets made of china, bunches of heather, bits of lace, pipe stems. But the ribbons were mostly not new and Carrie decided they would not do for the quality of hats in her shop.

Avery bought her a sprig of heather to pin on her coat for luck while she bought him a handkerchief that likely had been stolen. They laughed about their purchases, vowing they would keep them as mementoes of the day. A baker ringing a bell caught Avery's attention. He had a tray of delicious-smelling meat pies balanced on his head.

'Are you hungry?' Avery asked.

'I am,' she said. 'It must be all the fresh air.'

The baker lifted the tray down so they could make their choices.

'I am not sure I can eat a whole one,' Carrie said. Her stomach gave a little grumble as if to deny her words and they collapsed laughing.

The baker looked at them as if they had run mad.

'Two pies, please,' Avery said, handing over some coins, and they wandered along side by side eating their treat. A small dog appeared and danced along beside them. It leaped up and down all around them, begging.

A small boy charged over as if to claim the animal and stumbled into Avery, who caught him by the arm and gave him a little shake. 'Go play off your tricks somewhere else, lad,' he growled.

The boy gave him a cheeky grin and dashed away, calling the dog as he went.

Carrie blinked. 'What was that about.'

'He was trying to pick my pocket.'

Avery didn't seem angry.

'Is he not a little young to be involved in crime?' Carrie asked.

'Not these days. Most of the crime committed in London is committed by children.' His voice was grim.

'Something ought to be done about it.'

'There are things being done, but not nearly enough. Wipe your hands on this.' He passed her his handkerchief, not the one she had given him, but another. 'It is clean.'

She chuckled, did as he suggested and handed it back. 'I suppose he was trying to steal this.'

'Likely. And that lace you were looking at earlier was likely cut from the bottom of some poor unsuspecting lady's petticoat, so you had better watch out for yours.'

'This way, lady and gentleman,' a greasy-looking man called out to them. 'In here you will see the most amazing sight of your life. Take a peep at the bearded lady. It is as real as the hair on your face, sir. Pull it if you don't believe it.'

Carrie grimaced. 'I don't think I really—'

'Nor me,' Avery said. 'I am much more interested in the fortune teller.'

Carrie's heart sank. She had been hoping to avoid that too. But it seemed that it was inevitable. They wove their way between the people flocking around the stalls and avoided the flocks of geese and the man offering to box anyone who would like to try to win a shilling and found the little red-and-white-striped tent on the outskirts of green.

There was no evidence of the barker, but a sign pinned to one of the flaps proclaimed that Madame Rosie was in and willing to read palms, tea leaves or look in her crystal ball for a variety of prices.

'Come in,' a hollow-sounding, foreign-accented voice said.

'There are two of us,' Avery said.

'That is fine,' Madame Rose replied from the dark inside of the tent. 'Come in, my lord.'

Avery winked. 'It seems the lady knows her business.'

Avery held back the canvas for Carrie to enter. Perhaps this wasn't such a good idea after all. He'd been teasing her when he suggested they have their fortunes told, but he had a sense that Carrie, while she had agreed, was apprehensive.

He leaned close and lowered his voice. 'Don't take anything she says seriously. It is all a hum.'

Once the tent flap closed, it took a moment or two for his eyes to adjust to the dim light inside. To his surprise, the woman sitting at the table on the other side of the room was not some old crone, but a rather attractive girl with dark brown eyes and black hair pulled severely back under a kerchief. She seemed to be draped in brightly coloured scarves. Her idea of a gypsy costume, no doubt.

She waved towards the chair placed on the other side of the table. 'Sit, please.'

Her heavily accented voice made the hairs on the back of his neck stand up for some reason. Ignoring the strange sensation, he led Carrie to the chair and stood behind her.

Madame Rose held out her hand palm up.

Carrie glanced over her shoulder at him. 'She wants her money.'

Avery handed over a coin. The woman looked at it closely, then it seemed to disappear, no doubt up her sleeve. She must think him a Johnny Raw if she expected him to fall for those sorts of tricks. He realised she was staring at him. When she saw that she had his attention she jerked her chin. 'Stand over there. I wish to be private with the lady.'

'I'm not leaving.'

'I did not say leave.' She glared at him. 'Move over there.'

There was another chair in the corner adjacent to the opening into the tent. Carrie nodded. 'I'll be quite safe with you there.'

Safer than she likely knew. His travels had taught him to be alert for danger and to always be prepared. He therefore never went anywhere without a knife in his pocket. If the woman was really some sort of seer, she would know that already. More likely she would have guessed he would not come to a fairground completely unarmed. He didn't believe in her nonsense, but he had no doubt she would be skilled at judging people. He retired to his corner and kept a close eye on the woman as well as the entrance.

After a moment's discussion, it seemed that Carrie had decided to have her palm read. As the gypsy's voice dropped into a low mutter, Avery discovered he could not make out a single word. There was some chatter back and forth as if the woman was asking Carrie questions. The woman bent over Carrie's palm, turning it this way and that to catch the light and muttering in a low monotone. He felt his eyelids droop. Damn, it was warm in here.

Carrie gasped at something the woman said.

Avery straightened, his gaze flying to her face, but while she had pulled back a little, she did not seem to be in any danger. Madame Rose said something that sounded comforting and non-threatening and Carrie leaned forward again, peering intently at the finger tracing the lines on her palm. The muttering began again.

A few moments later it was over and Carrie was getting up.

Avery rose and strode forward. 'Is everything all right?' he asked Carrie. She looked shaken, but not exactly scared.

'Yes. Everything is fine.'

'What did she tell you?'

She laughed. 'Not to tell anyone what she said. Really, it is nothing but a lot of nonsense.'

The girl grinned. 'You wait and see, my lady. You will know I am right and you will thank me.'

'She will never see you again,' Avery said firmly.

The girl shook with silent laughter and the bangles hanging from her ears and festooning her wrists jingled. 'Take your seat, sir.'

Carrie started to move away.

'You may stay, my lady,' the girl said. 'There is nothing for him to know that he does not already know. Bring her the chair, if you would, sir?'

These people always talked in riddles. It was part of

their stock in trade, but he carried the chair over, then sat in the one vacated by Carrie and held out his palm.

'No, no, my lord. It is the cards for you, I think.'

More mumbo jumbo. He shrugged. 'As you please.'

She began laying out a deck of large cards with a strange design on their backs. Once she had them set out in rows, she began turning them over one by one and muttering. After she turned the last card over, she gave him an odd look. 'Your fortune intertwines with this lady's, but the path is not straight.'

She sat back.

'That's it?' he asked. 'That tells me nothing. Clearly, this lady and I are friends. Anyone could tell me that. What about the first race of the Season at Newmarket? Do you have a prediction?'

She wrinkled her nose and peered at the cards. 'A black horse with a white flash on its nose.'

'What about it?'

She stared at it again. 'It will change your fortune.'

'How? Good or bad?'

She shrugged. 'It depends on what path you choose before then.'

He laughed. 'You really are a charlatan, aren't you? Hedging your bets very well, my dear.'

Carrie shifted uncomfortably. He took her hand in his. He didn't know what the woman had told her, but he didn't want her taking it too seriously.

The gypsy girl gave him a cold stare. 'I can only tell you what I see, but estrangement from someone important in your life is a key turning point. Only by swallowing your pride will you ever know true happiness.'

His pride? He was not the one who was proud. If it wasn't impossible, he would have said his father had paid her to tell him this nonsense. He laughed. 'You know who I am, don't you?'

'I have no idea. I am only telling you what I see.'

'Rubbish. Anyone who knows me would have said just what you said. Your barker discovered who I was and told you, so you could pretend to know what you are talking about. I have met your sort before. Many times.'

'The cards tell me that it was once your dearest wish to be a soldier when you were a lad. But you chose a darker path.'

His stomach fell away. No one knew of his youthful dream. Absolutely no one. Apart from his father, who had refused to allow it. He swallowed the sudden dryness in his throat. 'A lucky guess. Every boy wants to be a soldier.' Why did he sound unconvinced?

The woman touched one of the cards. 'You are coming to a fork in the road of life, my lord. Choose wisely. At the moment, you appear poised to head in the wrong direction.'

'What are these choices you speak of?'

Her voice changed to an odd sort of monotone. 'The cards have spoken.' She shook her head as if to clear it. She gathered up her cards.

'I hardly call that speaking. I have more questions than answers.'

'It is in your hands.' The woman got to her feet and Avery stood, too, out of politeness, though he hardly felt polite. He felt irritated.

The tent flap drew back, letting in daylight. He turned to see the barker gesturing them out 'This way out, ma'am, my lord. Madame Rose has spoken.'

When he turned back Madame Rose had gone.

Damn it all. Of all the ideas he'd had, this one was

likely one of the worst. He hadn't thought about his father's refusal to buy him a commission in the army in years.

He escorted Carrie out of the tent and into a day that had turned from reasonably bright to overcast. 'Where to now?'

Carrie glanced up at the sky. 'Do you think it is going to rain?'

'It is hard to tell, but it seems likely. Shall I take you home?'

'I certainly think we should head back in the direction of the carriage, don't you? We can look at the rest of the stalls on the way.'

They sauntered between the stalls. 'Don't take anything Madame Rose told you too seriously,' he advised. 'There is nothing of the occult in what they do. It is all trickery and clever guesses.'

She glanced at him, her eyes troubled. 'I suppose so.'

'No, truly. I know these—oh, will you look at that. Have you ever seen a sword swallower?'

'A—? No, what is that?'

Pleased to have found something to take her mind off the fortune teller, he grabbed her hand and hurried her through the gathering crowd around a man with several swords laid out on a bench at his side.

Carrie's eyes widened. 'You are not going to tell me he is going to swallow those swords.'

'He is. In a manner of speaking.'

'I suppose you are going to tell me this is another trick.'

'There is certainly a trick to it,' he agreed.

Carrie stared in horror at the young man who stood in the middle of the circle of curious people. Beneath a black cape, he wore his shirt open at the throat and tucked into a wide belt studded with shiny metal. A bandana encircled his forehead, giving him a piratical look.

Another man moved through the crowd, holding out a hat. 'Famous throughout Europe for his daring and skill, the Spanish Count will astonish and delight. Never will you see his like again,' the man shouted as he passed through the gathering.

Avery tossed some coins in the hat. The man bowed and winked. 'Thank you, sir.' He continued on, shouting his words of encouragement until he must have decided he had received enough donations.

Meanwhile, the performer stood, arms folded, looking imperiously down his nose is if all commercial transactions were beneath him. He reminded her of Westram.

She giggled.

'What?'

'He looks like my brother-in-law.'

Avery narrowed his eyes. 'That much of a tartar, is he?'

Oh, she really should not give him that impression of her beleaguered brother-in-law. 'He can be, when pressed.'

The barker returned to the performer's side and muttered something in his ear, then turned to the crowd. 'Ladies and gentlemen, I present the Count of Barcelona.'

The young man bowed and removed his cape with a flourish.

The crowd shuffled closer. Avery put his arm around her shoulders, holding her close and serving as a barricade against the press of people. She felt protected. Cared for. It was such a lovely feeling.

A feeling the fortune teller had warned her against, before she'd said her odd rhyme.

Trusting your head will ensure your safety, I confess.
Trusting your heart is taking a chance when.
Only one path leads to true happiness.

But oh, feeling protected was such a lovely sensation. It seemed to warm her all the way to her toes.

The young man picked up one of the blades and waved it around. 'I 'ave 'ere an ordinary sword.' He held it out so members of the audience could touch it, feel its sharpness and strength.

'It is all a trick,' a man behind them shouted. 'It folds up.'

The Count held the blade towards him and shrugged. 'You are welcome to make it fold up, if you can.'

The man stepped into the middle of the circle and pushed and pulled at the blade and twisted and pressed at the hilt. When he had finished he gazed out at the surrounding people. 'By Gad, it is real.'

'A plant.' Avery murmured in her ear.

'You mean he is part of the show. That it is all a hum.'

'Yes. But he is not lying. The blade is real enough.'

The man disappeared back into the crowd and the sword swallower lifted the blade point first high above his tipped-back face.

Carrie's mouth dried. She pressed tighter against Avery's side.

The sword slowly disappeared into the young man's mouth and down his throat.

The crowd cheered and clapped.

'One sword, ladies and gentlemen. Do I hear you call for two?' the man who had collected the money shouted. He began passing his hat again and people added more coins.

The young man slowly took down the second sword, but it seemed much more difficult and he had to pull it up and then push it down more than once. Finally, he turned in a circle with head back and two swords hilts projecting from his wide open mouth.

There was another sword remaining on the chair.

'Go on then,' someone in the crowd shouted. 'Let's see you do the other one.'

'No, no,' his partner cried, looking anxious. 'That is merely a spare. Three is far too dangerous. It has never been done.'

The crowd began chanting 'Three. Three. Three.'

'Surely he won't,' Carrie said, appalled. 'What if he cuts himself?'

'If he cuts himself, he will die,' Avery said drily.

'He can't do it,' a man behind them said. Carrie turned to see a big belligerent-looking fellow glaring at Avery.

'I wager he can,' Avery answered, grinning.

At his side, Carrie made a strange sound. A sob of protest.

''Ow much?' the fellow said.

'A shilling.'

'I don't want to watch this,' Carrie said.

Avery laughed at the horror on her face. 'There is nothing to fear. He can do it.'

She glanced over at the couple in the centre of the circle of people, where the barker was speaking to the Count with a worried expression. Whatever the Count said in response was not clear, but once more his helper passed round the hat. 'You want to see a man risk his life, you needs to show me your coin, ladies and gents. The man has a wife and children to support.'

Avery tossed another coin in the passing hat.

Carrie began to turn away. Avery held her tighter. 'You will never get through that crowd and I cannot run out on a bet. It will cause all kinds of trouble.'

'Give me your shilling now and you can run wherever you wants,' the big man said. 'Can't he, Jim?' Jim proved to be an equally large fellow with a broken nose.

Avery glanced around. Even if they wanted to leave, it would be impossible while everyone was crowding in so close. 'Close your eyes and don't look,' he said to Carrie.

When the barker held the third sword out to the Count, she buried her face against Avery's coat. The crowd fell silent.

He liked the feeling that she had turned to him for protection, even if he knew the so-called Count was perfectly safe. He gave her a comforting little squeeze.

The man slowly slid the third sword home. A cheer went up.

'I told you he could do it,' Avery said to the man who had taken his bet.

The man grumbled.

Carrie made a sound of disgust. 'That was horrible.' She started to push her way through the crowd, while Avery accepted his winnings.

He quickly caught her up. 'Hey! What is the matter? I've seen that trick hundreds of times. The man is simply trying to earn a living.'

'Are you telling me, no one ever dies?'

He winced. 'Once in a while maybe…but—'

'Once in a while is once too often for me.' She glanced up at the sky. 'Dash it. It is raining.'

He muttered something under his breath and then raised his voice. 'It would have been helpful if Madame Rose could have forecast a shower. Then we would not have got wet.'

The heavens opened and the rain began in earnest.

Sitting next to a damp and clearly unhappy lady was not exactly the way Avery had planned the afternoon to end. He still wasn't exactly sure why she was fuming.

'What did Madame Rose tell you?' he asked.

She turned away from the window and shivered. 'It was all very vague.'

Clearly, she didn't wish to tell him. He didn't like it that she was upset. He had expected her to see through all the nonsense at the fair.

He put his arm around her. 'Don't let her ramblings upset you. It really is all a sham. I bet she asked you some pretty pointed questions before she got around to telling you anything.'

'Not really questions. She said she saw that I was an only child and, when I agreed, she said my parents had wanted a son, which was true.'

'She is a clever one. The first is a guess and if she'd been wrong she would have seen it in your face and changed it. The second an assumption based on your reaction to the answer and her knowledge of human nature.'

Carrie looked unconvinced. 'She also said I had been married, but not to you.'

'Well, everyone knows I am not married and she had to know who I was.' He grimaced. 'Her man only had to have seen us getting out of this carriage. It has our coat of arms on it. He might have thought I was my brother, but since neither of us is married, it makes no difference. They make a point of knowing who is who.'

'Surely no one would have expected you to visit such a little place?'

He offered her a comforting smile and a squeeze. 'Please. It was intended to be a bit of fun. I really don't want you upset.'

'I am not upset about the fortune teller.'

He pulled her close and she leaned against him with a sigh. 'Well, I suppose it all ended well, but…' She took a deep breath and he thought she was going to say something, something important, but she didn't say a word. He thought it best to let the topic drop.

'Will you accompany me to the theatre tomorrow?' he asked to divert her mind to more pleasant topics.

Mouth agape, she stared at him.

Hurt by her astonishment, he shrugged. 'I had the feeling that if you hadn't been going home to Kent last week, you would have accepted my offer to escort you. So, I thought to ask you again. Mrs Siddons is playing in *Measure for Measure.*'

She hesitated. Damn it. Was she still fussing about the sword swallower? If he had thought there was the least danger the man would be injured, he would not have encouraged her to watch. Didn't she understand that? 'I bought the tickets thinking you would like to go.' Dammit, now he sounded sulky when he had intended to sound offhand. 'It will be very good for business,' he hastened to add. 'It will give you a chance to wear one of those evening headdresses.'

'May I think about it?'

What was there to think about? He gritted his teeth. 'By all means. Send a note round to my lodgings with your decision.' He handed her his calling card with a bow.

'Thank you.'

He wanted to press her to agree. He opened his mouth to do so. He also wanted her to decide to go, because it was what she wanted.

Damn it, when had he ever been so confused?

Chapter Nine

Avery had never enjoyed going to the theatre as much as he had this evening. Fortunately, he'd won the use of the box at the tables the previous night, something he'd deliberately set out to do. Not that he was going to mention that to Carrie, who had been delightful company. She didn't chatter during the performance, but instead watched and listened intently. In fact, she rarely chattered about anything. Something he really liked about her. Something else.

He gazed at her sitting opposite him in the carriage. There were a great many things he liked about Carrie Greystoke. If he hadn't sworn off marriage altogether, she was just the sort of woman he might have liked for a wife.

He recalled, with discomfort, the note he had received earlier in the day. A request from his father that he visit. When he had asked his brother what it might be about, Bart had looked grim. 'He's heard about your widow.'

'She is not *my* anything.' Even if he wished she was. A cold sensation had filled the pit of his stomach. 'Is the old fellow getting worse?'

Bart had sighed. 'Not really, but he did have a letter from a distant relative earlier in the week. Seems you've been seen all over the place with this woman.'

He gritted his teeth. And the gossips would have a field day with this evening's outing. He was going to have to bring his association with Carrie to a close before he ruined her reputation instead of helping her business.

'Is something wrong?' Carrie asked.

Damn. He'd let his thoughts show on his face. Since when did he let down his guard around one of his ladies? But that was the whole point. Carrie was not *one of his ladies*. She was different. Better. More important somehow.

'I had a bit of bad news today.'

'Oh, I am sorry to hear it.'

'I am sorry to let it spoil our evening. I don't have to ask if you enjoyed the play, I could see from your face during the performance that you did.'

'Mrs Siddons was really quite wonderful, I must say. She lived up to her reputation.' A lantern on the street caught her smiling and he tried to capture that expression in his mind. A memory to treasure. Bah, what nonsense.

'I have never been to the theatre before. I enjoyed it immensely, though I suppose it is terribly gauche of me to say so.'

'Not at all. It delights me that you are pleased.'

She laughed as if she did not quite believe him, but that the compliment was welcome all the same.

'I mean it,' he said, moving from his side of the carriage to sit beside her.

The atmosphere in the carriage seemed to change. It grew warmer and crackled with tension. The attraction between them had not diminished in the slightest. Indeed, it seemed to have flourished.

He took her gloved hand in his, stroking the cotton-covered palm with his thumb.

A little sound like a quick indrawn breath reached his ears. He smiled. 'You like that.'

'I do.' She sounded shy, her voice trembling a little.

'Palms are very sensitive, right here,' he said, circling his thumb in the centre of her palm slowly. 'Even with two layers of fabric between us.'

She let out a shaky breath. 'Apparently so.' She did not pull away. He took it as a sign that he should continue.

He shifted towards her, bringing his other hand up to cup her cheek and jaw, turning her face towards him. 'You look stunning tonight.'

Her laugh sounded embarrassed. 'It is kind of you to say so.'

He frowned. 'I mean it, Carrie. You drew a great many eyes.'

'I have Marguerite's creation to blame for that.'

'Not at all. It simply did you justice.'

'You are such a flirt.' The pleasure in her voice lightened his heart. While she clearly did not believe his compliment, it had nevertheless pleased her femininity. Somehow, he would convince her, he was speaking the truth. He dipped his head towards her.

She put a tentative hand on his shoulder, not pushing him away, but not encouraging him closer, either.

Good heavens, his bold widow was also shy. The idea made him smile. And since Carrie seemed incapable of subterfuge, he was positive it was a genuine emotion.

When was the last time he had actually flirted with a truly shy woman? He did not think he ever had.

He lowered his head, his mouth coming closer to hers, hovering where he could feel her rapid breaths on his cheek and mouth. He could feel the warmth rising up from her body, as if she was blushing.

He moved his hand so his fingers curled around her nape, but his thumb pushed gently upwards on her chin. 'Carrie, if you do not want me to kiss you, you had better say so now.'

She swallowed. 'I do.'

He stilled. Shook off the strange sensation that those two little words had given him and chuckled. To his own ears it sounded a little forced, but fortunately she did not seem to notice.

'I do want you to kiss me,' she said. The longing in her voice was shocking.

What was a gentleman to do except satisfy a lady's wishes?

He started with the briefest brush across her lips, felt them part under the gentle fleeting pressure. The pulse below her ear thrummed beneath his fingers. She was not lying when she said she wanted him to kiss her.

How nice when a woman, no matter how shy, knew what she wanted and told a man. A great asset to love-making. His body hardened.

The strength of his reaction startled him for a moment. Oh, he had no trouble getting aroused by a beautiful woman, but it was early in the game. He certainly did not want to rush her because he lacked control.

He brushed her lips again and felt her breathing quicken and she shifted, turning towards him, giving him better access, leaning into him. A completely unconscious gesture of interest.

He pressed his lips to hers, feeling their soft plushness give beneath his mouth. He savoured their ripe fullness, nuzzling gently. A small sigh escaped her and she relaxed into him. He raised his head, gazing down at her, unable to see her expression in the darkness inside the carriage.

He put an arm around her shoulders and pulled her closer. The magnificent plumpness of her bosom pressed against his chest. Once more he took her lips, tenderly moving his mouth against hers, until he felt her soften, a slight yielding of her body to his touch.

She was not a woman to easily give up control. She had an inner strength he could not help but admire.

He stroked the seam of her lips with his tongue.

A little promise of the taste of things to come.

Carrie couldn't actually believe she was kissing a man in a carriage, as bold as brass. Until Avery had come into her life, the only kiss she had ever received in her life had been a peck on the cheek or a fleeting brush of lips on the back of her hand by some overbold friend of her father's.

Her husband had not even done that. His salutation on the day of their wedding had been to the air beside her cheek.

This was extraordinarily delicious. Naughty, too. Her insides tightened at the thought of the wickedness of sitting in a carriage kissing a single gentleman. A man she had no intention of marrying, but had every intention of taking to her bed. Hopefully.

His tongue played along her lips, sending shivers

down her spine and making her squirm on the seat at the tightness deep within her. A pleasurable but somehow irritating sensation that made her seek something more. She gave herself up to the storm of desire running though her veins and leaned into him, slipping her hands around his neck and into his hair. Her gloves foiled her need to feel the silkiness of his hair and the warmth of his skin, but she was too entranced by the glorious feeling of his mouth on hers to break the contact and remove them.

She could scarcely breathe for the pounding of her heart in her chest as if it had grown too large to be contained within the space behind her ribs. This was not what she had expected to feel while being kissed. Not at all. It felt wonderful, but somehow not quite enough. The tips of her fingers tingled as if they needed the sensation of touch. Heat raced along her veins. It was as if someone had stoked a furnace deep inside her.

His tongue swept inside her mouth.

Her body went up in flames. She gasped with the shock of it.

He broke the kiss. 'Are you all right?'

An unsteady breath gave her the power of speech. 'I—I should think so.'

He chuckled huskily. 'We are almost at your street.'

Oh, no! This lovely deliciousness was going to come to an end far too soon. 'Would you like to come in for a cup of tea?'

Inside she groaned. Men didn't want cups of tea. They wanted wine or spirit.

'I would love a cup of tea.'

Why, when he said it with that growl in his voice, did he make it sound like so much more than tea? She shivered.

He gently withdrew his arm from around her as the carriage slowed and stopped. He jumped down and helped her out. 'No need to wait,' he called up to the coachman.

A little thrill curled up in her stomach. Excitement mingled with fear. What if it was really only tea he wanted? Why on earth would she think so after that kiss? He seemed to enjoy it as much as she had and they were already into the second of their agreed-upon two weeks.

The porter let them in without comment, though he did give her a rather narrowed-eye stare. No doubt he was reporting on her movements to Mr Thrumby. Dash it. She was a widow. If she wanted to discreetly entertain a gentleman caller, it was no one's business but her own.

She let them in to her apartment, removed her shawl and gloves, but when she went to fill the kettle he caught her around the waist and turned her to face him.

His expression held hunger and heat.

The slow burn in her veins flared to life in the face of such desire. She gasped.

'Hush,' he said softly, cradling her in his arms. 'Do not worry. I won't do anything you don't wish to do.'

She realised her spine was as stiff as a board. So stupid. She relaxed against him, forcing fear to the back of her mind. This was what she wanted. Had asked for. She trailed her palm down his cheek, felt the faint haze of stubble graze her palm. Prickles ran across her shoulders and down her spine.

Fear rose up once more to hold her in thrall. Fear of rejection. Of humiliation. 'So,' she said softly, bravely, 'have you decided where this attraction between us leads?' She winced. Why could she not sound flirtatious and sweet instead of blunt and matter of fact.

He grinned at her. He was one of the few men she did have to look up at. Her insides melted. Not only because he was so very handsome, but because he made her feel small and feminine. And the warmth in his eyes bolstered her confidence.

'I think we both know where this is leading,' he said, his voice a low deep murmur full of sensual undertones. He hooked a chair leg with his foot to bring it clear of the table and sat down, bringing her with him to perch on his knee. 'Now, where were we when we were so rudely interrupted?'

On our way to heaven, a voice inside her whispered. A foolish voice, but one she could not ignore, none the less. She yielded to the pressure of his arms enfolding her in his embrace and relaxed against him. She gazed up into his face and returned his smile. His gaze fixed on her mouth.

Yes, she wanted to say.

He needed no encouragement, or verbal permission. The next moment his mouth covered hers and was teasing and wooing with pliant expertise until she thought she might die of the pleasure. Her extremities tingled, her heart pounded loud in her ears and low in her belly her muscles tightened, causing pleasurable little thrills to ripple along her veins through her body.

When his tongue stroked the seam of her mouth, she parted her lips. And when he explored her mouth with gentle touches, what had gone before seemed innocuous, innocent. This was a sensual wickedness that set her body on fire.

Avery couldn't recall when he had enjoyed kissing a woman more. Carrie seemed so untutored, almost innocent in her hesitant enthusiasm. He could not quite put his finger on what made her so tantalising, but the desire to make love to her was beyond anything he had ever experienced. The fact that he was sitting on a chair with her delicious derrière squirming in his lap was not helping his control.

He broke the kiss and took a breath.

She stilled, gazing at him with concern in her eyes. The heat of lust was not making it easy to process what her expression meant, but instinctively he sensed she needed reassurance. He smiled at her and ran one hand down her arm and stroked her back. 'You kiss divinely, my sweet. I am almost undone.'

Worry changed to confusion. She swallowed. 'Should I make tea?'

He swallowed a laugh and managed a gentle smile instead. 'Tea is not going to ease my predicament.'

The blank stare left him wondering what sort of pillock her husband must have been. Was he one of those chaps who did his duty as fast as possible and left his wife unfulfilled and in the dark, figuratively and literally? If so, it was no bad thing the fellow had gone off to meet his maker.

She stared. 'Is something wrong?'

Damn. His thoughts must be showing on his face again. He stroked the shell of her ear with a fingertip and down her jawline to rest at the tip of her determined little chin. He traced her lips. 'Nothing could possibly be wrong, apart from my need to catch my breath for a moment.' To regain a little control, for surely she could feel how hard he was beneath her luscious bottom.

She took a couple of quick breaths. 'Oh, yes.'

Her lips were so plump. How would they feel on his

pulsing shaft? And…that was not helping in the least. Sensual she might be, and bold, but those sorts of intimacies would have to wait until later in their relationship. If there was a later. Occasionally, he had the sense she was not quite as bold as she had originally made out. If it turned out she was having second thoughts about wanting him to be her lover, he would have to find a way make a graceful exit. Ultimately, it was her decision.

'Let down your hair for me, love.'

Her eyes widened. 'My hair?'

'Mmm… I love your hair down around your shoulders. It makes you look even more desirable.' And wanton. He'd been hard pressed to leave the other night when she looked as if she'd just risen from her bed after a good tumbling. He'd wanted to be the one to make her look that way.

He spread his legs wider apart, which put her more firmly on to his crotch, but would also balance her while he began the task of pulling pins from her hair. With both of them at it, it did not take long for the beautiful mass of wild curls to fall down around her shoulders. He sifted his fingers through the silky strands and massaged her scalp.

Eyes closed, she sighed with pleasure. 'That feels so good.'

'I don't know how you ladies can stand all that ironmongery in your head.'

She opened one eye and looked at him askance. 'Fashion before comfort. Besides, who wants to see a woman going around with a bird's nest on her head?'

I do. 'It looks lovely like this.'

She didn't look convinced.

So he kissed her. Immediately, she melted into him,

kissing him back. This time her little tongue licked at his and he withdrew it slowly, giving her time to follow where it led. His groin tightened unbearably when she began a slow exploration of the inside of his mouth. The pleasurable pain of it had him lifting his hips, seeking friction against that plump little bottom that was moving to a gentle rhythm in his lap.

She wanted him just as much as he desired her.

He let her take charge of the kiss, responding to her touches, to her little sounds of pleasure and shifts of her body, bringing her closer, stroking her hair back from her face, touching her everywhere.

The bed in the alcove behind the so-discreet curtain called with a siren's song. As did her passion, the sighs and moans deep in her throat. He had thought perhaps to wait to fulfil his part of the bargain, to draw it out a little longer, for both their sakes, but now he found he could not, would not. It would not be fair to either of them.

Would it?

He pushed aside the question asked by his conscience, and, with her clinging to him, he rose to his feet.

'Oh,' she murmured, clinging tighter, then once again looking uncertain. She slid down his body to her feet and pulled back. That would not do.

With fingers that were skilled from lots of practice, he began unlacing her gown. 'We should make you a little more comfortable,' he said. 'You seem to be having trouble breathing. Perhaps your stays are too tight?'

She nodded, though she looked none too sure.

He eased the gown over her shoulders. Thank heavens for the fashion for tiny bodices and low necklines. A little push and it slipped down her arms and fell to the floor. She stepped out of it and he shoved it aside

with his foot. He took her by the forearms and took a
step back, letting his gaze wander over her lovely hour-
glass shape beneath her shift and stays. Her legs were
long and, while not slender, they were beautifully pro-
portioned and lightly muscled.

He smiled at her. 'My word, you are lovely. Now it is
time for those stays. Turn around, sweetheart.'

Her breath gave a little hitch and she turned her back
towards him. He leaned forward, peering around that
gorgeous mass of hair to see her face. He feared he might
have been too forward, but the expression on her face
said otherwise. There was a dreamy distant look on her
face and in her eyes.

A cold fist clutched at his heart. She looked as if she
was recalling something from her past. Perhaps her husband? Perhaps the man hadn't been a completely idiot
after all. He quelled the urge to ask. If she was thinking of her dead husband, he absolutely did not want to
know. He undid the bow at the bottom of her stays and
swiftly pulled the tapes free of the holes. The garment
fell free and he tossed it aside.

He glanced down at the way the featherlight fabric
of her shift skimmed the rounded globes of her bottom and fell just shy of her knees, leaving her pretty
shaped calves in their delicate stockings exposed for
him to enjoy.

She was better than any picture he had ever seen.

He caught her around the waist a handspan below her
fabulous heavy breasts and stroked over the magnificent swell of her hips and down her thighs to the hem
of her chemise.

She swallowed.

He smiled at her shyness. It was a delight to find a

woman who retained a little of her innocence after her marriage, despite his very real puzzlement over it. Most married women, in his experience, became bold and often assertive in a way that left a man trying to catch up. Not that he often had that problem, but he could see how some men might have trouble.

He spun her around to face him. She looked so adorable, so pink-cheeked, something welled in his heart. A need to bring her great pleasure and see her smile.

He caught her under her thighs, lifted her, while she clung on for dear life, the soft hazy look in her eyes, fading away. He managed to sweep back the drapery and expose a narrow cot. He almost groaned out loud, whether because it was so small or because it was a bed—finally.

It did not matter which. He lowered her to the pristine white cover and when she was sprawled there, looking up at him with eyes large and anxious, he knelt beside her on the floor and plundered her mouth.

Chapter Ten

Despite that she still retained her shift, the way Avery looked at her made her feel naked. Vulnerable. Exposed. What did he see when he looked at her like that? A large woman, who men did not usually find attractive? A chore he had contracted for that he would like over and done with as soon as possible so he could be on his way?

Her breathing, shallow and fast from their kiss, began to slow. Her heart that had been beating with excited anticipation only a few moments ago was now pounding with fear that he would walk away. That once more she'd be left, embarrassed, humiliated and alone.

There was nothing she could do except lie there and wait for his rejection.

'My word, but you are beautiful,' he murmured, his voice deep and husky. His gaze ran down her body, clearly seeing right through the filmy fabric that now was drawn tight across her breasts and draped over her hips.

She glanced down along her length, aware that her breasts rose like twin peaks in a mountain range and that the nipples were as hard as beads. They lifted the fabric in a most unseemly way. Instinctively she raised her hand to cover her lack of modesty, but he caught them in his. He kissed each of her fingers in turn, make her insides melt and those little nubs on her breasts tingle with anticipation that he might kiss her there, too.

Never had she had such an unseemly thought in her life.

'Carrie,' he said softly.

She forced herself to look into his face, braced herself to see the distaste, but found nothing but heat and sensual pleasure. It shocked her to the core. Her body tightened unbearably.

'Yes,' she managed, though her throat was dry and her voice sounded raspy.

'Darling,' he murmured. 'I want you so badly.'

A ripple of pleasure moved out from her core.

'I—' She cleared her throat. 'I want you, too.'

There, it was out in the open for him to do with as he willed. At least with her husband she hadn't said anything quite so foolish. She'd simply nodded when he'd said he was leaving. He'd apologised, for he had been a gentleman, but that hadn't made her grief any less painful.

The horrible thing was that she had been unable to grieve when she'd heard the news of his death, for she had already been dead inside. But now, it seemed as if this moment had washed all of that bitterness away and her body had finally come to life.

He rose to his feet, his gaze never leaving her face, and undid the buttons of his coat.

Oh, good lord, she was going to do this. She really was.

Her body began to shake, to quake as if the bed was

rocking beneath her. She gripped the covers to hold herself steady. To stop herself from fleeing.

Fortunately, Avery didn't notice her panic as he was stripping off his jacket and moving with an efficiency that brooked no turning back.

Carrie took a deep breath.

The bed might be small, but the woman laid out before him like a banquet was the most sumptuous morsel Avery had ever set eyes on. He could not wait to taste her delights. About to pull his shirt over his head, he suddenly became aware of her terror.

It chilled him to the bone, like a dip in a frozen pond.

What the hell had her husband done to her? Instead of leaping on her and devouring her, as he had been inclined to do, he sat on the edge of the bed and removed his shoes, stockings and after a quick glance in her direction, his breeches. Oh, she was definitely nervous. Leaving his shirt on, he stretched alongside her on the narrow bed. She shifted over to give him room.

Or to give herself space.

He rolled on his side. Clearly, for all her boldness, her willingness to say what she wanted, she needed careful handling. Something had happened in her past that made her skittish.

He cradled her face in his hands and kissed her lips, tasting her sweetness, feeling the rise of her passion as she gave herself up to pleasure. Against his mouth, her full lush lips felt like heaven. The way her tongue responded to his invasion of her mouth, dancing in perfect harmony with his, fuelled his desire.

She rolled towards him, wrapping her arms around him, a soft hum of pleasure vibrating against his chest, where they touched. He eased his thigh between hers and, a moment later, her leg was wrapped high against his hip, the heat of her centre scorching his skin, making him dizzy with lust as if he was some sort of schoolboy, not a man who had bedded some of the most beautiful women every country had to offer.

He had thought himself somewhat jaded. Instead, here he was panting after this woman as if she was his first venture into bed sport. Madness. And utterly delightful.

Slowly he broke their kiss and, gazing into her face, he saw the haziness of desire and longing, along with the signs of arousal. Flushed skin, parted rosy lips and heavy-lidded eyes. A beautiful passionate woman. Why any man would leave such a wife and go off to war he could not imagine. He ran his hand down her spine, coming to rest on the swell of her hip. Slowly he caressed every inch of her back, her bottom, her upper thigh, while nuzzling at her neck, learning the places that made her shiver and those that made her gasp, and those that caused that delightful little hum of pleasure in the back of her throat.

When his thumb touched the underside of her breast, her breath hitched, but it was not fear this time, or not really. It was more like nervous curiosity. He took his time stroking her creamy flesh, while he dropped kisses on her throat, the pulse point in the hollow of her throat, upper chest and finally at the top of the magnificent rise of her breasts. She shuddered with pleasure.

He palmed the luscious fullness, gently kneading the bounteous flesh until her hips undulated against his groin. He bit back a groan, but held himself still, leaving it to her to discover just how hard he was, while he finally achieved his goal with his mouth. He licked the hardened nub of her breast through the fine lawn fabric of her shift.

'Oh…' She sighed against his shoulder, her hands sifting through the hair at his nape and sending shivers all the way to his shaft.

He was going to…

Shocked, he took a deep breath, regained control and eased her on to her back the better to pay attention to her other breast, massaging and kissing to the music of her sighs and moans. Her hands wandered his back in light stroking circles. Her thighs parted and he nestled into the cradle of her hips. A perfect fit for once. Because of her height, they were groin to groin. A most pleasurable sensation. Intensified when she wrapped both legs around his hips. She wanted him closer.

But first there was the issue of their clothing. He stroked one hand down her thigh, until he found the hem of her chemise, easing it upwards until it would go no further. He knelt up.

Her eyes fluttered open, anxiety filling her expression as if…she expected him to leave? Or was she fearful of being seen in all her glory? Far more likely, she was simply a particularly modest woman. He let his gaze roam her body. 'Beautiful,' he said. 'Gorgeous.'

A hesitant smile curved her lips.

'Will you let me see all of you?' he asked, twitching the bottom of her shift.

A blush suffused her face, but she nodded and lifted her hips and then her shoulders to help him pull it over her head. Now all she had on were stockings that ended just above the knee, tied with little blue garters. The curls at the apex to her thighs were light brown and her rosy nether lips beckoned seductively. Her breasts were full and bouncy with rosy nipples. So erotic.

'That is the loveliest sight I have ever seen,' he said, glancing up at her face, but her gaze was focused on his torso, on the place with his shirt tented over his erection.

She licked her lips and his shaft jerked in response.

She started and her gaze shot to his face.

'He likes that you are interested,' he said. 'Do you want to see?'

A little jerk of her head he guessed was a nod of agreement. How very nervous she was, like a bride on her wedding night.

The thought shocked him. He was a man without illusions. He knew women liked to act innocent, but usually he could see right through their wiles. With Carrie, though, he never quite felt sure if it was an act or not. Mostly because she was always so brutally honest. Pushing the nonsensical thought aside, he grabbed the back of his shirt and leaned forward to pull it off over his head.

Then down his arms, exposing his chest.

He almost laughed at her disappointed glance at where the shirt lay in his lap. That pouting look he could certainly interpret. A woman deprived of a treat she had expected.

He bundled up the shirt and fired it off at the kitchen chair.

She came up on her elbows to look at his erection, providing him with a perfect view of her bounteous breasts. He reached out and gently cupped them from the sides, feeling their soft weight in his palms. A touch on his shaft had him hissing in a breath, but she was too intent on shaping the crown of it to notice. She traced a fingertip down his length and gave his balls a little poke. She frowned.

It all became as clear as day. Her husband had been one of those men who took his pleasure without thought for that of his partner. Which meant Avery would have to make up for the lack.

Carrie knew what men looked like—how could she not when there were naked statues all over the place? She just hadn't expected to be so entranced by the sight of him fully aroused. To find herself gazing at him in awe and wonder at the contradictions. His member was so much darker than the rest of him and jutted towards her in a most intriguing way, while the other parts were surprisingly soft and silky.

Now some of the things her aunt had said to her before her wedding made a lot more sense. But she really didn't see how there would be enough room for him inside her body. Or he was bigger than a normal man. Certainly, she'd never seen one on a statue that looked as if it could possibly grow to that size.

He reached down and took her hand in his, cupping her hand around the soft part below the…penis, she remembered it was called. He used his hand to stroke her palm against him and it felt like marbles inside a velvety sack. He released her hand and she continued to gently massage, feeling the rough hair against her skin with the silky softness beneath. She smiled shyly up at him. 'I love the way it feels. Do you like this?'

He was watching her with hooded eyes, his expression dark yet somehow soft. 'Yes, it is exceedingly arousing. I like this, too.' He grasped the shaft in his fist, stroking up and down.

She followed his example and he threw his head back with a groan of pleasure.

Then his fingers burrowed into her nether curls and parted her cleft. And suddenly she was melting from the inside out. She collapsed back on the pillows, unable to support herself. Something inside her tightened, then flew apart. Like magic. Blissful. Amazing. Otherworldly. Her legs and arms felt like lead. She gasped for breath.

A soft curse caused her eyes to open. His expression was ruefully amused. 'You came faster than I expected,' he said. He looked pleased.

The words made no sense to her.

He leaned over her, one hand beside her head, the other between them. For a moment, she thought he was going to work that amazing magic again, but he was pushing something into her and then, yes, that lovely sensation again, as he thrust his hips forward.

The part of him she thought too big.

A pinch of pain. She winced with a little cry of protest and opened her eyes. She'd been right.

Hanging over her, he was frowning like a demon. His expression gave the impression he was in pain.

'Does it hurt you, too?' she asked, though her mouth felt dry and the words seemed difficult to form, she was still breathing so hard.

He shook his head. 'It is not possible.'

Her heart missed a beat. Was this why her husband had left her? 'It doesn't fit?' Disappointment filled her.

He made a choking sound. 'Oh, it will, but we will have to take it slowly. Tell me if I hurt you.'

She lay frozen, rigid, waiting for pain, but then he started to move, slowly inching forward and back with

a kind of rocking motion of his hips and it felt…nice.
More than nice. And then he used his hand in that other
place and the tension she had felt before started to build
again. Higher, this time, with the stimulation on his hand
and his member inside her.

She closed her eyes.

'Carrie, look at me,' he said.

She forced her eyelids open. The intensity on his face
was almost scary. The tendons in his neck stood out
under his skin, his shoulders blocked the light from the
room and he continued to move, until she did not think
she could stand it any longer.

Again, that feeling of shattering some sort of barrier,
so much more intense than before, and she was flying
apart into a thousand tiny pieces. Sinking into some
sort of abyss where all she could hear was her breathing. And his. He made a soft sound and withdrew from
her body, rocking hard against her hip for a moment or
two and then sank down on to his side to lay beside her.

He drew her into his arms and kissed her forehead.
'Lovely, lovely girl,' he murmured into her hair. 'Oh,
my sweet child. Why didn't you tell me?'

Tell him?

His breathing deepened. He seemed to have fallen
asleep. She lay in the circle of his arms, her head on his
chest, her heart still racing as if she had run a mile. Why
hadn't she told him what?

Chapter Eleven

Avery slowly came to. Replete. Content. Blissful.

And then he remembered. Damn it all.

What an idiot he'd been not to recognise the signs. But honestly, when would any man expect a widow to be a virgin? It was almost beyond the realm of possibility. But apparently not entirely, since the evidence was right before him. And perversely he was pleased.

When he ought to be furious.

He glanced down at where she lay nestled against his chest. Her eyes were closed and she was breathing evenly, but she wasn't asleep.

'Well?' he asked.

'Well, what?' she responded in a very small voice.

'Why did your husband not do the deed?' Dash it, that didn't sound exactly right. He gentled his voice. 'I do not understand why a married woman would still be a maid.' That really wasn't much better. Hell, how did he ever end up in this situation?

A small sound struck him through the heart. Dear God, was she crying? He'd made her cry? He wanted to leap out of bed and run a mile. Instead, he drew back, lifted her face until she had no option but to look at him and wiped her eyes on the corner of the sheet. 'What is it, Carrie?'

She sniffled.

He didn't even have a handkerchief to give her. She pulled something out from the tangle of sheets and wiped her nose. Her shift, he realised. He gently stroked her arm. 'Hush. It is all right. It doesn't matter. I was surprised, that was all.' Shocked, more like it. Such a mess. 'I would have been a lot more careful had I known. I hope I didn't hurt you too badly?'

'Oh, no,' she said, her voice sounding watery and full of sadness. 'It was lovely.'

Then why did she sound so miserable? True, he could have done a whole lot better if he had not been blind-sided, but it wasn't that awful surely?

She sniffled again and mopped up her tears with the scrap of fabric.

What else could he say? Perhaps her husband had been unable. Hell, that would send a man off to get killed in the war, wouldn't it? And he could just imagine that scene playing out. A man's worst nightmare that.

'He left me the moment the ceremony was done,' she said softly.

He frowned. 'Right after?'

'He escorted me to the suite of rooms he had booked for us at the hotel, where I was to change before the wedding breakfast, and I never saw him again. Our few guests were waiting for us to make our appearance, but he never returned. The next day, I learned that he had gone to join Wellington's army.'

The forlornness in her voice nigh on broke his heart.

Something that should not be happening. Hadn't he heard enough sad stories from the ladies he escorted about to harden him to the vagaries of his fellow man? Of all the tales he'd been told, though...

'The man was an idiot.'

'I thought so, too,' she said with a wry little laugh.

He let go a sigh of relief. Brave to a fault. He gave her a squeeze. 'That's my girl.' His? He winced. Those sorts of statements would get him into more trouble than he already was. Yet he could not help offering comfort. 'May I say how honoured I am that you chose me to be your first lover.'

A little silence met his words and then came a beautiful smile. His heart gave an odd little lurch. Oh, yes. He was really in trouble. 'Um...' she said.

He clenched his jaw, waiting for the admonition he so rightly deserved. 'What is it, Carrie?' He sounded terse. What was it about her that drove his easy charm into hiding? He turned to face her. 'Was there something I can do for you?' Something else.

'I was wondering if you would like to dine with me tomorrow evening? Here.'

Oh. Instead of a bear-garden jaw she was inviting him to dine. Desire flooded his body at the thought of being alone with her again.

Now he had slept with her as she'd wanted, he really ought to say farewell and get back to his life, because since he'd become involved with Carrie and her business he had not been to one ball to find someone to replace Elizabeth or escorted one lady on a shopping expedition. He hadn't even spent much time at the tables either. His income was suffering badly and that meant Laura would also suffer.

He really should call a halt to this right now. 'Yes. I would like that very much.' The words were out before he could think them through. But then, she had just given him the most amazing gift of his life, one he would likely never receive again. Not to mention he enjoyed her company.

The glorious smile he adored broke out again. 'I shall look forward to it.'

And dammit, so would he.

He reached for his waistcoat in the heap of clothes by the bed, grabbed his watch and peered at the time. 'Oh, Lord.'

'What is it?' she asked sitting up, the sheets pulled tight across her mouthwatering breasts.

He forced his gaze away. That was not the direction his thoughts needed to go, and besides, since this was her very first time, she would likely be sore for a few days so he should keep that in mind when he came for dinner the next day.

'I promised to meet someone and I am already late.' He slid out of bed and pulled on his clothes. He glanced over at her, watching him and wanted to slide right back under the sheets. Grimly he forced himself to continue dressing. He glanced her way and saw her watching him, her gaze oddly pained.

'What is it?' he asked, despite knowing he shouldn't.

'Are you going gaming?'

The question was laced with disapproval and it hurt when usually he didn't care what people thought, but he wasn't going to lie like some naughty boy caught teasing the family pet. Gaming was how he made his living. 'I am.' He buttoned his waistcoat and turned to face her.

'Oh.' There was a world of dismay in her voice.

'Is there a problem?'

She flinched at his tone and he felt like some sort of ogre.

What the devil? 'What is it, Carrie?' He did not mean to sound impatient, but really? He didn't answer to her any more than he answered to his father. Why was it people were always wanting to control his life when they really knew nothing about him?

She shook her head, her hair moving like a waterfall about her creamy shoulders. 'I don't see why it is enjoyable for gentlemen to risk everything on the toss of a dice or...something equally foolish.' Sadness reverberated in her voice.

His jaw dropped. What? Did she think he routinely fleeced green boys of their fortune or ruined men down on their luck? Looking at him as if he was some sort of Captain Sharp, no less.

He never cared what people thought of him or said of him. So why would he care now? A chill entered his veins. He picked up his hat and gloves.

'It is how I make my living, madam. I bid you goodnight.'

The next evening, while tidying up from yet another extraordinarily busy day, Carrie caught a strange look from her assistant. 'Is something wrong?'

'No, ma'am, but...well, you are humming. You didn't do that when I first came here and I wondered what has made you so happy.'

Humming? Oh, goodness. Heat crept up her face. 'I suppose I am happy because the shop is doing so well.' Certainly not because she was expecting Lord Avery later this evening. She had half-expected him to cry off on their dinner after they had parted on such bad terms, but since she had not received a note cancelling their engagement, she could only assume he would arrive as promised. And, yes, that was making her happy. She shouldn't have said anything about his gambling. Gentlemen gambled. It was a fact of life. And they did not like to be criticised. Certainly, Carrie Greystoke was not going to change those facts of life.

'Yes, ma'am.' The girl sounded none too convinced.

Surely she could not have an inkling that Carrie was entertaining a gentleman in her rooms later that evening. No, it wasn't possible. She frowned. 'Why would I not be pleased that the shop is doing well?'

'Oh, I didn't mean it that way, ma'am. It is just that you work so hard and it seems to get busier every day. If this keeps up, we won't have enough stock to satisfy our customers. I expected you to be worried.'

It was true, there were a great many gaps on the shelves. 'I will bring more stock back with me when I return from Kent on Monday.'

A note she had received from Marguerite indicated that they had managed to gain the services of several women in the village, but that until they were fully trained, she and Petra were working long hours to meet the demand. Hopefully they would have enough stock on hand for the following week at least. And in a few more weeks it would be the height of summer and the *ton* would be departing the city for cooler climes and they would have enough of a hiatus to prepare for the Little Season. They would also need new autumn designs if they were to maintain the interest of their customers. After all, while many of the ladies had come to take a look at the shopkeeper who had caught Lord Avery's eye, they had fallen in love with the hats. And it was the hats, and the naughty nightwear, that would keep them coming back.

The girl finished tidying the drawers and glanced around. 'I think that is everything.'

'It is indeed. Off you go home and I will see you first thing in the morning.'

The girl smiled. 'Yes, Mrs Greystoke. If there is anything else I can do to help, please let me know. I love working here. It is so much nicer than being a housemaid. It means I can go home and help my mum with the little ones while she gets dinner, but if you needs me to stay late or to do anything at all, I will be happy to help out.'

'Thank you. I will be sure to let you know.' But please right now…just go. 'My goodness, is that the time? You don't want to be late, or your mother will worry.'

The girl shrugged into her coat and with a cheery wave was gone. Carrie locked the door behind her and leaned against it in relief. At last. Now she could bathe and get ready for Avery. This must be their last night together. Since the shop was doing so well, it would not be fair to her sisters-in-law to continue with their arrangement when it was no longer needed. He'd helped her get started and that should be an end to it.

While she had honestly not expected him to make love to her once he'd explained he did not do that sort of thing for money, the fact that he had, made her want to make this evening as special for him as he had made this time with him special for her.

But first she needed to get ready.

Excitement rippled through her belly. She had decided on a very wicked plan. She hugged her arms around her waist, but did she dare follow through on it?

Yes, she had to do this. Avery had taught her she was not a complete failure as a woman. He had called her lovely. He had made her feel utterly feminine. A feeling she would treasure for the rest of her life. And this was one thing she could do for him and bring him some measure of pleasure.

On his way to visit Carrie, Avery dropped in at Laura's lodgings. Having let himself in as usual, he stopped short at the sight of his older brother seated in the armchair by the fire. He almost turned tail, but that would be cowardly.

'Bart,' he said warily. 'What are you doing here?'

Laura put her needlework aside and rushed forward to greet him. 'Now, now, Avery. No need to sound so unfriendly.' She gave him a peck on the cheek. 'Bart came to see how we did and to report on Father's health.

Avery set his hat on the table and shook hands with his older brother. 'Good of you, Bart. How is the old fellow?' He tried to keep the bitterness out of his voice, but clearly had not succeeded when his brother gave him a narrow-eyed stare, then shrugged. Only Avery could solve the bad blood between him and his father.

And to be fair on his brother, the Duke kept his heir so short of funds there was little he could do to help either of his siblings. The best he could do for Avery was loan him his carriages on the odd occasion. And for his sister? Laura never said anything, but no doubt he did what he could. Unfortunately, most of the care for Laura fell on Avery's shoulders. Or it would until her husband was able to earn a decent income.

Bart glanced at Laura and back to Avery. He heaved a sigh. 'Sometimes he is the way he always was and sometimes I am amazed he is still with us he is so fragile.

Quite honestly, I don't see how he keeps going. Strength of will, I suppose.'

Avery's stomach dipped. The longer time went on the less likely he would ever be reconciled with the Duke. And, despite everything, that did not sit well in his gut. 'I am sorry you have to bear the brunt of it.'

His brother looked grim. 'It is truly pitiful to see.' He took a deep breath. 'Which brings me to the reason I called here today.' Again, a look passed between him and Laura.

What the hell? He glared at them both. 'What are you two plotting?'

'Nothing,' Laura said, sounding anxious. 'It is just that…'

'Father is extremely agitated about the female you now appear to be…courting.'

Avery froze. 'I am not *courting* anyone.'

'Damn it, Avery—' His brother's cheeks coloured. 'I beg your pardon, Laura, but devil take it, Avery, a widowed shopkeeper?'

'She is a business associate,' Avery snapped. 'Nothing more.'

'Well, whatever she is, Father's not pleased you are still seeing her.' His mouth tightened. 'He nigh on had an apoplexy thinking you'd be trapped in marriage to such a one when you can have your pick of half the nobility in England.'

'I have no intention of marrying anyone and so you may tell our father.'

His brother snorted. 'Driving in Hyde Park? Taking her to the theatre. Smelling of April and May is how he has heard it.'

Laura frowned. 'Avery, surely you are not toying with

the lady's affections? I told you before that Harriet's godmother saw you in Hyde Park, too, but apparently she reported to Harriet that she had never seen a lady so much in love.'

Avery's jaw dropped. *In love?* 'Nonsense. We are simply good friends.'

'I'll wager you are,' his brother said morosely.

Avery shot him a grin, because he knew it would annoy his brother. 'You are just jealous.'

'Avery—' his brother growled.

'But what of the lady's reputation?' Laura asked. 'You know how people talk.'

After running off with a man society considered beneath her, Laura had suffered her share of gossip.

'She doesn't care about such things. She is a milliner.' Avery mentally crossed his fingers that no one had discovered her relationship to Westram. If that ever came to his father's ears he might be singing a different tune about her suitability as a bride. Maybe it was just as well their *association* was due to end shortly. The thought scoured a hole in his gut. He forced himself to ignore it. 'I take a commission on sales resulting from my recommendations to her shop. That is all there is to it.' On a financial level, anyway.

Laura frowned. 'That might be all it is to you, but are you sure she feels the same way?'

Now they brought it to his attention, he wasn't at all sure, given her actions. He inhaled a deep breath. 'Whatever the case, I am not marrying her or anyone else. Besides, why is Father so concerned about me? You are the heir, Bart. It is your *duty* to marry and provide the next heir. I suggest you get on with it post haste.'

His brother's face hardened. 'I am doing my duty. As you well know, I am betrothed.'

'You've been betrothed for nigh on five years. Why haven't you married the girl?'

'That is why, you idiot. She's barely out of the schoolroom.'

Avery winced. Their father had chosen a girl from an excellent family for his brother. Unfortunately, she'd been fourteen to his brother's twenty-five at the time. Her family had signed the settlements, but had insisted the wedding not take place until after she'd had her come out. Thank God.

For Laura, the Duke had chosen a man in his fifties. Of the three of them, the woman chosen for Avery had seemed on the surface the most acceptable in terms of age. Except that Avery had been in love with someone else, Alexandra. Or had thought so anyway. All the young bucks new on the town had been in love with Lady Alexandra Wellford. She'd been the most beautiful of all the debutantes that year, although her family's pockets were largely to let.

Avery had thought she loved him in return, until his father bought her and her family off. When Avery had discovered what the Duke had done, they had had the most awful row. It was then that he'd told his father he was never going to marry and they hadn't seen each other from that day to this.

'I'm sorry. I forgot she was so young. How much longer do you have to wait?'

'Until next year.'

'I hope she is worth it. I really do.'

His brother's expression became blank. 'I will do my duty.'

Avery frowned. 'Surely—'

'I am not going to discuss my intended with you, Avery. I merely came to ask Laura if she knew anything of this shopkeeper before I approached you about it.'

'You don't need to worry about me, I can assure you.'

'You know, if you would just settle down with someone reasonable, Father would reinstate your allowance. He has mellowed considerably over the past few years.' Bart looked so damned hopeful, Avery almost weakened. But he knew his father. It would never be enough. He'd want to rule his life completely. First the wedding, then he'd be relegated to managing one of the family estates and answering to his father for every aspect of his life. He'd tried to appease his father all through his boyhood until he'd almost lost sight of himself as a person. He was not going to subjugate himself again.

'Thank you, but, no.' He pulled his purse from his pocket and emptied the contents on to the table. 'Laura, this should keep you going for a few days. I will bring more in a week or so.'

Bart curled his lip. 'I suppose that is payment from your widow for services rendered?'

'And?' Avery said icily.

His brother grimaced.

Avery punched him lightly on the shoulder. 'What a stuffed shirt you are becoming. It is actually my ill-gotten gains from the tables.'

'Hardly any better.'

Laura looked upset. 'Please, both of you, do not fight. You are the only family I have left. I hate to see you so at odds.'

Inwardly Avery winced. He hated it, too, but he wasn't going to buckle to his brother's pressure. 'We would not be at odds if he didn't think he had the right to tell me what to do.'

'I am trying to save you from yourself, Brother. And if you think gaming is a good way to make a living, it is not. Sooner or later it will lead you into trouble.'

Why did everyone want to run his life? He bowed. 'Please excuse me, Laura, I cannot stay. I have another engagement.' He stalked out.

He wasn't feeling exactly good about things. He hadn't lied to his brother, but he hadn't been truthful either. Damn it, the man was almost as bad as their father. He didn't deserve to be told the truth about Carrie.

Outside in the street, Avery let go a breath. It wasn't true. His brother was a good man. Too good.

Chapter Twelve

Carrie glanced at her clock for about the fifth time and ran her hands down the front of her gown. Even with the addition of the negligee it was so sheer... What if he took one look at her trying to be seductive and laughed? Oh, this was such a stupid idea.

She ran to the clothes press. She still had a few minutes before he was due to arrive. The gown she had worn to the theatre would be better than this, surely?

A creak behind her. She jerked around. Too late. He was here and looking so handsome and well dressed. She swallowed. She really should have worn something more appropriate.

His eyes widened as they ran down her length. The smile on his face broadened. 'My word, you look good enough to eat. Was this what you meant by dinner?'

Her nervousness fled. She smiled back, though she knew from the heat in her cheeks she was also blushing. 'No. I promise I do intend to feed you.'

He closed the door behind you. 'You know, that doorman let me in without a word. I am sorry if I surprised you.'

She let out a breathless laugh. 'I told him to send you straight back here.'

A brow tilted up. He glanced at the evening gown she had pulled from the clothes chest, still gripped in nervous fingers. 'Am I too early? Shall I come back? Though I must say what you are wearing is absolutely enchanting. No wonder the ladies of the *ton* can't get enough of them.'

He knew just the right thing to say to set her at ease. She dropped the gown back into the chest and closed the lid. 'I was putting it away.' As lies went, it was fairly white. It certainly wasn't going to do anyone any harm and it was certainly better than admitting she had started to panic. She had wanted to wear this outrageous robe for him. After all, she'd bought it and would certainly wear it again.

'Ah, I see,' he said. He hung up his hat and tucked his gloves inside it. He raised his chin and gave a sniff. 'Something smells good? And not only your perfume.'

The man knew just how to make her feel at ease. He was lovely and kind and generous to a woman most men considered as plain as a pikestaff and not worth their time. She just wished she had more to offer. Her heart ached a little, knowing he could never be hers, but she had intended this evening to be for him and pushed such thoughts aside. There would be time enough later for regrets.

'Mrs Thrumby's cook kindly prepared enough for two.' She gestured to the armchair beside the hearth. 'Please, sit. May I offer you some sherry?'

'Will you join me?'

'I will.' She smiled.

'Then, yes, please.'

She poured them both a glass of the sherry she had bought earlier in the day and, having given him his, she took the small stool opposite.

He raised his glass. 'Your health.'

'And yours.' They sipped.

'Very nice,' he remarked.

Relief filled her. She had spent rather more on it she should have. She rose. 'No, please. Do not get up. Finish your drink while I put the first course on the table. Soup to start.'

She ladled the soup into bowls and placed them on the table. 'Whenever you are ready.'

He came to the table at once. 'Pea soup. How did you know it is one of my favourites?'

She laughed. He would have said that about any soup, she was sure, but she wasn't going to spoil things by being practical. She was determined she would not. 'A lucky guess.' They took the seats opposite each other.

He tucked in with obvious relish. 'How was your day?' he asked. 'Was the shop very busy?'

How normal it sounded. How like family. Her heart gave a little squeeze. This sort of family would never be hers.

How could she let such regrets enter her mind, when she had her sisters-in-law? It was wrong of her. Terribly. But she could not seem to help it.

'Extremely.' She hoped she sounded more cheerful than she felt.

'I am glad to hear it.'

Good, he had noticed nothing of her longings in her voice. 'Me, too. Mrs Buxton-Smythe came in today and she brought Lady Carstairs with her. I think our reputation is assured among the ladies of the *ton*.'

He paused in his eating to look at her. 'Then you no longer need my assistance even though our two weeks are not quite up.' His face was grave.

She managed a smile, even if it did feel false. 'I believe you are right. But I really must thank you for your help in putting us on the road to success.'

'You would have got there by yourselves eventually,' he said cheerfully.

'It would have taken a great deal longer and…and we might not have been able to survive long enough, to be honest.' She had his share of the profits ready for him, of course, but she did want him to understand how very much she appreciated his help, though he seemed determined to brush it off.

She cleared away the soup bowls and took two plates out of the oven where she had put them to keep warm. The roast beef didn't look as if it had dried out. Not too much, anyway. And the vegetables looked fine, too. Mrs Thrumby's woman had explained how to keep the meals warm for half an hour.

Once they were both served she sat down again.

'My compliments to the cook,' he said after a couple of mouthfuls and a sigh.

She frowned. It was almost as if he did not usually eat proper meals. 'I am glad you are enjoying it.' Oh, heavens, she had forgotten the wine. She shot up from her chair.

He rose, too, looking worried.

'Oh, sit, please.' She ran to the pantry and fetched out the decanter of red wine she had put there to keep cool. 'I nearly forgot this.'

He took the decanter from her. 'Allow me.' He poured them both a glass.

He raised his. 'To the most beautiful woman I know.'

She tried hard not to show disbelief on her face or in her laugh. 'To my most favourite gentleman caller.'

He frowned fiercely. 'Your only gentleman caller, I hope?'

Her jaw dropped. 'I was jesting. The only other men who call here are Jeb and Mr Thrumby.'

'Hmmph. I am glad to hear it.'

Oh, even his pretence at jealousy made her heart beat faster and her skin feel warm. 'Eat,' she urged, hoping that such thoughts did not show on her face. She did not want him to realise his departure would hurt her terribly. Far more than she'd been hurt when her husband left. Because her heart hadn't been involved. Only her pride.

She stilled. Every nerve in her body tingling with awareness. Her heart? Surely not. The man made his living from ladies who paid him for his services and, worse, from gambling. He lived on the edge of ruin and seemed to enjoy the risk. Look at the way he had wagered money he could ill afford on the life of the sword swallower.

It all left her feeling terrified. And fascinated at the same time. She could not help staring at the way his throat moved when he swallowed, at the even white teeth when he bit into his meat, at the way his fingers curled around the stem of his glass when he lifted his glass to drink. Such long clever fingers.

He glanced up and caught her watching him. She dropped her gaze to her plate and forced herself not to hide her heated cheeks beneath her palms. Why on earth had she acted like a schoolgirl? It was perfectly ridiculous. 'I hope the beef is not too dry,' she said. 'It was in the oven a bit longer than it should have been.'

'I thought I was right on time,' he said.

When she glanced up at him, she saw that his eyes were alive with amusement. At her. Oh, she was so hopelessly gauche when it came to this flirting stuff. 'Is it?' she asked. 'Too dry?'

He carved another piece from the slice on his place and gravely chewed. 'It is perfect.' A flash of those lovely white teeth as he smiled. 'Just like you.'

'Hardly,' she said, attacking the slice of meat on her plate. Did he think she was a fool? That she did not look in the mirror and see the truth?

'And that gown of yours is enough to drive any red-blooded male insane.'

She could agree about the gown, but not what it covered. 'I am glad you like it. My sister-in-law Marguerite came up with the design.'

He leaned back and gave her what she could only describe as a rakish stare. 'With you in it, the gown quite takes my breath away. Though I expect that was your intention.'

Inside she cringed. 'I thought you might want to recommend them to your special ladies.'

His expression darkened. 'There is only ever one special lady at a time, you know.'

Was he saying…? 'Are you classifying me as one of your special ladies?' Her heart gave an odd little thump. She put down her knife and fork and took a fortifying sip of wine.

'You are very special.'

'That was not my question.'

He straightened his knife and fork on his plate, then lifted his gaze to meet hers. 'You are not one of my special ladies, you are my only special lady.'

She blinked. 'You do not sound happy about that.'

He gave a little grimace and a sigh. 'It is somewhat bad for business.'

'Oh.' What had she been thinking? 'I have your money.' She leapt to her feet.

He caught her wrist. 'I do not want your money.'

Something inside her shrivelled. He meant he did not want her. 'Oh.' She glanced around the kitchen, sifting through her mind for something to say that would not sound like he'd hurt her feelings. 'I do not expect anything more from you,' she said. At his look of shock, she continued on quickly. 'You have fulfilled the terms of our arrangement to the full.' Oh, that didn't sound quite right. 'I mean the increase in trade is quite remarkable and it is all down to you.'

'Is that what you mean?' he said drily.

'I—yes, of course. What else would I mean?'

He pushed back his chair.

An ache filled her chest. He was going to leave and he hadn't even had dessert.

He tugged on her wrist. She hadn't realised he was still holding it. Off balance, she lurched towards him and, a moment later, she found herself perched once again on his knee. He tipped her face up to meet his gaze. 'Carrie,' he murmured. 'I find myself quite at a loss. It is not your money I want, it is you.'

'Oh,' she gasped.

'And that, my dear, is very bad for business.'

She wasn't sure whether to laugh or cry at the way his words made her feel inside. 'But we have decided to bring our arrangement to an end,' she said, deciding it was better to feel nothing at all, because if this was really the end of their association, she did not want him to leave with the recollection of her crying all over him. Instead, she would prefer him to recall her with a smile on her lips. 'So, should we not make the most of it?' Oh, goodness, where on earth had that come from? 'But first you must let me serve you dessert.'

His arm tightened around her waist. 'Dessert? I thought *you* were dessert.' He pulled her close and nuzzled in her neck. Shivers coursed down her spine. Her brain turned to mush.

'Oh, no. There's…' What had he said? She was dessert? Goodness '…um…trifle,' she finished saying. Oh, how wretched! Once more she had missed the opportunity to meet his seductive flirtation with some witty response. No doubt Mimi Luttrell would have known exactly what to say. Bother.

He laughed and let her go. 'Trifle, hmmm. That reminds me of something my sister said.'

She popped to her feet and cleared away the dirty dishes to hide her discomfort. 'Really? What did she say?'

'She wanted to know if I was trifling with your affections.'

When she glanced up, he was watching her intently. waiting for her reaction, despite that he'd asked so nonchalantly.

She served the trifle and smiled. 'I think we both know that is not possible.'

'I told her that was so, but people are talking and—'

Her heart seemed to still. 'And we have reached the end of this venture.'

'Indeed.' There was an odd note in his voice. She wasn't sure if it was relief, or something else. His expression gave nothing away, however. It had to be relief. What else could it be?

Her poor heart felt bruised and sore. She managed to breathe around the pain. 'It makes perfect sense.' She shot him what she hoped was an arch look. 'And then people will wonder what happened, so curiosity will continue to bring them to my shop.'

He gave her a faint smile. 'Smart girl. Naturally, I will continue to advise the ladies of my acquaintance to patronise your shop. Why would I not? You have the very best bonnets in London.'

'Then everything is just as it should be.' She smiled while inside she felt as if she was dying. 'Now eat your dessert and tell me if that is the most delicious trifle you have ever tasted.'

He gave her an odd look, but picked up his spoon.

Avery ate as he had been ordered. 'It is excellent.'

Everything was going exactly to plan. The civilised ending to their arrangement by way of a delicious companionable meal served by a woman so gorgeous he would certainly never forget his first sight of her in that filmy robe as long as he lived. He'd been fighting his arousal since the moment he'd walked in her door.

Everything about this evening was perfect.

Then why was he feeling so damned discontented?

Surely it wasn't because she was accepting his departure from her life with such equanimity? He usually hated scenes and female tears when it came to a parting. Another reason he preferred his dealings with females to be strictly business.

No, he should be delighted with the way the evening was going, but despite everything he had said, he felt uneasy, as if he was making some sort of mistake.

The spoon part way to his lips he stilled, glanced

across the table at her, where she was watching him, her chin cupped in her palm. She looked lovely. Alluring and not simply because of the extraordinarily sensual gown draping her luscious curves. She was lovely inside and out. Honest yet sweet, self-sufficient yet completely feminine. Undemanding. So different to any other woman he'd ever met.

She'd make any man a wonderful wife.

Any man but him.

He couldn't afford a wife. While he did well at the tables, nothing was ever certain about gambling. He'd sometimes had weeks of poor luck which was why he had set up his arrangements with various shopkeepers. And that was not something he would continue if he was married. And while Carrie was Westram's sister-in-law, she was still a merchant's daughter and completely unsuitable so there would be no help from his father. His gut clenched. If the old fellow decided to buy her off, the way he had with Alexandra, or tried to do her professional damage as he had with John, well, Avery might just end up committing patricide and that would help no one.

'You don't like the trifle?' she asked.

He started, realising he'd been staring at her instead of eating. 'It is nearly as delicious as you.'

As usual she gave a self-conscious little grimace as if she didn't believe him. He wanted her to believe him. He wanted her to realise her self-worth, to feel confident in her femininity. If he could give her nothing else, surely he could give her that?

He took her hand across the table. 'If this is to be our last night together, it seems a shame to waste it speaking half-truths. You are a very desirable woman and I want you more than I could ever want dessert.'

She blushed prettily and met his gaze head on. 'Thank you.'

Yes, that was what he had wanted, her acceptance of his compliment. Still holding her hand, he got up from the table and brought her to her feet. 'And while I love looking at you, Carrie, I would much rather be holding you in my arms.' He suited the action to the words, drawing her close, feeling the gorgeous soft wells of her generous figure flush with his body. 'I'd much rather be tasting you.'

He kissed her, gently at first, a merest brush of their lips, but as she melted into him, he deepened the kiss, making it firmer and more insistent.

Her lips parted and he tasted the sweetness of custard and the tartness of raspberry, but most of all he tasted Carrie. A far more exotic flavour to him than any confection. The way she yielded beneath his touch made him almost dizzy with desire.

His hands wandered over her familiar swells and hollows, stroking her in ways that made her press closer into him, while her hands trailed up from his chest to work their way around his neck and winnow through his hair.

The pleasure of her gentle touch aroused him more than the sight of her in the clinging gown had done. The scent of her filled his nostrils. Something spicy and clean. A scent he never wanted to forget. He kissed her, until they were both breathless and trembling with pent-up need and he was forced to stop before his legs gave out.

He rested his forehead against hers, breathing hard. 'I want you.'

'I want you, too,' she said.

He nodded and shrugged out of his coat. She attacked

the buttons on his falls while he undid his waistcoat. He toed off his shoes and tore off his waistcoat. She sank to her knees, pulling down his pantaloons until he could step out of them. She flung them over a chair and sank back on her heels with a smile, waiting for him to remove his shirt.

'I think it is your turn to remove an article of clothing,' he said, raising her to her feet and tugging at the pretty red ribbon that held her robe closed at the neck.

She swallowed as the delicate fabric fell to her feet, revealing the nightgown beneath. If one could call it that. It was the sauciest garment he had ever seen. It tied at the back of her neck and dipped all the way to below her navel. The fabric barely covered her nipples and only stayed in place because of the narrow plaited belt around her waist. The skirts fell to the floor, but a slit up the sides revealed her glorious long legs and her feet encased in high-heeled slippers.

She peeped up at him from slightly lowered lashes. 'Is it—?'

'You are the most sensual sight I have ever seen.' His voice rasped in his dry throat. His erection jutting upwards, tenting his shirt, should be proof enough of his words, but in case she had not noticed, he whipped off his shirt and flung it aside. 'I want you. I need you.'

He swept her up and deposited her on the bed. 'And right now I am going to have you.'

Her delighted smile filled his vision.

Held in his arms, her head resting on his shoulder as he carried her to the bed, Carrie realised that, despite everything she knew about him, she was head-over-heels in love with him. Not because he was handsome and charismatic, though he was all of that and more. And not because he had proved himself a wonderful lover and was about to do so again, but because underneath all that swaggering bravado he was one of the kindest people she had ever met.

It was going to be so very hard to let him go.

Never in her life had she felt the pull of her heart. She'd never been in love, not once, so it wasn't surprising that she would fall for him. It was what he did. He made women fall for him. She knew it meant nothing. So then why did she feel so wonderful and so wretched at the same time?

She knew he didn't love her back and he had never lied about it, but she did think he liked her and she wanted to make this evening memorable. Their last time together.

She smiled when he paused at the little alcove containing her bed. With his arms full of her, he did not have a free hand to draw back the curtain. She reached out and pulled it back and he gently deposited her on the bed, gazing down at her, his body gloriously displayed to her wandering gaze.

For a man who spent his days escorting women around town and his nights at the gambling tables, he really was amazingly fit. His chest was broad, his shoulders deeply muscled, his waist and flanks narrow and firm. And his erection was proud and aggressive.

She licked her lips.

His member jerked.

Pleased, she glanced up at his face.

He grinned at her, his teeth a flash of white. 'Yes, he wants you also.'

She swallowed. Hopefully she wasn't going to spoil

this by doing something stupid. She wanted this evening to be perfect, something she could remember all her life, for there would never be another man in her life. She would not dare do this again. Besides, no man could ever live up to Avery, not in her mind or in her foolish heart.

A heart that must be ignored. *Trusting your heart is taking a chance.*

She leaned back on her elbows, sprawling, so the gown would leave her legs bare to his gaze. When she had tried the pose earlier, she had thought it looked inviting. When he didn't move, she thought perhaps it was too much. Too eager, too demanding.

She shifted, trying to make herself less...less something.

'No,' he rasped. 'I just want a moment to remember the way you look right now.'

Oh. A smile pulled at her lips. A surge of happiness swelled her heart. He always said the most lovely things. As she had planned earlier, she pulled free the strategically placed comb and her hair tumbled down around her shoulders.

'You little minx,' he said approvingly. 'You planned that.'

He looked pleased.

As she had hoped. She tossed him a saucy glance. 'I'm glad you liked it.'

A serious expression flitted across his face. 'I like everything about you.'

And she adored him. Loved him. Stunned at the admission, she took a deep breath, forcing the words back where they belonged in the deepest reaches of her heart where she would treasure the memory of having loved and been loved, if only for a brief time.

She held out a hand to him. 'Are you going to stand there all night, or are we going to make some more memories together?'

In a moment, he was on the bed, kneeling astride her, leaning down and kissing her lips, his tongue delving deep into her mouth, sending tingling sensations out to her fingertips and in the deepest regions of her body. Breathless and trembling, she lay back against the cushions and twined her arms around his neck, pulling him down with her, feeling his weight on her body, pressing down on her breasts, his erection hard against her belly. Yes, this was what she had been missing, the feeling of belonging, of sharing, of being close.

When he broke the kiss and gazed down into her eyes, she stroked his hair back from his face with her palms. She would not say the words, they were buried and his rejection of them would hurt far too much, but she could fill her gaze with that love and give him the gift of her body, and bring him pleasure.

His hand came to her breast and swept the scrap of fabric aside. His gaze left her face and dropped to where his thumb was slowly circling her nipple.

Her nipples hardened to stiff little points, one bare, the other hidden, but obvious beneath the fabric of the nightgown.

'It seems they are ready for you,' she said softly, tilting her hips at the pleasure of his touch.

'It would seem so,' he said. His eyelids drooped a fraction as he gazed down at the tight little nub. He swooped down and licked it.

She gasped.

He looked up at her with a piratical grin. Then he lowered his head slowly. She waited for the lick that held such shocking sensations. It never came. He opened his mouth and took in the peak of her breast. Heat rushed to her core where little pulses sent waves of heat through her body. She moaned at the sheer overwhelming deliciousness of the sensations rippling along her veins.

And then he sucked.

The painful pleasure blanked her mind to everything except the tight drawing sensation on her breast and all the way down to the apex of her thighs. Her hips ground against him, seeking to ease the pleasurable ache. This time she knew what it was she wanted, what he would bring her. She tried to part her thighs, to encourage him closer, to bring him into the cradle of her hips, but he ignored her attempts, continuing to kneel astride her, his erection brushing her belly, but not going where she wanted it.

Indeed, if anything, he lifted himself up, further away.

She made a sound of protest.

He released her nipple on a hard little suck and pressed a brief kiss on her lips. 'Patience, little one. Let us not rush this.'

Little one? Was he talking to her?

But when he loomed over her like that, when his shoulders blocked her view of everything but him, yes, she did feel a whole lot smaller and vulnerable. And he was right, much as her body protested, she did want to savour every second of this last time.

She sighed. It was so lovely. She never wanted it to end. And yet she wanted him to bring her the release her body craved.

Chapter Thirteen

Never had Avery had so much trouble controlling the animal urges roaring through his blood. It might be knowing this would be the last time they would ever make love. Or it might be her inexperience exciting him more than it should, but the only way to stop himself from racing to the finish was by keep physical distance between them. For a while longer, at least.

If she would let him. Her legs came up around his waist, her heels digging into his buttocks as she lifted her hips to rub her sex against his groin, while she pulled his head down to kiss his lips and dance her tongue around his. Delicious. Seductive, yet innocent. He didn't know what aroused him the most, her hesitant touch or her boldness in demanding what she wanted.

Once he'd learned the way of it as a youth, he'd always been the one in charge in bed. Always set the pace, controlled the flow. Carrie set things end over end, leaving him running to catch up. As he was now. Breathless, bordering on driving into her and losing himself in her slick heat and to the devil with the consequences.

That was not going to happen.

Breaking off the kiss, her pushed backwards, breaking her hold around his neck and his hips. He pressed first one knee then the other between her thighs and, smiling her approval, she parted her legs to accommodate him. She reached out to pull him back to her.

He ignored the invitation and sat back on his heels, letting his gaze wander over the salacious sight of her white smooth thighs, the damp curls at their apex that gave him a little peek of her feminine rosiness. He skimmed upwards to her waist with the plaited belt and the rumpled fabric of her nightgown hiding her belly. He undid the tie and pulled it free, sweeping the scrap of material aside to view her slightly rounded belly and the magnificent globes of her breasts with their hard-tipped peaks.

His mouth watered at the utterly scrumptious sight she made. He pressed a kiss to her navel, swirling his tongue around it, enjoying the way she squirmed at the pleasure of his touch. Her hands roamed across his shoulders, her fingers combed through his hair, her moans of encouragement filled his ears. Slowly he worked his way up to tease and lick each nipple, moving from one to the other in quick successions, taking her sensual defences by storm, until her hands lay limp on his shoulders and he could see the rapid beat of her pulse in the hollow of her throat and feel her hips stirring restlessly beneath him.

Once more, he sat back. Her heavy eyelids lifted a fraction or two.

'Is something wrong?' she whispered hoarsely.

'Everything is perfect.'

She frowned at his erection as he scooted backwards, looking lost and confused. Then gasped as he lowered his head to her sex. He swept his tongue up the sweet little cleft, tasting her essence, feeling the heat of her desire.

She made a noise in the back of her throat that he was sure was a denial and he lifted his head, looking past her beautiful breasts to take in her shocked expression.

'No?' he asked. 'You don't like it.'

'I don't—'

He pulled away.

'No! I mean, I have never felt anything so—'

He waited. He had known this would be a shock to her, but he wanted her to know the pleasure of this. She deserved to know the pleasure of this. But he would not force it on her. She was too new to the art of lovemaking. But he did hope her boldness would not let her down. 'So?' he questioned, pressing her, intrigued, wanting to hear what she thought.

'So wicked,' she gasped. She rubbed her hands up and down his forearms where he braced himself beside her hips. 'I—' She cast him a shy smile. 'I liked it.'

'There is more,' he said.

She hissed in a breath and the little sound caused his groin to tighten. He was in trouble all right. 'Show me,' she whispered.

Big trouble.

He dipped his head and swirled his tongue around, flicking it back and forth across her most pleasurable spot. She cried out and shuddered. 'Avery,' she murmured. 'Oh.'

She lay lax beneath him.

He should have expected her swift response. She was a very sensual female aroused quickly by touch. He leaned over her and kissed her lips. She flicked out her tongue, licking at him, tasting herself on his mouth and looking surprised and very pleased.

'That was so nice.'

'Only nice?' he teased, grinning down at her.

'Amazing. Wonderful.'

'Better.'

'Out of this world.'

He nodded his approval and took her lips in a long heart-stoppingly lovely kiss.

When it was over and he rose above her, holding himself up on his hands, she looked worried.

He gave her a questioning look.

She blushed. 'What about you? Are you not going to take your pleasure?'

'Giving you pleasure is my pleasure.'

That did not seem to please her. 'But I want to give you the same kind of pleasure you gave me.'

His shaft jerked in response to her words. 'Are you sure?'

She glanced down between their bodies, her gaze seeking out his erection, and licked her lips.

'You don't have to, you know.'

He certainly didn't expect it, given her inexperience. 'Do you like it?'

She sounded so serious, he wanted to smile. 'I most certainly do.'

'Then I would like to.'

Who was he to argue with a lady, especially when she wanted to give him such an incredible gift? Except—

'Well?' she said, sounding almost cross.

Too delighted for words, he stifled a grin and rolled over on to his back. 'Have at it.'

She gazed at him as if what she was looking at was

the most wonderful thing she had ever seen and licked her lips. He almost came apart.

A small secret smile curved her lips. 'I don't think I have ever seen anything so tempting as this.'

He groaned as her delicate hand curled around the base, squeezing ever so lightly. He forced himself not to push into her hand, holding himself still by gritting his teeth until they hurt. As she leaned over him, her hair fell forward, hiding her and what she was doing from view. All he could do was feel the heat and wetness of her tongue as she gave an experimental lick at the head of his shaft.

He bit back a groan of frustration. He did not want anything to call a halt to these proceedings.

Then she took him fully into his mouth and his vision blanked. He swallowed hard, reaching for a scrap of control, while she used her mouth and tongue to explore his shape and size.

Finally, she gave an experimental suck and he almost came apart.

Quickly, before he succumbed to her teasing, he reached down and gently lifted her up towards him and kissed her senseless.

When he broke the kiss, she smiled with a little cat-like smile. 'You liked that.'

'More than I can say,' he managed to gasp hoarsely.

He rolled her on her back and came over her, gazing down into her lovely face. 'But we do this together, this time.'

Carefully, he pressed the blunt head of his shaft into her body, circling his hips while he watched her face, probing for the spot that would bring her the most pleasure.

She moaned, her hips writhing, her body tensing as if pulled as tight as a bowstring. He rocked, moving against that spot until her head was thrashing and her heels were trying to press him deeper into her body.

The base of his shaft tingled with the urge to drive deeper. He slid deeper into her and withdrew. She groaned her pleasure. Lifted her hips, sought to bring him deeper still.

And then there was no more waiting or teasing, he could do nothing but thrust into her, pound against her, while caressing her breast with one hand and kissing her lips, sucking her tongue into his mouth.

Her inner muscles seized around his shaft, tightening so hard, it was like being held in a hot hard fist. His vision filled with white light and he exploded into darkness as he felt her shudder with the force of her own climax. His body pulsed his seed into hers.

Only when the shattering ceased and the pieces of him came back together did he realise that he had not withdrawn from her body as he had intended.

Damn it all. Not for years had he made such a foolish mistake.

Wrapped in Avery's arms, Carrie had never felt quite so...treasured. It was more than the lovely sated feeling after their lovemaking. It was a feeling of belonging. As if she had found her true home. She snuggled closer and he tightened his arm around her, stroking her back. She cracked an eyelid and peered at his face. He was still asleep. The caress had been instinctual, rather than deliberate, and that pleased her more than it probably should.

The man certainly knew how to make a woman feel precious, even in his sleep.

The haze of pleasure slowly drifted away and she put her thoughts in order, instead of letting her heart rule her head. Yes, the lovemaking was amazing, but tonight was their last night together. It had to be. The longer he remained as her lover, the harder it was going to be to let him go.

There was no future for them. He was a reprobate, a charming one, but a reprobate none the less. He made his living as a ladies' escort and, worse yet in her eyes, by gambling.

Besides, while her sisters-in-law would happily close their eyes to a love affair, as they had all agreed that they would, that was all it could ever be. They had agreed to stick together, to help each other through thick and thin. None of them was ever going to marry again. As wonderful as this was with Avery she could not see herself being a man's permanent mistress. She only had to imagine how horrified her father would be, were he alive, to have guilt and shame making her go hot and cold by turns.

No. This would definitely not continue after tonight.

Avery rolled over on to his back and put his arm over his eyes. She raised up on her elbow. 'Are you awake?'

He sat up, his bare torso reminding her again just how young and virile he was. He placed his elbows on his bent knees and scrubbed his hands through his hair.

She frowned. He seemed…unhappy about something. The wonderful warmth she'd been feeling, even though it had been tinged with loss, dissipated and left her feeling cold. 'What is it?'

'I fear I got a bit carried away,' he said. He rubbed at the back of his neck. 'I didn't take proper precautions.'

What?

'I could have got you with child.' He looked at her, his face thoughtful. 'When did you say your husband died?'

Oh. He was worried about her having a baby. Oh my word, that would certainly complicate matters. 'Over a year ago. Surely it isn't possible? Not so quickly.' Everyone said it was not. Couples often tried for many years before the wife fell for a child.

'Anything is possible.' He sounded rather off-hand. 'We can hope not, I suppose. But I will do right by you, Carrie, should we be unlucky.'

Oh, dear, he was not happy about the idea at all.

There was a scuffling sound outside the door.

Avery's head came up. With a sudden premonition, Carrie clutched the sheets to her chest. Had she locked her door after—?

The door slammed open. Westram stood framed in the doorway staring into the room. His gaze found the bed. His expression went from angry to furious.

'Well, madam?' he snapped.

Avery glanced at her, eyes wide. His surprised expression disappeared in an instant and was replaced by dawning understanding and then a bored smile as he turned his attention to Westram. 'Someone you know, Carrie?' he drawled.

'I am her brother-in-law, sir. Westram,' the Earl said, his voice full of menace.

'Lord Avery Gilmore, Second son of Belmane at your service,' Avery replied.

Carrie had never heard him sound so regal.

He spoiled the effect by flashing an insolent smile. 'You will forgive me if I do not get up?'

Was he trying to make Westram more annoyed than he was already?

But Westram's demeanour changed in an instant. He looked—pleased. 'I see.'

What? 'Why are you here, Westram?' Carrie asked.

'I received a letter from an interested party about what was called your goings on.' Westram looked down his nose. 'You said nothing to me about opening a shop, Carrie Greystoke. But that is only part of it, isn't it?' He glared at Avery. 'If you don't care for your own reputation, you could give some thought to those of my sisters.'

Avery made a sound like a growl.

Westram glared at him. 'And as for you, sir, what are your intentions towards my sister-in-law?'

Beside her, Avery shifted uneasily.

Oh, no. Westram was not going to do this. 'How dare you, Westram?' Carrie cried. 'What I do is none of your business. I am an independent—'

'You live under my roof, madam. I feed you and clothe you and you are my brother's widow. Therefore you are my responsibility. If I had gleaned any idea you planned to drag my sisters down to the level of—'

'Enough, sir,' Avery thundered. 'Mrs Greystoke has done me the honour of agreeing to become my wife and if you say one more disparaging word about her, I shall be forced to thrust them down your throat where they belong.'

Carrie froze. At the words. At the fury in Avery's voice. At the longing filling her heart.

Westram's demeanour changed in a moment. 'Your wife, you say?'

'I do,' Avery bit out, putting a hand over hers to still her protest.

Westram scanned her living quarters and his lip curled. 'I hope you intend to keep her in better circumstances than this?'

'Now look here, Westram,' Carrie said. 'There is no need to ridicule what we have done here. Our shop—'

'We, madam?' Westram said. 'You turned my sisters into shopkeepers?' He shook his head. 'And I thought you were the sensible one.' His gaze returned to Avery and spoke harshly. 'You, sir, will be expected at my lodgings tomorrow morning to speak of the settlements. I assume eleven of the clock will suit you? In the meantime, allow me to use my carriage to deposit you at your lodgings, forthwith.'

'No need,' Avery said, equally tersely. 'I will walk.'

'Then I will see you off the premises.' Westram turned his gaze on Carrie and there was a coldness in his eyes Carrie had never seen there before. 'I will send my carriage round in the morning to return you, madam, to Kent. When you arrive, you may inform my sisters that I will be calling on them in a day or so. You may also inform them that you are to be married within the fortnight.' He smiled at Avery. 'I assume that will suit, Lord Avery.'

It was not a question.

Avery inclined his head.

'Very well. I will wait outside for you, my lord.' He turned and stalked out.

As he left, Carrie got a glimpse of Mr Thrumby hopping from foot to foot. She buried her face in her hands. 'Everything is ruined.'

She should never have let herself be entranced by

Avery. Never let the desires of her heart overcome the sense of her mind. Her sisters-in-law were going to be so unhappy at this outcome.

The moment the door closed, Avery shot out of bed and, grim-faced, began dressing. Despite everything, she could not stop admiring his lean narrow flanks and firm buttocks or the breadth of his shoulders, or the feeling of disappointment when all that glorious male disappeared beneath his clothes.

'Avery,' she said her voice catching, 'I am so sorry.'

He left off buttoning his falls to give her a hard smile. 'Never mind. We shall manage, my dear.'

She didn't want to manage. 'Surely you don't intend to go through with this plan of Westram's? Let me talk to him in the morning. I am sure I can smooth things over.'

He shot her a look of such incredulity, she recoiled. 'Are you sure this is not exactly what you wanted?' he asked.

'I—I beg your pardon?'

He let go a breath. 'Never mind.' He shrugged into his coat and picked up his hat.

'I do mind.'

'Let it go, Carrie. We will discuss this some other time, when Westram isn't pacing the hallway outside the door. It isn't the first time I have been thrown out of somewhere and I'll wager it likely it won't be the last.' His chuckle sounded hollow. 'Care to bet on the odds?'

Carrie froze. Here they were in the direst of circumstances and he was making one of his awful bets. Exactly the sort of bet her husband had made before departing for the Peninsula.

'I don't care to bet,' she said stiffly.

'Good thing, too. You would lose.'

He walked out of the door and closed it behind him.

Carrie leaped out of bed and turned the key. She gazed around her, seeking some sort of divine inspiration. The only thing that occurred to her was that she had messed it all up. Dash it all. The shop she might have been able to explain to Westram, but Avery had added a whole level of complication she could not explain away. If only… If only she hadn't been so curious.

It was all Jonathan's fault. If he had done his husbandly duty… *Argh*. She could not place the blame anywhere else. It was her fault. She had ruined everything.

Westram was right, she was not good enough to remain with his sisters. And what was she to do about Avery and his talk of marriage? She didn't want another marriage of convenience. Another man forced to the altar.

Her heart squeezed in longing. Her throat felt as if she had swallowed something large and dry. The backs of her eyes burned.

Oh, no. She was not going to cry over something she never intended and had no wish for. No wish at all.

Tomorrow she would have to find a way to sort out this whole blasted mess. Hopefully Westram's temper would have cooled somewhat and Avery could be brought to see sense.

Avery, at his lodgings and still in his dressing gown the next morning, gazed into the maelstrom within his cup as he stirred his tea. Engaged to be married, by God. There was absolutely no way around it. Carrie had been wrong when she said Westram took no interest in what his sisters did. He also should have known better than to believe it. Perhaps it had been wishful thinking on his part, damn it. Not that there was anything Westram could do to him if he did not come up to scratch. His reputation was already as black as it could be and he had not a penny to his name.

He should have stuck to his principles. Never got involved with a single lady. And if for one moment he thought Carrie had actually engineered that scene last night, if he for one moment thought that she had either written to Westram or had her landlord do it, he'd be on the next boat travelling to India, or China. But upon reflection, he realised Carrie was incapable of such deceit and felt awful for having suggested as much. No. It wouldn't be Carrie. She wasn't like that. It had to be the Duke. And while he wasn't quite sure what the old man might be trying to achieve, Avery should have expected something of the sort after his conversation with Bart and taken the necessary precautions.

But Westram insisting on marriage was likely not the outcome the Duke hoped for, surely? More likely he'd be hoping Westram would set Avery to the right about. Papa certainly wouldn't want him marrying the daughter of a merchant. Would he? Perhaps he didn't know Carrie's exact circumstances.

But despite what Avery had said to Carrie the previous evening, when his temper had been high, he wasn't even all that displeased about Westram's demand. He hadn't wanted to say goodbye to her after their lovemaking last night. He wasn't ready to bid her farewell. And Westram wasn't wrong to sneer at the way she was living in that little shop. She deserved so much more.

His gut tightened. And just how was *he* going to provide more?

He closed his eyes and leaned back. He'd have to play for higher stakes, which increased the risk of higher losses. With luck, John would soon start earning enough to support his family so Avery could leave Laura to him. Avery certainly wouldn't be playing escort to anyone else's wife. He hadn't done so since meeting Carrie and he could not see himself ever doing so again. And while he had no problem with his wife being a shopkeeper, a husband should be the breadwinner.

A scratch at his door brought him upright. Had Bart heard the news? It wouldn't surprise him. His brother had an amazing network of suppliers of intelligence. It was the only way he managed to keep the Duke from committing some new folly.

'Come.'

The door opened and Carrie stepped in. 'Lord Avery, I have come to thank you for your kind proposal, but I am afraid I cannot accept.'

Shooting to his feet, he stared at her blankly. As the words made sense, a sharp pain pierced his heart. 'Why?' It was the only thing he could think of to say. His mind went back to that day when he'd been twenty-two and still green about the gills and another lady had said almost the same thing to him. Had Father bought this one off, too? But then why bring Westram into it at all? None of this made any sense. He was missing something.

Carrie lifted her chin. 'I do not think we should suit. You never wanted to be married and nor did I. I value my independence.

Last night, Westram had indicated he had no intention of allowing her to maintain that independence. Had something changed? He gestured to the chair on the opposite side of the little table. 'Please, sit down. Have you breakfasted? Would you like tea?'

'I—' She gazed longingly at the toast rack.

'Help yourself.' He went to the cupboard beside the hearth and brought back a fresh cup and saucer. He sat down and proceeded to pour tea while she buttered a slice of toast. 'I don't have any jam, I am afraid.' It was a luxury he could do without.

She nibbled at the toast, then put it down on the plate and clasped her hands in her lap. 'I came early so I could catch you before you went to your appointment with Westram.'

There were shadows around her eyes. She'd clearly spent a sleepless night worrying. Dash it all. 'Carrie, I told Westram we were affianced. There is no way I could in all honour go back on my word now.'

She drew in a deep breath. 'I did not give my word.'

'You did not deny it.'

When she opened her mouth to object, he shook his head. 'Think about it. Would it be so very bad?'

She glanced around his lodgings. 'I don't think I can keep the business going. Thrumby was most distressed when he came to see me this morning. He said if he had known Westram had not approved of the venture he would never have allowed me to rent the shop. And besides, Westram will not allow Marguerite and Petra to have anything to do with it any longer and so, without any more hats to sell, it must close.'

'Quite honestly, I am not surprised that Westram would put a stop to it. But that is no reason for us not to marry.'

She frowned. 'How would we manage?' Her frown deepened. 'On your gambling?'

He shrugged. 'What else?'

She nodded slowly, frowning at the toast. Finally, she pushed the plate away, her grey eyes lifting to focus on his face, thoughts, like shadows, swirling beneath the calm surface. 'We were both very clear at the start of this adventure that neither of us wanted to marry. Nothing has changed.'

He wanted to howl with frustration. Bang his fist on the table. He took a deep breath. 'Nothing? A great deal has changed. Do you think Westram will not insist on this marriage? If I renege, do you think he won't ask for satisfaction?'

She looked shocked.

Hah. Got her. A feeling of triumph filled him. She was right, he had not wanted to get married when they first met. But that was then and now things were different. Warmth spread through his veins at the idea of Carrie as his wife. He was definitely fond of her. And she seemed fond of him. Perhaps it was love, of a sort. Perhaps love did exist?

She gave a little jerk of her chin. 'Do you think your father will be happy at you marrying a cit, as you nobles call us?'

Blast it, he really wasn't sure if the old man was behind this turn of events or if he would be opposed to it. 'It is none of the Duke's business what I do and I neither know nor care what he thinks.'

She narrowed her gaze and took a deep breath. 'All right, let me stop beating around the bush and get down to brass tacks. I am not going to be forced into marrying anyone, not by Westram or anyone else.'

Forced? He felt as if he had been stabbed through the heart. The pain left him speechless.

Her chin came up and she looked him straight in the eye. There was a glassiness about her gaze that looked suspiciously like tears. 'I will not marry you, Avery, and

I wanted you to know this, because that is what I intend to tell Lord Westram before you call on him at eleven o'clock and I will ensure that he listens.' She rose to her feet and headed for the door.

'Carrie,' he said, giving her a smile that ought to soften her anger. 'Be reasonable.'

'I am being reasonable. Reasonable and sensible. Please, get this through your head. Our little fling was wonderful, but it is now at an end and we are not getting married.' She strode out.

He started after her, but he could hardly chase after her through St James's in his dressing gown. He rubbed at the growth of beard on his chin. And he could hardly turn up on the Earl's doorstep in disarray if he wanted to make a good impression.

His gut dipped. Nor could he force Carrie to wed him if she didn't want to.

He actually had the strange feeling she was trying to give him a way out of the whole mess. Instead of feeling pleased, or grateful or relieved, for the second time in his life he felt desperately hurt.

Only this time, he wasn't going to run away the way he had after what happened with Alexandra. This time he was going to fight for the woman he loved.

Loved?

Dammit all. He did love her.

And he did not believe she cared nothing for him, not after last night. Apparently, he was going to have to find a way to convince her of his love and to woo her into loving him back.

Oh, no, Carrie Greystoke, this was definitely not the end of their affair. Not if he could help it.

Chapter Fourteen

Only an idiot would be tempted to marry a man like Lord Avery.

And Carrie counted herself an idiot. She stopped a few yards from Westram's hotel and dried her tears with her handkerchief, then blew her nose.

She took a deep breath. She was not going to allow Westram to force Avery into marriage. He had forced her first husband up to the mark, she certainly would not allow him to do the same thing to Avery. If she had known more about Jonathan, she would never have agreed to his proposal.

Although with the pressure from her father to accept after Jonathan had offered for her—well, it was no use going over old ground…it was the present she had to deal with. She had her sisters-in-law to think of now, too. They had agreed to stick together. To renounce the married state and help each other. The idea had been to take a lover should the opportunity present itself, not end up in church marrying the man.

So what if Avery had stolen her heart? It was the sort of thing men like him did. He made a living by making foolish women fall for his charm. And foolish men, too.

At the gambling tables. Unlike the situation with Jonathan, whom she knew little about before they married, she *did* know all about Avery. Even if Westram wasn't pressing him to marry her, she could not be with a man who loved the thrill of a wager.

What if he promised to give up his gambling? The strength of that hope took her aback. Oh, she really did need her head examined if she thought he would keep such a promise.

When the next wager came along that offered the chance of easy coin, he'd be off risking his life by swimming across the Thames or climbing a steeple. That was the sort of thing her first husband had done she had learned after his death. People had spoken of his exploits with awe and fondness. It had made her so very angry.

She certainly wasn't going to sit at home waiting for the news of Avery's death in some misadventure. She simply could not do it.

Her mind kept running in circles. Tossing up what ifs and maybes until she could not think at all. This was so unlike her. But oh, she did so wish things could be different. They couldn't. And even if Avery gave up gambling and wagering on ridiculous outcomes, she would not marry a man who had to be forced to the altar for the sake of his honour.

What had that gypsy fortune teller said, something about the head ruling over the heart if she wanted true happiness? Then that was her answer. Logic and reason, not sentiment.

She strode into the hotel without hesitation. She knew exactly how to go on. She had visited merchants who had come to Nottingham on business with her father. In those days, her father had been a force to be reckoned with among the merchants and no one had taken any notice of him bringing his daughter along.

Here, the porter looked at her askance.

Well, he would. Young women did not usually call on gentlemen unescorted. Blast, she should have thought of that and brought Tansy with her, but she needed her to mind the shop. 'I am here to visit my brother-in-law,' she said firmly. 'Lord Westram.'

The man's eyes widened. 'What name shall I give, ma'am?' His expression was polite enough, but his eyes held doubt.

'Mrs Greystoke.'

He wrote a note and gave it to a lad in livery standing at attention near his desk. 'If you would take a seat for a moment or two…' he suggested.

She nodded and perched on one of the chairs scattered around the lobby. She chose one with a good view of the stairs.

A few moments later, Westram ran down them, looking harassed and flustered. He had a brief word with the porter before coming to her side. 'There is a private parlour we can use.' He took her arm and escorted her up to the second floor. The windows of the small room looked out over the Strand where not long ago she had gone to visit an elephant.

'What are you doing here, Carrie?' he asked once they were seated.

'I have no intention of marrying Lord Avery, so it is absolutely pointless you meeting with him this morning.'

He reared back. 'So the blackguard got you to do his dirty work for him, did he? Well, it won't wash. I will not allow such an insult to my family name to stand—'

'Enough.' She inhaled a deep breath and calmed herself. 'Please, Westram. Believe me when I say the blame is mine. I approached him. I am sorry if you are disappointed in my behaviour. I certainly did not intend to cause you any anxiety. I can assure you nothing like this will ever happen again, but I am not marrying Lord Avery.'

She could hardly be any plainer.

'*You* approached *him*?'

Dash it, why was he focusing on that part of her apology? 'I am a widow, Westram. I assume that has not escaped your attention? He came to my shop with another lady and I found myself charmed.' She launched into the other thing she had hoped she would not have to say, but now felt obliged to offer. 'If you are concerned about *my* lack of decorum somehow tainting the reputation of your sisters, I will leave Kent immediately and break off all contact with them.'

Westram stared at her. 'I must say I am surprised at you,' he said his voice gruff. 'I thought you were the most sensible of the three of you.'

At the sight of the pain in his expression, she felt bitterly ashamed that she had let him down.

He reached out and patted her hand. 'I wish you had talked to me first. That sort of fellow, well, charm, it's his stock in trade,' he said heavily. 'But then I should have realised you weren't as up to snuff as you seem.'

She wasn't sure if he was insulting her or being kind, he spoke so gently. Why would he be kind? 'No doubt you think because I am of common stock, I do not know how to go on.' She ungritted her teeth and forced a smile. 'As I understand it, as a widow I am permitted some licence to pursue my own interests.'

He stiffened. 'I believe I made myself clear that you

were all to look for husbands,' he snapped. 'Lord Avery is a well-known philanderer. You cannot believe how many people couldn't wait to tell me my widowed sister-in-law had taken up with the *ton*'s most idle rake. And if you think I am happy about the idea of having to hand over blunt in settlements to that fellow who will likely just gamble it all away in a single sitting just as my—' He ran a hand through his hair and closed his eyes briefly.

'As your brother did,' she finished his sentence. 'Which is why I will not marry him, despite his kind offer.'

Westram sagged back in his chair. 'This is all my fault. I should have insisted you all came with me to live at Castings.'

Worry and sorrow filled his normally austere expression.

'You have had the care of your family for a very long time, Westram. You did your best to protect your sisters and now me. I honestly regret causing you this worry. To be honest, I made a mistake in marrying your brother. I had no idea he was wedding me in order to pay off his gambling debts, leaving nothing for my future should he die. I should have been told beforehand.'

He opened his mouth to speak.

She put up a hand. 'The past is the past. It need never be spoken of again, but I hope you will not insist I marry another ne'er-do-well.' Inwardly she winced, for she did not really think Avery anywhere near as bad as Greystoke, but it seemed strategic to use Westram's overdeveloped sense of responsibility against him in this particular instance.

'Devil take it, Carrie,' he said on a sigh. 'All right. If you are really opposed to the match, then I will get rid of the fellow. I'll pay him off.'

'No need,' she said, feeling very sad inside, hollow and achy. 'I have been to see him. He will not call.'

'You went to see him?'

She nodded.

'Alone at his lodgings? Are you mad?'

'No one saw me.'

'Someone will have seen you,' he said heavily. He straightened his shoulders. 'Well, I'll just have to do my best to scotch any rumours that arise.'

'Why not return to Gloucestershire as if nothing had happened. I shall not be seeing Lord Avery again and everything will die down soon enough.' The same way the drama over the deaths of Westram's brother and brothers-in-law had died down. 'By next Season it will all have been forgotten.'

Westram gave her a sharp look. 'You are a very intelligent woman, Carrie. It is a pity you were not as perceptive when it came to being charmed by a blackguard like Lord Avery.' He waved a hand. 'Never mind. I agree with your suggestion. But this shop thing must stop.'

She pressed her lips together, trying to marshal her arguments. 'I do not—'

'If you want me to forget about this affair with Lord Avery, then this is my price.'

Damn him, he was not at all a stupid man. She and his sisters would have to find another way to earn an income. That was if the other two would even welcome her back into their fold. She inclined her head. 'As you wish.'

He nodded sharply. 'It is what I wish. I will send round a note to Thrumby, asking him to send me his outstanding bills.'

She drew herself up straight. 'You need not do so. Mr Thrumby's bill is paid in full.'

His jaw dropped. 'You mean you actually made enough to pay your rent?'

'We made a healthy profit. Which is why you should let us continue with the endeavour.'

He shook his head. 'I cannot have it said that my sisters have gone into trade.'

Heat scalded her face.

He had the grace to look chagrined. 'I apologise. There is nothing wrong with being in trade, per se. It is simply that if my sisters are to marry again, they will need to see that their reputations are spotless. It is the way of the world, Carrie. There is nothing I can do about it.'

He was a good brother and he cared about his sisters. She could not fault him for that, much as she resented his high-handed interference. But then that was really her fault, wasn't it? If she had stuck to selling bonnets, instead of getting involved with Lord Avery, they would not be having this conversation.

But without Lord Avery, their little enterprise would not have been nearly so successful.

Oh, dear. What a pickle it all was to be sure. But there was clearly no gainsaying Westram on the matter. He was determined to have his way and she had given him all the ammunition he needed to shoot down their plans. 'I will need one day to close up the shop and dispose of the stock.'

His sisters were going to be so disappointed. The thought made her heart sink even further.

Westram nodded. 'I'll send my carriage around first thing in the morning.'

'Westram has no right to interfere in our business,' Petra said, pacing to the drawing-room window and back. 'We should simply ignore him and continue on as planned.'

Carrie, who had arrived the previous evening to deliver her news, could not remember seeing her sister-in-law so agitated. 'We cannot. Mr Thrumby will not allow us to keep the shop without Westram's approval. I do not think your brother will change his mind, do you?'

'He tends to be one of the more stubborn sort,' Marguerite said. 'My concern is all the women we employed to help us. We will have to find a way to pay them.'

At least she had a bit of good news on that front. 'This past week was surprisingly successful. We had almost no hats left and the nightgowns were exceedingly profitable as the ladies paid top prices for the few that were left. There is definitely enough to pay for their work. There will be little left over for us, though.'

Not enough for them to show Westram they could manage for themselves and did not need his support.

'And what are we to do with all the bonnets and nightgowns they made in the meantime? There has to be something we can do.'

'I suppose we can give them to charity,' Marguerite said. 'I must say I did not expect Westram to take a pet over an affair with a gentleman.' She turned her gaze on Carrie. 'Surely you were not terribly indiscreet?'

Carrie shrank inside. 'We were not exactly circumspect. The idea was to bring customers to the shop.'

'While I can quite understand why the son of a duke would be interested in you, Carrie, I don't understand why he would involve himself in helping our business.'

Startled, Carrie stared at her. 'I believe you have it the wrong way around. His interest was primarily in our commerce. It is how he earns his living.' That and gambling. 'He is cast out by his father.'

'Then he must have done something dreadful,' Marguerite said. 'And you are better off not associating with him.'

So Carrie had told herself repeatedly. Telling herself and believing it were two very different things, though.

Petra's face grew thoughtful. 'He is need of funds, then?'

'He is. He has arrangements with several shops in town. If the ladies he brings to them buy their wares, he receives a commission.'

'Ladies?' Marguerite said sharply.

Carrie ignored the stab of pain in her heart and the realisation dawning on her sister-in-law's face. The look of pity.

Petra came back to the sofa and perched beside Carrie, looking at her intently. 'I have an idea.'

'Someone needs to have an idea,' Marguerite said on a sigh.

'You said he offered for you,' Petra went on. 'Marry him. Then Westram can have nothing to say about the shop.'

Carrie gasped. Her heart stilled. Her stomach fell away. Longing filled her. She shoved it away. 'Marry him? Certainly not.' She hoped she sounded convincing, because the fluttering in her stomach was internally giving her the lie.

Petra made a dismissive gesture. 'You must like the fellow. And it will simply be a business arrangement. We will have to include him in the partnership, of course. But we cannot let our business go, when it is just beginning to be successful.'

'No!' Carrie exclaimed. 'We agreed we all wanted our independence from husbands. That we would stick together in this matter.'

Marguerite nodded, giving her sister a frown.

'Besides,' Carrie continued, 'while Lord Avery is everything that is charming, he has an unsteadiness of character that I cannot like. And,' she added for good measure, 'I would never marry again out of convenience.'

'Oh, pooh!' Petra said indelicately. 'You cannot mean to say you expect to find true love a second time? If indeed you found it the first time.'

The hurt in her voice was hard to hear. But it was more than that, a sort of disillusionment.

'Enough, Petra,' Marguerite said, clearly noticing nothing amiss, which made Carrie think perhaps she was imagining something that wasn't there.

'We agreed when we set up house that *none* of us wished to marry again,' Marguerite said. 'Marriage is nothing but a disappointment. This independence of ours was supposed to relieve us of the necessity of relying on men.'

While Marguerite never spoke of her husband, she was certainly the one who had been the most vocal of the three of them about never wanting to marry again. Setting up house here in the country had been her idea. Carrie had really let her down. 'I am so sorry.'

'It is not your fault,' Marguerite said.

'No,' Petra said, her blue eyes flashing. 'It is Westram's and we are left still relying on his support.'

'That is different,' Marguerite snapped.

'I don't see how?' Petra said. 'And if Carrie was married, then she could act as our chaperon and we would never have to be answerable to Westram for anything again.'

Unfortunately, Petra was right. But she was not the one being asked to marry a man who had been forced up to the mark.

'I am sorry,' Carrie said. 'Truly I am. But I cannot marry Lord Avery. Not after—' Her voice broke.

Petra drew in a breath, her eyes wide, and full of sympathy. 'Oh, I am sorry, too, Carrie. I did not mean to hurt you. I know you loved Jonathan, but I thought if you had taken a lover, you were ready to move on. I did not mean to be unfeeling. And besides, you are right, we did agree we would stick together no matter what. Please, forget I so much as mentioned it.'

Argh. Now she felt like a complete fraud. She should have scotched their romantic notions at the very beginning, but she had felt like such a fool when they had both appeared so happy in their marriages.

'It was a fling, nothing more.' The words hurt dreadfully. 'Neither of us wishes to marry and I won't have him forced into it.'

Petra sagged back against the chair cushions. 'Since Westram won't entertain our names being associated with at shop, mayhap we can find someone to run the shop while we are silent partners. Westram never said anything about not making hats, did he? His objection is purely about trade, I believe. What about the young woman you hired to help you, Carrie? Do you think she could manage it alone?'

Carrie winced. Tansy had been devastated to learn she had lost her position. Carrie had convinced Mrs Thrumby to take her on as a chambermaid.

Marguerite put up a hand and shook her head. 'No.

We are not going behind Westram's back again. We have to find something less objectionable.'

Carrie felt her shoulders stiffen.

Marguerite looked conscience-stricken. She put her arm around Carrie's shoulder. 'Oh, my dear, I did not mean that the way it sounded. It is not me who finds trade objectionable. It is Westram and he is being an ass. But he is doing his best according to his lights, that is all. And sneaking around behind his back again will be just the ammunition he needs to insist we return to living under his roof.'

'Oh, Lord,' Petra said. 'I never thought of that. It is the last thing we want.'

Carrie hugged Marguerite back. 'I just wish I had more to offer. My portion is so small it hardly helps at all.'

'Having you here with us is enough,' the older girl said. 'Never fear, we will think of some way out of this conundrum.'

An idea occurred to Carrie. 'Perhaps Lord Avery would buy the business. We could put him in touch with the ladies who have been making the hats and the night-gowns. They would be glad to work for him, I am sure. And we would be solvent for a time.'

'Oh, bravo,' Marguerite said. 'If that were possible, it would give us some breathing room to find another way to support ourselves.'

Chapter Fifteen

Carrie tossed the third sheet of paper into the fire in the drawing room. Her sisters had gone about their own chores and left her to it. The note to Thrumby had been easy. She hadn't given him any details—she couldn't until she had Avery's answer—but simply requested that he not rent out the shop to anyone else until she'd had a chance to sell the business to someone who would need the premises.

After almost a week, he had replied in the affirmative.

The letter she now had to write to Avery was proving much harder. She'd been pretty scathing in their last meeting. And while she didn't mind humbling her pride for the sake of her sisters-in-law, she was worried that she'd be tempted to throw herself at his feet and beg him to make his proposal again—if he would still have her. And that would never do, despite that her stupid heart kept telling her she was making a terrible mistake by letting him go. Her head was very sure she was doing the right thing.

Trusting your head will ensure your safety, I confess.
Trusting your heart is taking a chance when.
Only one path leads to true happiness.

Doing the right thing should not make one feel so miserable. Should it?

Besides, though she had agreed to write this letter, Avery had made it quite clear he intended to continue with his travels and his gambling at some time in the future. He had never intended anything more than a short-lived affair and nor had she. The more she had thought about it, the more she kept thinking she had got her sisters-in-law's hopes up for nothing.

She swallowed the lump in her throat.

The door opened and the maidservant gave her a beaming smile. 'Lord Avery to see you, mum,' she announced and gestured him in.

The breath caught in Carrie's throat. It couldn't be. But it was.

Somehow, she had forgotten how handsome he was. All she could do was stare at him as if he was a vision.

He bowed. 'Mrs Greystoke. How glad I am to have found you in.'

Where else would she be? And what on earth was he doing here? She glanced down at her letter. Writing to him was one thing. Greeting him in person was another altogether. Her tongue felt awkward. Her mouth dry. She gestured to a chair. 'Won't you sit down?' The words were little more than a breathless whisper.

'Thank you.' He took a straight back chair near the hearth. She sat on the sofa a little distance away.

Marguerite bustled in, followed by Petra. 'Lord Avery, how delightful of you to call.'

A shadow passed across his face, but he rose to *his* feet and gave the two ladies an easy smile.

Carrie made the introductions. Petra joined Carrie on the sofa, while Marguerite sat close to Avery. Too close.

'I believe Lord Avery came to have private words with me,' Carrie said pointedly.

Marguerite cocked an eyebrow. 'Indeed. That is hardly proper.'

What sort of game was she playing? Had her sister-in-law changed her mind about asking him to take over the shop for them? Carrie felt all at sea. Indeed, she felt rather unwell. Thinking about Avery was bad enough, but seeing him here in the flesh was almost more than she could bear.

'Did you have a good drive down from town?' Petra asked.

He inclined his head. 'I rode. It was very pleasant.'

'You are lucky it did not rain,' Marguerite said. 'The weather has been exceedingly inclement recently.'

'I was indeed fortunate,' he said, smiling. 'It seems my luck is holding.'

Luck. What was he saying? Fortune smiled on the brave? Hardly. Who could have been braver than her husband and his two companions if reports of the battle were to be believed? And look what had happened to them. Believing in luck was no way to live. So why had he come?

'I hope the stables were able to accommodate your horse?' Marguerite went on. 'We rarely have visitors.'

'They were most accommodating. Thank you.' His smile was so charming both of her sisters beamed back at him. Of course they would. All the ladies fell at his feet. She wanted to bash them both over the head. She wanted to flee.

'Excellent. You will stay for dinner, of course,' Marguerite said calmly. 'I have asked the housekeeper to prepare a room for you, where you may refresh yourself.'

Carrie stared at her, mouth agape.

Avery also looked bemused, but he recovered in an instant. 'That is most kind of you, my lady.' He glanced at Carrie as if seeking her agreement. 'I would not wish to impose, however?'

What could she say? It was getting late. He would never make it back to London before dark and there wasn't an inn for miles. Not a decent one, anyway.

'It is no trouble at all,' she said, but her tone was a little terse and he grimaced.

She had not meant to sound unwelcoming. Indeed, her heart was thumping so loudly at the very sight of him, she was sure he must hear it. But having made up her mind to never see him again, having him here, under the same roof, was just too unsettling. The longings she was sure she had under control were now struggling to the fore, doing battle with all the good reasons she had lined up to defend her decision to refuse his offer of marriage.

'Naturally, it is no trouble,' Marguerite said. 'If you would care to follow me, I will take you to our house-keeper who will show you up. We keep country hours here and dinner will be ready in an hour.'

Again, Avery glanced her way, as if seeking guidance, but she gave a little hitch of her shoulders. Clearly Marguerite had something in mind and, until Carrie knew what it was, there was nothing she could say.

Perhaps she intended to tackle him herself about their idea. Indeed, it might be the best way to get him to agree. A man who was well fed and content was more likely to be accommodating.

She just wished she knew what his intentions were in coming here. Surely he did not intend to pursue his suit? She didn't think she could bear it.

* * *

Despite Carrie's obvious discomfort in his presence and monosyllabic answers to his questions, Avery found himself glad he had come. Her sisters-in-law were lovely women and thoroughly charming. How could their husbands had gone off to war and left them to fend for themselves? Idiots.

Likely that was why Carrie seemed so averse to marriage. Well, she needn't worry. He would never abandon her, if that was her fear. He would make her understand this. Somehow.

If only he could get a few minutes alone with her.

He had talked to Laura and John before leaving to come here. John's clientele had picked up remarkably over the past couple of weeks and he had been very clear he and Laura no longer needed anyone's financial help. John had also given Avery a bit of a bear-garden jaw about finding sensible employment and settling down.

You would think the man was a saint instead of the cheeky blighter who had run off with a duke's daughter. Still, Avery was pleased to see his sister so happy and his brother-in-law finally finding his feet, leaving Avery free of the financial burden of his sister.

'Would you like another helping of compote, Lord Avery?' Petra asked.

He leaned back in his chair. 'No, thank you. I could not eat another bite. Your chef has excelled himself.'

'Oh, we don't have a chef,' Marguerite replied.

'Then you have an excellent cook.'

The woman seemed to swell with pride. Good. He needed these women on his side. 'And may I say that the hats you ladies produced for your shop were amongst the most well made and creative any of the ladies of the *ton* have seen for a long time.'

Marguerite beamed.

'Lady Marguerite designed them,' Carrie said. 'She has a great deal of talent in that regard.'

'It is a great deal too bad her talent is to be wasted,' Petra added.

'Westram is determined the shop is to be closed, then?' Avery asked.

'He is determined that none of his sisters shall become shopkeepers.' Carrie was looking at him oddly. She glanced around the table. 'I suppose now is as good as any time to put our proposition to you.'

The other two ladies nodded their agreement.

Avery straightened. Another proposition? His body heated, remembering her earlier proposition. The one he'd initially turned down. But this could not possibly be that sort of proposition, this was something else entirely. He forced his mind to focus.

Carrie blushed and hung her head as if she'd guessed his thoughts and was ashamed.

Dash it, that was not what he wanted at all.

'Tell me,' he urged.

She straightened her shoulders as if bracing for a rejection. 'We wanted to offer you the chance to buy the shop and the millinery business.'

She wanted him to become a shopkeeper.

Why was he surprised? She would likely see shopkeeping as infinitely preferable to his current modes of making a living. And it would provide the ladies with some additonal finances.

It would certainly infuriate both the Duke and Westram. Just for that reason alone he was tempted.

Carrie was watching him closely, as were her sisters-in-law.

Was there something here he was missing? He'd learned to study his hand closely before he made a wager. 'I need to think about it.'

Carrie looked disappointed, but Marguerite smiled sweetly. 'You can let us know your decision in the morning.'

He frowned. 'Why the rush?'

'We employed women in the village to make more hats and nightgowns because we were not able to keep up with the demand by ourselves,' Lady Petra said. 'We have paid them for their work, but they are relying on the future income. We have to inform them one way or the other.'

'I see.' If he did this, he would have to come down to Kent all the time and would likely see Carrie, too. See her and be kept at arm's length, the way she was keeping her distance now. No, he would not be able to live with that.

He needed her answer to his proposal, if he could ever get her alone. Unfortunately, he had a feeling he already knew what her answer would be. She had not been pleased to see him. Not one little bit. He would simply have to change her mind.

'If you do not wish to buy the business,' Carrie said, tightly, 'perhaps you might know of someone who will.'

That did not bode well. Something in Avery's chest gave an unpleasant squeeze.

'Carrie,' Marguerite interjected. 'It is perfectly reasonable for Lord Avery to request a little time to think about our offer.'

She nodded, but her jaw hardened. 'Very well.'

Had he been wrong about her having deeper feelings for him?

Damn it all. Why was he surprised at her indifference? Or hurt? She had been quite clear that she wanted to use him right from the very beginning and the only reason she was entertaining his presence now was because he could be of further use.

The pain of that knowledge went far deeper than he would have expected. Could he really feel that strongly about a woman who wanted nothing to do with him? It seemed so. And yet he couldn't really blame her. He was a man who lived by his wits. Did she think he could not provide for her adequately? It was ironic, after he had been providing for Laura these many months.

'I will also try to think of who else might be interested,' he said, smiling despite the pain in his chest.

Lady Petra and Lady Marguerite exchanged glances.

'I think it is time for us to retire to the drawing room and leave you to your port,' Lady Marguerite said, rising.

'I think I would prefer to take tea with you in the drawing room, if you ladies would not object,' Avery said, standing. 'I plan on leaving early in the morning.'

And before then, he needed a private word with Carrie. No matter how much it hurt, he wanted to hear her answer when he laid all of his cards on the table.

Avery followed the ladies to the drawing room. At the door, Carrie hung back. 'If you don't mind, I will not join you. I seem to have a headache.'

She walked briskly away.

Oh, this was not going well at all.

Carrie paced up and down her bedroom. Why on earth had Marguerite put Avery in the chamber next to hers when there were two other guest rooms to choose from.

Once the maid had left, Carrie had been indulging in

a good cry as a way of saying goodbye to Avery—again. A painful never-ending endeavour, when the sound of men's voices had penetrated her wall. First Jeb, then Avery.

The words were indistinct, but since no doubt Jeb was there to ready him for bed, Avery must be undressing.

Her mind's eye imagined his coats coming off. Jeb hanging them over a chair, ready for him to take away and brush while Avery disposed himself on the sofa in that masculine sprawl she so adored. Now attired in his shirtsleeves, he looked deliciously informal.

Jeb knelt, removing Avery's boots and rolling off his stockings.

The manservant's voice rumbled again. 'Been a fine summer so far, my lord,' Carrie imagined him saying.

'It has indeed.' Avery's charming smile would be in full effect as he held out his wrists for Jeb to remove his cuff links. Avery lifted his chin and Jeb removed the ruby pin that had winked and glittered in the candle-light at dinner.

A light metallic tinkle made her think of the tray on the dressing table. No doubt Jeb placing the valuable items there.

Avery, meanwhile, unwound his cravat from around his throat and tossed it on top of the coats, white on black.

Avery's tenor now, quite distinct from Jeb's baritone. 'Have you always lived on the Westram property?' She imagined him saying in that polite charming way he had.

'I have, my lord,' Jeb replied. 'Born in a cottage not far from here.'

'It is a lovely corner of England.'

Jeb grinned, looking pleased. 'Ah, that it is.'

He reached out to help with the shirt buttons, but Avery waved him off with a genial smile. 'Unpack my valise, would you, there's a good chap. I've a couple of clean shirts in there.'

While Jeb emptied the valise, Avery pulled the shirt off over his head, revealing that mouthwateringly broad torso.

Carrie collapsed on the sofa, breathing fast at the image her mind was so vividly recalling. A pair of wide shoulders, a smattering of crisp dark hair and the heavily muscled arms of a horseman—or a swordsman.

His strong large hands went to the buttons of his falls. He paused, looking at her from beneath lowered lashes, tempting and teasing with his eyes.

Her breasts became full and heavy, the place between her thighs tingled and pulsed. Unable to help herself, she cupped one breast and her other hand drifted between her legs, gently circling, imitating the way he had touched her on their last night together. Heat rippled along her veins.

Her eyelids drooped, her body warmed, breaths became shallower, faster. She wanted…

The voices next door silenced. A door closed. Footsteps whispered along the corridor in the direction of the servants' stairs. Now alone, Avery lounged on the sofa in the glorious dressing gown he'd worn the day she went to his chambers looking relaxed, at ease yet as lithe as a cat.

She moaned softly, imagining kneeling beside him, untying the belt. Letting the robe fall open to reveal the strong column of his neck and the dark hollow at the base. The bones a sharp contrast to the smooth male skin displayed so openly.

She leaned forward to kiss that tender spot, feeling the warmth of his skin against her lips, his cheek resting lightly on the top of her head while he stroked her back.

Her lips cruised from his throat to his neck to the shell of his ear. He sighed with pleasure at her kisses. She stroked her hands over his chest, revelling in the heat of his skin against her palms, the rough texture of the hair, the tight little nipples beading beneath her touch, the way hers tightened now beneath her fingers.

She pulled the dressing gown down over his arms and he helped her take it off, leaving him naked to her view. His wide chest and narrow waist and jutting erection.

She collapsed back on to the sofa, her fingers delving into her core, stroking and circling and… A wave of gentle pleasure and heat rippled outwards, leaving her limp and panting and…disappointed.

She dragged herself out of her trance. Emptiness filled the space behind her ribs. How foolish to have thought that, in discovering what every wife should know, she would find some contentment with her lot as a widow. Instead, she had found only greater longing and deeper despair than ever she had felt at the loss of her husband.

His death had only left her feeling cheated and angry. This new loss made her feel sad. And alone.

She sat up, clenching her hands in her lap. This must never happen again. She had to stop her foolish imaginings about Avery. She had her sisters-in-law to think about now. They had made a pact to support each other in their bid for independence. They had agreed none of them wanted marriage. She would not go back on her word.

Certainly, Avery, no matter how much desire she felt

for him, was not the sort of man she would ever wish to marry. He spent his life taking risks at the card tables or on the throw of a dice or—she shuddered—on the ability of a man to swallow yet another sword.

With a man like him, a wife would spend her life expecting the bailiff at the door or, worse yet, discovering he'd died risking his life for some nonsensical wager.

She had to do what she'd promised herself she would do and put him out of her mind.

For ever.

She climbed up into bed and pulled the covers up under her chin. She would not think about Avery sleeping in the bedroom next door.

She definitely would not.

Chapter Sixteen

Finally, Avery was alone. He'd thought the lad assigned to assist him would never cease his chatter and go. At least Lady Marguerite had pointed out Carrie's chamber, so Avery didn't need to go prowling around trying to discover her whereabouts. He could have kissed the woman when she let that bit of information fall from her lips, though why she had done so, he was not exactly sure. If it was to trap him into making an offer to Carrie, she needn't have bothered. It was the first thing on his agenda.

And if she would not see him alone, then he was damn well going to do it with a house full of sisters and servants looking on. Because he wasn't leaving here until she agreed to their marriage. Or until she gave him a good reason as to why she would not. He poured a glass of the brandy someone had thoughtfully left on the dressing table and swallowed it down. He shrugged into his dressing gown, pulled the belt tight and squared his shoulders.

Now to accost the lioness in her den. Hopefully, she didn't have her door locked.

Having checked there was no one lurking in the corridor, he strode the few steps to Carrie's door. The handle turned easily and the door swung back at a push. He breathed a sigh. One hurdled crossed.

Once inside, he closed the door behind him. The air in here seemed warm and somehow sultry. Sensual enough to stir his blood. A slight whisper of air caught his attention. There. In the bed, half-hidden in shadows, propped up on her elbows. Carrie. Watching him. Yes, a lioness in her den. He could not help but recall her magnificent anger the last time they'd met when her voice came to him in a fierce whisper. 'What are you doing in here?'

Not the welcome he'd hoped for, certainly, but at least she wasn't screaming or running to the bell pull to summon a servant. He held up his hands in a gesture of surrender. 'I came to talk.'

She muttered something under her breath.

'I beg your pardon?' he asked, stepping further into the room.

'I said, how like you to take such a risk.'

He frowned. 'Don't tell me you have a pistol in your hand and were about to shoot me for a burglar.'

'All right, I won't.'

'Won't what?'

'Tell you—'

'Never mind that. Will you give me leave to talk to you?'

She heaved a sigh. 'I don't suppose you would leave were I to say no?'

He winced. Apparently, her mood was no better than it had been at dinner. He lit a candle from the banked fire in the hearth and moved nearer the foot of the bed. She blinked at the light.

She looked warm, deliciously flushed, almost as if… Could she have been…? A surge of hot blood made him lose focus. He reined in his lust. If she preferred to seek solace alone, that was her right.

But dammit all…

He stepped back. 'I beg your pardon. I assumed this might be a good way to catch you alone, since your sisters-in-law made it impossible downstairs. Perhaps you will grant me an audience tomorrow?'

She grimaced. 'Not like you to be so formal, my lord. Now you are here, I suppose it is as good a time as any other.'

She swept a glance over him. 'I hope Jeb made a satisfactory valet?'

Off balance at the change in topic, he glanced around for somewhere to sit. There was a chair beside the window, but it was a little far away. He opted for perching on the end of the bed. 'Jeb was most attentive.'

She glared. 'Give me that candle, before you drip wax all over the counterpane or set the bed curtains afire.'

He handed it over and she put it in the candlestick on the bedside table.

Now he could see her properly. Her hair neatly plaited and laying over one shoulder. Her plain cotton nightgown buttoned up to her chin. Her eyes wide and unfathomable.

Clearly aware of his assessing gaze, she folded her arms across her chest and shot him a glower of what looked like resentment, but not before he noticed that her nipples had tightened and pressed against her nightgown in a most interesting way.

'What did you want to talk about?' she asked.

'Us.'

Her gaze slid away. 'There is no us. Our personal arrangement is at an end.'

Was he really going cast his pride aside to profess his love like some callow youth or would he be better off appealing to her practical side and work on gaining her trust?

The latter might be more successful, since there was nothing to suggest she held him in any great esteem and certainly there was nothing to suggest her heart was involved.

That was something he would work on. If she would allow it.

'Why not extend our arrangement? It was profitable for us both.' He grinned. 'On more than one front.'

She clearly caught his meaning because her frown deepened. 'Westram wouldn't like it. He has made that very clear.'

'He made it clear, he expected a wedding. Perhaps a betrothal would satisfy him for the nonce.'

She looked unimpressed. 'I had no intention of marrying and nor did you until Westram arrived on the scene.'

'I have missed you.' Hell, where had that come from? She'd been gone barely a week, but the subtle change in her expression told him this might a better tangent. He recalled his first impressions when he stepped into the room and—'I think you have been missing me, too.'

She dropped her gaze to the counterpane and picked at a non-existent thread. 'Nonsense. Why would you think so?'

He leant forward and tilted her chin with one finger. 'Haven't you?'

Slowly she raised her gaze to meet his. No coward, this woman. It was what had impressed him from the very first, the way she squared up to him.

'I've missed some things about our liaison,' she admitted bravely.

He couldn't stop himself. He kissed those luscious lips and, after a small resistance, a slight stiffening of her body, she made a low groan in her throat and kissed him back, pulling his head down with feverish gasps and moans that had him hard in an instant.

He flung the covers back and shrugged off his dressing gown, aware of her greedy gaze on his already responding erection. A feral triumph filled him at the heat in her gaze and the evidence of her arousal, the flush of her cheeks, the hardened peaks of her breasts lifting the soft cotton of her gown.

A growl rumbled up from his throat and in seconds he had the nightdress over her head and flung aside so he could feast his gaze on his sensual Amazon lover.

She opened her arms to him with a smile so seductive and welcoming a breath caught in his throat. Unable to resist the invitation, he fell upon her like a ravening beast.

Apparently, he had not merely missed her, he had been starving for her, for this. She wrapped her legs around his thighs and he slid into her slick heat in a dizzying rush. Ready. She was so damned ready.

His mind darkened. His lips found her full ripe breasts and he latched on, suckling as her bucking hips urged him to drive home deeper and harder.

Her cries of pleasure were sweet music to his ears and her urgent desire for his body sent a hammer beat of blood through his veins.

For a brief moment, he tried to pull back, to slow things down, but her sheath was so tight around his shaft, and the feel of her hands wandering his skin so very urgent, that he followed her lead, drove into her in time with the upward thrust of her hips and, when he felt her come apart, only a long-honed instinct for self-preservation had him withdrawing at the last moment before he followed her into bliss.

He wasn't exactly sure how he managed it. Likely because he'd been more ready for the onslaught that had completely ambushed him last time.

Thrills rocked him, drained him and lasted for ever, yet was over far too soon. He rolled clear and cleaned off her belly with a corner of the sheet. Replete and overwhelmed by the power of the orgasm that had ripped through his body, he basked in the warm haze of satisfaction. Never had he been so shattered.

Or felt so good.

He pulled her close, nuzzling her ear, stroking whatever part of her he could reach. 'Lovely,' he murmured. 'You are lovely.' Warm darkness enveloped him as he heard her sigh.

'Oh, Avery.'

With her firmly entwined in his arms, positive she could not leave him before he had a chance to have his say, he let himself drift.

A slight shift of Carrie's arm drew a sleepy sound of protest from Avery. He tightened his grip. She abandoned the thought of getting up and tried to process what had just happened.

Whatever it was, it was her fault. She had no doubt if she had told him to leave he would have done so. Instead, when he had slipped through her door, all she could think of was that she had not worn her pretty nightgown.

What on earth was the matter with her? Did she have no sense when it came to men? First, she married a totally unsuitable man because her father had wanted it so badly. Only to discover Jonathan had only married her to pay off his debts and to have him reject her as a person. Now she was considering marriage to one who had the power break her heart. One, for that matter, who seemed in no hurry to leave her bed. Good lord, what would the maid say if she found them? Or, worse yet, what would her sisters-in-law think.

Well, they wouldn't mind the bed part, that had been agreed to, but the fact that she was so very tempted to let him convince her to marry him, that was a whole other story. She could not be married after she had sworn to stand by them through thick and thin. She certainly could not marry a man who—

Dash it. Why did he have to be a gambler?

Her heart sank. If she was honest with herself, that was the real reason she had rejected his offer. The only reason. Because her sisters-in-law would understand. And even him being forced up to the mark wasn't an impediment. Because even if he didn't love her the way she loved him, they liked each other and it was possible that it could grow into something stronger.

No, it was the gambling, the recklessness of it that held her back.

Yet the thought of not accepting his offer and imagining him going off and finding another lady on whom to lavish his affections had her heart in a permanent spasm.

'What is going on in that head of yours?' Avery yawned. 'I can hear the wheels turning.'

For a moment, she considered blurting out her fears. How he would laugh. After all, everyone gambled. It was *de rigueur*. Only the merchant class frowned upon wagering.

She turned on her side to face him. 'You said you came to talk.'

'I did, *chérie*. Somehow I got sidetracked.'

He flashed her a wicked grin and her insides tightened. Oh, he really was a naughty man. Not at all the sort of man her far more serious nature needed. 'I hope you are not here to try to convince me to marry you.'

'I am here to explain why it would be a good idea.' He kissed the tip of her nose and brushed a strand of hair back from her face.

At least he wasn't spouting poetry and other such nonsense. But oh, she could understand why women fell for his charm.

'If you must say your piece, I will listen, but do not expect me to change my mind.'

He gave her a look of admonishment. 'Please do me the courtesy of hearing me out *before* you decide.'

She pressed her lips together, determined not to let him charm her into doing something she would most certainly live to regret.

'Think about it, Carrie. If you were married to me, you could continue operating your shop and your sisters-in-law could continue selling their wonderful hats and Westram could say nothing about it.'

She thanked heaven she and the others had already had this conversation. 'They will not go against Westram's edict. The millinery business is not an option. So we are right back where we started.'

'Surely Westram wouldn't object to a hands-off approach? Provided your names are not known, what could possibly be his objection?'

The dear man, he really wanted to help. She placed a hand flat on his cheek. 'He is adamant.'

'So how does he expect his sisters to maintain themselves?'

'He doesn't. He wants them to marry again.'

'Understandable.'

'Is it?' A little flash of disappointment took her by surprise. Why would she have thought he was different to any other male of the species, thinking that all women needed a man to rely on.

He gave her enquiring look.

'The reason we came here was that none of us wanted to marry again. We wanted our independence.'

He frowned. 'Then why did you ask me to be your lover?'

'You know why. I was curious about something that had been denied me. Besides, the three of us had agreed that being widows meant that we were free to enjoy lovers if we so wished.'

'Lovers.' His tone was heavy.

'Surely you are not judging me when you flit from one lady to another on a whim.'

He had the grace to look chagrined.

'Besides,' she continued, 'I have no intention of taking any other lovers.' She could not even think about it, not when there would only ever be one man she loved.

He rose up on one elbow, looking down into her face, his gaze searching her face intently. 'Am I to understand from that admission that you do care for me? At least a little.'

'Of course I care for you,' she almost snapped at him.

'You don't think I would do this...' she waved a hand to encompass them, the bed, the room at large '...if I did not care for you.'

He lay back down. 'Good. Very good.'

She frowned, but he seemed to be thinking and it was a long pause before he spoke again.

'So now you can no longer gain income through the shop, apart from selling it to me, how do you plan to support yourselves on an ongoing basis?'

'We haven't come up with a solution yet.' She sighed. 'And if we do not solve the problem, Westram will solve it for us.'

'By marrying you off.'

'Yes. And that is not an option.'

He did not seem disturbed by her vehemence. Indeed, he seemed almost pleased.

'Then why not pre-empt the fellow and marry me? We get along well. We like each other. And to be brutally honest, I have never enjoyed a lover the way I enjoy you.'

A marriage of convenience in other words. 'You plan to support a wife on your earnings from gambling when you do not make enough to afford decent lodgings?' She didn't mean to sound scornful, but she could not keep her feelings out of her voice. 'I have nothing to bring to such a marriage. I am honour bound to continue to pay my portion into this household. Without my contribution, they would have no choice but to return to Westram. We worked it all out very carefully. I cannot do that to them.'

He stiffened. 'If I can support my sister, I cannot see why I cannot support a wife and her sisters-in-law.'

'You support your sister?'

'I did until recently. Very handsomely, too, I might add. Thankfully, her husband can take up the reins now that his clientele has picked up.'

'You supported her with your winnings at the tables?'

'That and… Well I have given up my other source of income.'

'Your special ladies.'

'Yes. It wasn't all that profitable and I only started it to help out an old friend. It added a bit to the coffers, but I won't miss it.'

The man was nothing if he was not resourceful, but… 'I cannot see myself relying for room and board on the results of a game of *vingt-et-un*.'

'Pooh. That is a game for novices. I don't play games of luck. I play whist. It is a game of skill and I rarely lose.'

'But it also has an element of chance. You must lose sometimes.'

'Of course.' He sat up, forearms resting on his bent knees. She ran a hand over his lovely naked back. How would it be to have this lovely man in her bed all the time? As her husband. Oh, she wanted to say yes so badly it hurt.

A hot hard lump rose in her throat. 'I can't do it.' She hated how weak she sounded. She swallowed, hating the burn behind her eyes. 'I cannot marry a man who risks everything on the turn of a card. My first husband spent all my money paying off gambling debts and then he died because of some stupid wager and I cannot live day to day wondering if you might do the same.' She sniffed.

He was looking at her over his shoulder, his eyes grave, his lips unsmiling. He said nothing.

'There. Now you have it. The truth. I am a coward. Please do not ask me. I am sorry.' She buried her face in her hands. 'You must think me such a plebeian to concern myself with such things.'

'I did not know that about your husband.' His voice sounded cold. Remote. 'I knew he went off to war and got himself killed, but I did not know it was because of a wager.'

'Hardly anyone knows and Westram asked us not to speak of it. No one actually seems to know the full details, but what is undeniable is that all the money from my settlements was used to pay Jonathan's gaming debts. They were huge. Westram was nearly ruined keeping us out of debtors' prison. The day after our marriage Jonathan made some sort of stupid wager, I presume to recoup his losses, and went off to war and got himself killed, along with his two best friends. No doubt he lost the bet into the bargain. How can I place my future in the hands of another man who lives by taking those sort of risks?'

He stared at her. 'You think he got himself killed because he didn't want to be married to you or because he lost the bet?'

She flinched. Pain twisted in her heart. 'Probably both. What am I to think when…when he did not even come to my bed before he left?'

His mouth became a thin straight line. 'I beg your pardon for asking you to take such an unwarranted chance on marriage to me.' He got up and threw on his dressing gown in silence. 'I fully understand your reticence and can quite see why you think we might not suit.'

'I am sorry,' she whispered.

'You cannot be sorrier than I.' He bowed.

Only Avery could bow while wearing a dressing gown and make it look like the most elegant movement in the world.

She was still warmed by the thought when he left the room and closed the door behind him.

Then, cold, alone and lonely, she let her tears run free until she was too exhausted to remain awake.

In the morning, she learned he had left at first light.

It had taken Avery two days to get an appointment to see his father. Finally he knew exactly what he had to do to ensure Carrie's happiness. Heavens, her first husband had been an absolute bastard. Now he understood some of the things that had puzzled him about Carrie. Her withdrawals. Her frowns. They'd all occurred when the subject of gambling had come up.

And no wonder.

He'd sent Westram a note rescheduling their meeting. Westram's reply had been stiff, bordering on insulting, but Avery had swallowed his pride.

Westram was simply doing his duty, protecting the women of his family, no matter how much the idea stuck in Avery's throat that the other man had the right to protect Carrie while he did not.

Pride swallowing was the order of the day, apparently, for he was now in the company of a man he'd sworn he would never again have anything to do with.

Shadows lurked in the corners of the room, because the curtains were drawn against evening drawing in. The chamber smelled like old dust and old man. With his brother standing at his shoulder in a show of support, Avery tried not to stare at the father he'd not seen for five years. To his dismay, the Duke had shrunk in on himself in the intervening years, grown older, his dark hair completely white now. He hunched into a shawl someone had placed around his shoulders as if he felt cold, despite the heat from a blazing fire. Yet the old man still had the same piecing glare that had always made a youthful Avery feel like an insect under a microscope.

'So, finally, you decided to do your filial duty,' the old man grumbled, sipping at his glass of port. He groaned and shifted the bandaged foot propped on a padded stool.

Avery gritted his teeth, both in sympathy at the old man's obvious pain and annoyance at the truculent tone. Ah well. He'd sworn to Bart he would not let the old fellow get under his skin. 'I came to tell you to stop interfering in my business.' Damn, he'd meant to approach this a little more tactfully.

'Hah,' the old man said, rolling the stem between gnarled fingers and watching the way the light played on the ruby liquid. 'Why would I bother?'

'You bothered before, remember.'

The old man shot him a glare from beneath white bushy eyebrows. 'I was right, wasn't I?'

Avery hesitated. If his fathered hadn't interfered, he would have been married these past five years. To a woman only interested in his money whom he'd barely given a thought to in a very long time. And he would never have met Carrie. But that was beside the point.

'I know it was you who went to Westram. Telling tales.'

The Duke glanced at Bart and back to him. 'You should know better than to lift the skirts of one of the nobility. Even if she is widow.' He glowered at his port.

'I hear she's a cit, to boot.' There was a slyness in his gaze when he lifted it to meet Avery's glance.

Damn him. 'You will speak of the woman I intend to marry with respect.'

His brother moved to his father's side. Took the glass of port from his shaky hand and set it on the table.

'Why would you marry the girl?' the Duke asked. 'Seems you are getting what you want without it?'

'I am marrying her because that is what she deserves. And I do not care what you have to say about it, quite honestly.'

'And how do you plan to support a wife? She happy about your philandering with every married woman in town? Likes the idea of being married to a man who spends his nights in London's hells, does she?'

'I will support her by way of my birthright.' Hell, this was coming out all wrong.

'Will you now?'

He reined in his anger. He was angry because he'd had to come here cap in hand, but this was for Carrie, not for him. She deserved the best he could give her and this was it.

'I acknowledge you were right about Alexandra.'

The old man leaned back in his chair. His eyes widening. 'Well-a-day! I never thought I'd hear such an admission fall from your lips. A right stubborn one, you always were.'

Avery relaxed somewhat. This was the father he remembered. Irascible. Outspoken. But not completely unreasonable. Except when it came to the marriage of his offspring.

'I came to ask you to sign over the estate of Fenward to me, as Mother requested and you agreed.'

'It wasn't part of the settlements.'

'But it was her intention.'

The old man shook his head. 'Only if I thought you were ready to take on the responsibility. Even she knew you for a harum-scarum. What do you know about managing an estate? You've spent your life in ladies' boudoirs or at the tables and have nothing to show for it.'

'I haven't forgotten anything I learned as a boy under your tutelage.' Indeed, the very idea of having his own estate was one of the things that had kept him going all these years. If he hadn't needed to help Laura, he would have bought one by now.

The Duke glanced up at his eldest son, who gave him a grin. 'I told you he'd come around.'

'You did. Took him long enough. I tell you this, my boy, I was beginning to despair of you. You always had a good head on your shoulders. I couldn't believe it when you wanted to marry that dizzy-headed puss. I hope this widow of yours has a bit more sense.'

'She does.' He hesitated. 'Are you saying you accede to my request?'

'Of course. Been keeping Fenward for you, boy, if you ever decided to come to your senses. Runs along beside Wrendean. You'll also manage that one. For your brother if you'd rather do it for him than for me. I'm not long for this world. Your brother will need all the help he can get.'

Avery didn't like all this talk of death. But he wouldn't put it past the Duke to play on feelings of guilt. He was a cunning old so-and-so. He narrowed his eyes. 'I'll expect a wage, if you want me to take on Wrendean as well.'

The old man waved a hand. 'I will leave all that to your brother.'

Bart nodded. 'There is nothing I would like better.'

'And Laura?'

He knew he shouldn't be asking. He'd got far more out of this interview than he ever expected or even hoped. But he hated that his father had cast out his sister.

'Another stubborn one,' his father said, reaching for his port.

Bart put the glass in his hand.

The Duke took a sip. 'Well, I ain't dead yet. Had that jackanapes of a husband of hers not come here demanding I agree to their wedding and laying out all kinds of conditions about what I would and would not do, I might not have lost my temper. Damn his eyes. Sent him to the right about, as he deserved.'

Avery closed his eyes. Of course, that would have set the Duke's back up no end.

The old man fixed him with a stare. 'Don't think I don't know you and Bart have been helping the pair of them behind my back.'

'Mostly Avery,' Bart said. 'Since you've made it too difficult for me to do much.'

'Then you shouldn't go behind my back.'

Avery rolled his eyes. 'What else were we to do?'

'Nothing,' the Duke snapped. 'You are her brothers. I am glad to see you have at least that much sense of duty. I've been keeping an eye on that husband of hers, too.'

Argh. Now they would be in for a lecture.

'He'll make a fine barrister,' the Duke said.

Avery gaped at his father, who seemed oblivious to his surprise.

'Going to do well for himself,' the Duke mused as if surprised. 'I've already had some old friends send business his way.'

So that was why things had recently turned around

for John. Avery sank on to the edge of the seat in front of his father, the fondness he'd tried to bury for so damn long welling up. 'You really are an old curmudgeon.'

The Duke ruffled Avery's hair, the way he had when Avery was a boy. 'And you will be just like me if you aren't careful.' He leaned back in his chair with a sigh. 'Send for Sprake. I'll take that damned medicine now, my boy,' he said to Bart. 'Makes me so damn sleepy. Needed my wits about me, dealing with the likes of you two.'

'Yes, Father,' Bart said.

'You can't be thinking of cocking up your toes,' Avery said, feeling a sudden sense of panic at the weakness his father was showing. 'You have yet to get either of your sons to the altar.'

'Not thinking any such thing,' his father said wearily. 'See him out, Bart, and make whatever arrangements are needed. You have carte blanche.'

Clearly surprised by this magnanimity, Bart rang the bell and Sprake rushed into the room with a bottle of tonic and a spoon. 'You see, your Grace,' the elderly valet said. 'I told you, you needed this, but, no, you weren't going to take it. Too proud.' He shoved a cushion at the Duke's back and loosened his collar.

Avery hated seeing his father so fragile.

'What are you still doing here?' the old man asked. He curled his lip. 'Thought you had a lady to see.'

Avery narrowed his eyes for a moment. There was a glint of amusement in his father's eye and, yes, triumph. Damn the old man, he had finally got what he wanted. An acknowledgement that he was right. And a wedding in the offing.

And Avery discovered it was like a weight off his

shoulders. If not for meeting Carrie, he might never have swallowed his pride and made peace with his father before it was too late. Something he now knew he would have regretted for the rest of his life.

Carrie. A pain pierced his heart, for his own pride might yet have caused him to lose her.

He must now convince her to change her mind and set his whole world to rights.

He hoped she would listen. He had never felt this nervous when betting on a mediocre hand of cards with a hundred guineas on the outcome. But then cards were games of skill and he knew what he was doing.

In the game of love, he risked losing everything.

Tomorrow he would learn his fate.

Carrie's umbrella did nothing to keep her skirts dry, the wind drove the rain so hard. The weather had been fair when she'd caught the stagecoach from Sevenoaks. Jeb had been far from happy dropping her off at the inn, but she had insisted. She didn't want anyone witnessing her embarrassment should Avery turn her from his door.

What she would do if he did so, she wasn't sure. Throw herself on Westram's mercy, she supposed, assuming he was still in town.

Evening was already drawing in when she turned the corner on to Avery's street. She hesitated. Stopped. The street was empty except for a lad huddled in a doorway with his broom and one or two gentlemen holding on to their hats as they hurried on their way.

Turn back, her mind whispered.

This might be your only chance, her heart argued.

Squaring her shoulders, she marched the last few

yards to the house where Avery lodged. More doubts assailed her.

She swallowed them down and banged on the door.

The same porter who had opened it to her the first time opened the door with a glare.

'I am here to see Lord Avery.' She had certainly learned how to be imperious from her sisters-in-law. The thought bolstered her courage.

The porter bowed her in. 'You know where to find him.'

Heart thumping hard in her chest, she walked up the stairs to the first floor. Obviously, her heart wasn't quite as brave as it had pretended to be out on the street.

Only one path leads to true happiness.

This had to be right. She'd chosen with her mind once. She had to give her heart an opportunity.

She knocked. Scratched, really. Was she hoping he would not open the door? That he would be out and she could scurry away telling herself she had tried?

She raised her hand to knock again, more loudly.

The door opened.

Avery stood there, looking sartorially splendid as he always did, clearly dressed to go out.

A pain cramped her chest. Was he off to meet one of his special ladies?

His face lit up and her fears disappeared.

'Carrie?' He scanned her up and down. 'Good Lord, you are soaking wet. Come in. Take off your wet cloak.' He whipped it from around her shoulders. Took her by the hand and led her to a chair. 'Sit here, by the fire. Warm yourself.'

He was on his knees building up the fire, no sooner had the words left his lips.

A long sigh escaped her. She had been so worried about his reception. This was all she had hoped for and more.

'What the devil are you doing out on a night like this? And how did you get here? Not in that open gig, I hope.'

'I came on the stage.'

'What? Is Westram so nip cheese he will not afford you a post chaise?'

'Westram knows nothing of this journey.'

He frowned, sitting back on his heels as the flames of the fire took hold. 'Your sisters-in-law? Do they know?'

'Of course.'

Indeed, they had encouraged her when she had explained her dilemma and asked if they would be terribly upset if she pursued her suitor.

'You should have at least brought a maid if you are going to visit a single gentleman in his lodgings. Though really you should not be doing that at all.'

How else was she to speak to him? Send him a note and hope he might reply? 'La, sir, it is not the first time.'

He rearranged the coals in the fire. 'No,' he agreed, watching the flames take hold. 'It is not. What message of importance do you bear for me this time?'

Her heart stumbled. This was it. Taking the risky path and hoping for happiness.

'I changed my mind.'

He looked startled.

Dash it, where were all the elegant words she had rehearsed in the long hours on the stage? Left behind in that cramped little box, it seemed.

'I mean, I will accept your proposal of marriage if it is still on offer.'

Not exactly elegant, but to the point.

His brow cleared. 'I see.'

'I quite understand if you have changed your mind,' she hastened to add. 'You are under no obligation, of course. But...' she looked at him shyly '...you were right—there are some great advantages to be had in our union.'

At that he looked a trifle disappointed. 'Yes, indeed. As I said.'

'Of course the disadvantages may outweigh them now you have come to think about it a bit. I am a little long in the tooth. I am a widow who comes with baggage. I will always do my best to help my sisters-in-law, howsoever you earn your living. My settlement is small and you cannot expect anything from Westram, he was quite done up paying for his brother's debts as I told you.'

'Are you trying to talk me out of my offer?' He sounded amused.

Oh, dear, she really was making a mull of this. 'I simply don't want there to be any misunderstandings and I shall quite understand if you have changed your mind.'

Understand and be devastated.

He glowered. 'If that rapscallion husband of yours hadn't got himself killed, I would be ready to murder him about now.'

'If Jonathan was still alive, none of this would be happening.'

He chuckled. 'Ever the practical one.'

She swallowed. Was that good or bad? 'Someone has to be practical. I am hoping we can make enough from the shop—'

He frowned. 'So you changed your mind about that. Why?'

Cold fingers travelled down her spine. This was the question she dreaded. 'Remember the fortune teller?'

He looked surprised. 'I do. But surely you are not basing your decision on her words.'

'Not really. Well, perhaps in part. These were her words to me. *Trusting your head will ensure your safety, I confess, trusting your heart is taking a chance when only one path leads to true happiness.*'

For a moment he looked hopeful, then the frown returned. 'So is it your head you are trusting?'

She knelt down beside him and, leaning against him, put her arm around his waist.

His own arm crept around hers.

'I trusted to safety when I married Jonathan. Father was right about Westram being a good provider for his family, though he had no idea Jonathan's debts were so outrageous. I am safe, even as a widow, with Westram in charge, but it is not true happiness. My heart tells me you are the man meant for me.' She hesitated. 'Something in my heart also tells me you feel the same way about me.' She gave a little laugh and it broke in the middle. 'Of course if you do not—'

He turned towards her, gazing into her eyes. 'How could you doubt it, my dearest darling Carrie? I love you. I think I have since the moment I saw you.'

'You were too bosky to know anything,' she said, her heart filling with a bubble of joy she did not know how to contain.

'I most certainly was not.' He gave her a look. 'And you? How do you feel?'

She sighed. 'Oh, Avery, I thought my heart was broken when you left Kent. I realised a while ago that I loved you, but I thought I was doing the right thing, knowing I could never be happy marrying a gambler. But without you, being safe and secure seemed like so much dross after you left. I fell in love with you, the man who is kind and generous and caring. I do not want to change you.'

He picked her up in his arms and settled himself on the sofa where he commenced kissing her silly. When they finally broke for breath, he twirled one of the strands of hair that had escaped her pins around one finger and gave it a little tug.

'I was coming back down to Kent tomorrow to give it one last shot,' he said.

Shocked, she gasped. 'You were?'

'You made me see things I refused to look at before.' He gave a small laugh. 'You see, I am not really a gambler at heart. I never bet on anything unless I know I can win. Even so, I fully accept that no woman wants to live her life worrying about whether her husband will lose everything they own. So, I went to see my father.'

'The Duke?'

'We came to an agreement.' He sounded grim.

'Was it so very dreadful? You know you do not have to do this for my sake.'

'Turns out I am doing it for my own sake, too. Without a reason on which to hang up my pride, I would never have gone to see him and I would have regretted that deeply.' He swallowed. 'He's aged terribly in the years I have been absent.' His voice softened. 'Though he's still as autocratic as ever. It seems we both regret our row, though of course he is positive he was in the right.' He smiled fondly. 'He was, actually. But he could have found a less unpleasant course of action.'

He let the strand of hair spring free and kissed her

cheek and then her lips, before continuing. 'I went to him to tell him to stay out of my business, since I thought he must have learned you were related to Westram and set him on us. He denies the latter, but I am still not so sure. I also insisted he hand over the estate my mother left me.'

She could scarcely believe it. 'You have your own estate?'

'Yes. He also offered me the position of land agent for one of the nearby ducal properties, one I know well and that will bring a good income.'

Her head was spinning. She could not quite believe all he was saying. 'Are you saying you intend to give up gambling? For me?'

'For us, love. Though I believe the odd gentlemanly wager is not a crime.'

'No. No, of course not. Avery, I love you. And I trust you to do what is right.' She did. How could she not have realised that before?

He smiled and his face took on a boyish cast. 'The estate is in a lovely part of England.' He glanced at her intently. 'That is if you do not mind burying yourself in the country.'

'I love the countryside. Living in Kent for more than a year, I have come to realise how much I prefer it to the city, though the city is where I grew up.'

He breathed a sigh of relief, lifted her off his knee and settled her on the sofa. He went down on one knee before her and her heart did a little dance of happiness.

'Dearest Carrie, will you do me the very great honour of becoming my wife?'

She reached for his hand, took it in hers, kissed it and rubbed it against her cheek. 'Yes, Avery, I will.'

He kissed each of her hands in turn. 'Then you make me the happiest man in all of England.'

He rose to his feet and pulled her to hers. 'Now we must get you to the Westram town house. I'm not having the gossips saying this marriage was forced on you. Everything is going to be absolutely above board.'

Avery looked so happy, it was only now Carrie realised that there had always been shadows behind his mischievous flirtatious gaze. Those shadows were gone, replaced with a light she could only describe as love. The fact that the light was for her was the most amazingly wonderful thing in the world.

The fortune teller had been wrong. Following her heart had also led to the safety and security of her one true love's arms.

'I do love you so,' she said, unable to contain her happiness.

He whirled her about with a laugh, then gazed down into her face. 'I wasn't sure you would take the risk. I have not been the most stable of fellows, these past many years.'

'It is no risk at all when love is involved. We will face whatever comes along together.'

Gravity filling his face, he cupped her cheeks in his hands. 'That, my darling, we will.'

We. It was such a wonderful word when compared to you and I and them. 'I do have one favour to ask.'

'Anything, my sweet. I'll never gamble again. I'll buy you the moon. Ask, it is yours.'

'If we are going to observe all the proprieties now that we are engaged, can we get married tomorrow? I really don't think I can wait any longer to, er…have you as my husband.'

He looked startled. Then laughed. 'If that is your true wish, then it shall be done. I am certainly happy not to wait. I will go to Doctors' Commons for a special licence right after I speak to Westram.'

'Thank you.'

She flung her arms around his neck and kissed him.

Epilogue

Sunbeams filtered through the window in the bedchamber where Petra and Marguerite were helping Carrie dress for her wedding. She'd chosen a simple gown of pale primrose and wore flowers made by her sisters-in-law in her hair.

Petra retied the bow at the back of the dress. 'That is better. Now you are perfect.'

Strangely enough Carrie felt perfect. It was the way Avery looked at her that had made her feel that way. Avery. Today they would be wed. She could scarcely believe it.

'You are sure you wish to go through with this?' Marguerite said, her expression one of concern. 'Do not let Westram force you into something you do not want.'

Her palms grew damp inside her cotton gloves. This was the only part of marrying Avery she had been dreading. Saying goodbye to her sisters-in-law.

After the ceremony she and Avery were travelling north to one of the Duke's properties and from there, in two weeks' time, they would move on to their new life together.

'I am going to miss you both terribly,' she said and swallowed the lump forming in her throat. 'But I do love Avery and he loves me.' It sounded so wonderful to say those words and to mean them and feel sure.

'I should say so,' Petra said with a teasing smile on her lips. 'I have never seen a man so besotted as he has been these past three weeks.'

Carrie puzzled over the words. Surely Petra's husband—

'I know,' Marguerite said almost too briskly. 'Yesterday Westram grumbled that he could no longer walk around the house without tripping over him.'

Carrie chuckled. It was true. And she loved it.

Her eyes went a little misty at the thought of Avery's impatience to get their wedding over and done. Not that she had felt differently, but Westram had insisted there be nothing havey-cavey about the marriage and had vetoed their intention of getting a special licence.

While their wedding was to be a small affair in the Westram town-house drawing room, everyone who ought to be invited had been, including the Duke. They had all accepted, too. Waiting three weeks for the banns to be called had been the longest weeks of Carrie's life and yet they had also flown by, she had been so busy. Petra and Marguerite had come to town to help with the preparations and to help her shop for her trousseau. A new one. Avery wanted nothing of her first marriage to haunt the beginning of theirs. For once, she had agreed with the extravagance.

Petra briskly twitched at Carrie's skirts. 'I must say, though, this bridegroom of yours is not one to let grass grow beneath his feet. The ladies in Westram village were delighted to hear they are to continue supplying the shop now that the Thrumbys have taken it over.'

'I was so pleased that Thrumby agreed,' Carrie said. 'Tansy was thrilled, too, now she's going to help them in the shop again. She hated being Mrs Thrumby's chambermaid, despite being grateful for the job.' She gave her sisters a regretful smile. 'Now the only people my departure inconveniences are you. I feel so badly for letting you down.'

In a flash, both girls put their arms around her and they clung together for a moment. 'Nonsense,' Marguerite said, her voice a little hoarse. 'Your happiness is more important than anything. Petra and I will find a way to keep ourselves busy and earn some money to boot.'

They drew apart. Carrie took a deep breath. 'About that.'

Marguerite raised a brow. 'You know we agreed you were not to worry about such things.'

'I haven't. I promise. Avery has. He went to see Mr Thrumby and finally convinced him that since he will continue to use Marguerite's designs, he must give you a share in the profits from them every quarter.' She did not think it worth mentioning that Avery upon his third visit had told Thrumby what a mistake it would be to annoy the son of a duke. Avery hadn't wanted to play the ducal card, as he had put it, but needs must. 'Oh, and should you happen to show something you have designed to the village ladies and they make it then you are to receive a commission for that too.'

Petra and Marguerite gasped. 'But what about Westram?' Marguerite said.

'These are royalties, Marguerite,' Carrie said. 'Your name will never be attached to the shop in any way. Avery spoke to Westram and has agreed it is not the same as being in trade.' She shook her head. 'Though to be honest I really feel you ought to be credited with your work. And you, too, Petra, for you taught the ladies how to turn the drawings into beautiful hats.'

Both sisters looked pleased. 'It's fine,' Petra said. 'We don't need recognition, but we could certainly use the funds.'

Carrie let go a breath. She hadn't been sure the women would accept the arrangement with or without Westram's approval.

'I don't know how to thank you, Carrie,' Marguerite said, giving her another hug. Petra put her arms around both of them.

'It is what sisters do,' Carrie said and received a very tight squeeze from both of hers.

A knock sounded at the door. They broke apart, smoothing their gowns and dabbing their handkerchiefs beneath watery eyes.

'The guests are all assembled, ladies,' the butler said, smiling broadly.

As they started down the stairs, Carrie's heart started to pound. What if Avery wasn't there? What if she was fooling herself and he left her right after the ceremony?

No. Not Avery. He would never do that to her. They loved each other.

They walked in procession across the hall and into the drawing room. At the fireplace the minister was waiting with Avery before him in a beautifully fitting dark blue coat with silver buttons and buff pantaloons. His brother standing beside him was similarly attired.

Carrie knew the room was full of people, knew the Duke was there, and Avery's sister, and Westram and other relatives, but she only saw Avery. It was if her vision had narrowed to encompass only him. She hesitated.

He turned and gave her such a heartfelt welcoming look, she felt utterly beautiful. Then he was walking towards her with his hand outstretched. She reached out and took it. Together they walked to the front of the room.

'Dearly beloved,' the minister began…

Beloved. Yes. Those words described her feelings to the full and the love and pride and joy in Avery's face told her he felt the same way, too.

* * * * *

If you enjoyed this story
you won't want to miss these other great reads
by Ann Lethbridge

More Than a Lover
Secrets of the Marriage Bed
An Innocent Maid for the Duke
Rescued by the Earl's Vow

HOME on the RANCH

YES! Please send me the **Home on the Ranch Collection** in Larger Print. This collection begins with 3 FREE books and 2 FREE gifts in the first shipment. Along with my 3 free books, I'll also get the next 4 books from the Home on the Ranch Collection, in LARGER PRINT, which I may either return and owe nothing, or keep for the low price of $5.24 U.S./ $5.89 CDN each plus $2.99 for shipping and handling per shipment*. If I decide to continue, about once a month for 8 months I will get 6 or 7 more books, but will only need to pay for 4. That means 2 or 3 books in every shipment will be FREE! If I decide to keep the entire collection, I'll have paid for only 32 books because 19 books are FREE! I understand that accepting the 3 free books and gifts places me under no obligation to buy anything. I can always return a shipment and cancel at any time. My free books and gifts are mine to keep no matter what I decide.

268 HCN 3760 468 HCN 3760

Name	(PLEASE PRINT)	
Address		Apt. #
City	State/Prov.	Zip/Postal Code

Signature (if under 18, a parent or guardian must sign)

Mail to the **Reader Service:**

IN U.S.A.: P.O. Box 1341, Buffalo, New York 14240-8531
IN CANADA: P.O. Box 603, Fort Erie, Ontario L2A 5X3

Get 4 FREE REWARDS!

We'll send you 2 FREE Books plus 2 FREE Mystery Gifts.

Harlequin® Special Edition books feature heroines finding the balance between their work life and personal life on the way to finding true love.

FREE Value Over **$20**

Get 4 FREE REWARDS!

We'll send you 2 FREE Books plus 2 FREE Mystery Gifts.

Harlequin Presents® books feature a sensational and sophisticated world of international romance where sinfully tempting heroes ignite passion.

FREE
Value Over
$20

Get 4 FREE REWARDS!

We'll send you 2 FREE Books plus 2 FREE Mystery Gifts.

Harlequin® Desire books feature heroes who have it all: wealth, status, incredible good looks... everything but the right woman.

FREE Value Over **$20**

READERSERVICE.COM

Manage your account online!

- Review your order history
- Manage your payments
- Update your address

We've designed the
Reader Service website
just for you.

Enjoy all the features!

- Discover new series available to you, and read excerpts from any series.
- Respond to mailings and special monthly offers.
- Browse the Bonus Bucks catalog and online-only exculsives.
- Share your feedback.

Visit us at:
ReaderService.com

RS16R